D1602572

LINEAR TACTICAL SERIES
ECHO

USA *TODAY* BESTSELLING AUTHOR
JANIE CROUCH

ECHO: LINEAR TACTICAL

This book is dedicated to Anu-Riikka.

You might recognize this story from the first time around.
I am here today as an author because of your encouragement.
Thank you, my friend.

Chapter 1

Five Young & Naive Years Ago

THE THREE WOMEN in the gas station started screaming.

Peyton Ward would've been more concerned about the commotion if the screeching hadn't been followed by jumping up and down, clapping, and hugging.

And if the same sort of behavior hadn't been happening for the past week—ever since Cade Conner's song first got airplay on the radio.

It was playing again now.

"It's Cade! It's Cade! It's Cade!"

Brittney and Melinda Sumter's excitement pretty much mirrored the entire population—slim as it was—of western Wyoming . Cade had graduated from nearby Oak Creek High three years ago. The Sumter twins had barely known him since they'd gone to Sublette County, Oak Creek's rival.

But that didn't stop them from folding their hands over

their hearts, and letting out almost comical sighs as Cade's baritone poured through the speaker.

"I love Cade. I've *always* loved him," Melinda gushed.

Apparently, not knowing someone didn't make a difference in true love, especially when that someone had a hit song on the radio.

Time to live by my own rules. Separate the strong from the pack of fools.

The girls sang along with the upbeat country lyrics. The fact that Mrs. Sumter was dancing around the gas station with her daughters, obviously equally as enthralled with the thought of Cade as her teenagers, was a little weirder.

Peyton rolled her eyes. *Cougar much?*

Melinda and Brittney were both Peyton's age—eighteen—so that made Mrs. Sumter at least in her super-late thirties. Cade was twenty-one. Peyton rolled her eyes again.

Brittney caught her eye roll but misunderstood it. "Oh, come on, Peyton, you have to remember Cade O'Conner. I know you were too artistic," she air quoted the word as she continued to dance around, "to ever deign to come to football games, but you had to have at least heard of him."

"He was a senior when we were freshmen," Melinda chimed in. "But he was super-hot."

Brittney gave her sister a little push. "Still is. Even hotter now."

Peyton studied the register in front of her rather than make eye contact. "I guess I must have missed him."

She hadn't missed him.

She knew Cade O'Conner better than the Sumter women ever would. He could've completely destroyed her future but instead had kept her secret.

And because of that, her entire life was about to change. She was about to get out of this town. Out from under…everything. From this job at the gas station that regularly left her warding off unwelcome advances and wondering if she was going to need to grab the shotgun hidden under the counter, to her situation at home.

Which was much worse.

But not for long.

Time to get out. Not look back. One step at a time.

Mrs. Sumter handed Peyton the cash to pay for their gas as the lyrics continued around them.

"He's in town, you know," Melinda said. "Maybe we can meet him. Or at least catch a glimpse of him if we drive into Oak Creek."

Peyton thrust Mrs. Sumter's change back at her. "Cade's in town for his father's funeral. He's probably not interested in signing autographs right now."

Damn it. She shouldn't have let out that she was aware of that. She'd just claimed not to know Cade at all.

Fortunately, the Sumter women were too busy singing to catch Peyton in her lie. They grabbed their sundries and headed out to their car.

And Peyton had to admit, she was still humming Cade's song under her breath as she got off from her shift a couple hours later.

Of course, she had heard it before it ever made it onto the radio.

She dashed to her car through the rain, the setting sun nowhere to be seen in the Wyoming sky. The Gas and Go wasn't a particularly convenient location for her to work at any more since she'd graduated from high school three weeks ago. It was too far from her house in Pinedale. Was actually in Teton County, rather than Sublette.

That had been a godsend Peyton's freshman year. Had changed the course of her life.

Thanks to the Gas and Go's Teton County address,

and a lot of hard work over the past four years, she was getting out of here. Getting away from Pinedale. Getting away Dennis's fists.

She was going to London, baby! Three months and counting.

She pulled out of the station carefully in the deluge and began driving toward her house. Once she left Pinedale, she was never, *ever* coming back. If she had to work four jobs waiting tables in Los Angeles until she got her break in the film industry, she would do it.

But attending the prestigious London Film Centre, on a full scholarship no less, would surely help open doors.

If not, she'd knock until they opened.

She had a gift, a true talent for visual storytelling. She knew it. Her teachers had seen it, and the dream of London had begun.

Peyton's smile was huge with the thought right up to the point where her car began to sputter as she drove along the back roads toward Pinedale. She gave it more gas, but that didn't seem to do anything at all.

"Come on, girl. I only need you to last three more months." She wouldn't be taking her car to school with her.

But her old Buick wasn't interested in lasting even three more minutes. Peyton pulled over to the side of the road as the engine gave a deep rattle—death throes—before quitting completely.

Damn it, why hadn't she taken the highway? At least she would've been able to flag someone down. The four minutes the back roads would save her definitely didn't seem worth it now. And her cheap cell phone wasn't going to get coverage out here.

Although who would she call? Definitely not Dennis.

And her mom may or may not be sober at this point in the evening.

She turned the key again, but the engine didn't turn over. Cade's baritone came crooning over the radio once again, barely winning the battle of volume against the rain pummeling her rooftop.

I want to be. I want to know. I can't wait for life to find me.

She banged her head back against the seat. "Your sexy voice isn't going to do me any good here, Cade."

But she sang along with it anyway. She might have played it off with Melinda and Brittney like she wasn't a fan, but the truth was, she might possibly be Cade's biggest fan.

And had been before he'd ever left Oak Creek for Nashville.

And for way more than just being the hot senior quarterback from her freshman year.

He'd noticed her. He'd been the only one who had.

I'm done waiting. Time to live by my own rules…

She'd kept a low profile at Oak Creek High School. The special visual and musical arts academy had only been available for qualifying students. It required a talent and a passion for the arts and a Teton County address.

Her abilities had given her the first, the Gas and Go address had given her the second. Peyton had forged her mother's signature and since she could pick up mail any time she needed at the gas station…a new Teton County student had been formed.

She'd kept her head down, trying to stay invisible at Oak Creek as much as possible. Teton and Sublette counties weren't very populous—she didn't want anyone putting two and two together. So, no friends.

Not that her home situation would've allowed it anyway.

Her plan had worked fabulously almost her entire freshman year. Except for a certain popular quarterback senior who'd discovered her in the film editing suite one day and hadn't left her alone for the entire remaining two months of school.

Cade had been friendly and compassionate to the girl who jumped at her own shadow and worked every spare second toward a filmmaking dream that had seemed way beyond her reach at that time.

He'd been part of the music division. Maybe the entire reason the arts program existed at all since it was based on equipment donated by the O'Conner family.

When he found out she lived in Sublette County not Teton, he could've turned her in.

Instead, he'd kept her secret. And for the last two months of her freshman year and his senior one, they'd become friends. As unlikely as that seemed.

And for her...more than friends. Not that she'd ever let him know the way she felt.

They'd been a pair of artists. She'd encouraged him in his music, and he'd sat by her in the editing suite. She'd like to think maybe she had a little bit to do with him deciding to go to Nashville, and now his song was playing on the radio.

"Getting Cade to Nashville is not going to get you home," she said out loud as the song ended.

Not that she really thought Cade remembered or ever thought of her anyway. And it didn't matter now.

She hopped out and opened the hood, searching under it for anything that seemed wrong. Immediately, she realized what a terrible plan that was. She didn't know what she was looking for, and now she was soaked. She gave up after a couple minutes and got back inside the car.

Damn it. She was miles from anywhere and this storm

was supposed to last all of tonight and most of tomorrow. There was nothing around but a few lake cabins, and she had no idea where any of them were.

Wait. Peyton jerked her head up, straining to see out into the gathering darkness. She'd just passed the Emerson Creek bridge when her car trouble started. So she knew where at least *one* cabin was.

One that happened to belong to the O'Conner family.

"Thanks, Cade," she whispered, tapping the front face of her radio. She pulled her keys from the ignition. She'd make a dash for the cabin. Most of these vacation houses didn't have a land-line phone, but at least it would be warm and dry.

Mom and Dennis probably wouldn't notice if she didn't come home anyway. The current bruise across her cheekbone from Dennis's backhand, hidden by makeup, meant that he was probably back to the ignoring-Peyton stage. It would be another couple of weeks before he was itching to use his fists again.

Three more months. All she had to do was keep her head down, make as much money as she could, and survive for three more months. Then she'd be gone.

Any dry part of her body was drenched fifteen seconds after she'd made a break for it. She dashed back along the road and over the bridge, then took the footpath that provided a shorter route to the cabin—glad she didn't have to explain to anyone why she happened to know about this shortcut.

It had absolutely nothing to do with occasionally looking in from a distance when Cade had thrown a few small parties at the cabin.

He'd invited her to one, but of course, she hadn't gone.

But watching from a distance had been sort of nice.

Like she'd been included even if she hadn't really been part of it.

She was shivering by the time she made it to the front porch but forced herself to sit on the swing as she wrung out her clothes. She'd always loved the thought of porch swings—the serenity of them. Plus, if she was going to break into a house, she wanted to be a considerate criminal and not drip all over the floor.

Not that this place was so fancy that it would be immediately noticeable. The O'Conners may be multi-millionaires, but nothing about this place—nothing about *Cade*—had ever been pretentious.

The O'Conner family would make wonderful subjects for a film documentary. She'd love to be the one to tell their story. That's what she wanted to do more than anything: tell people's stories through film.

Of course, being half in love with the subject probably wouldn't make her an impartial storyteller.

Once she was at least not dripping wet any more, she moved to the front door, not surprised when she found it unlocked. Theft wasn't a big problem around here, and unless someone was going to steal kitchen utensils or a bed, there wasn't much inside to entice a burglar.

And at least this way, she'd only be arrested for the entering part of breaking and entering if she got caught.

The cabin wasn't big—a couple of bedrooms, bath, kitchen, and open living room. She dashed into the bathroom, thankful to find a towel and dried herself off the rest of the way.

She slipped off her shoes and grabbed a paper towel to wipe up where she'd dripped on the floor. The storm was still beating against the side of the cabin. She'd go outside and sit on the porch swing and listen to it for awhile.

A lot of eighteen-year-olds wouldn't be interested in

spending a Saturday evening doing nothing more than listening to rain on a porch roof. Peyton wished she had her camera with her. It never hurt to have some stock footage of a storm tucked away to overlay with something else at a later date.

She wrapped the towel around her head and opened the door to step outside—

—letting out a shriek when she saw someone sitting on the swing.

Cade.

Chapter 2

Five Young & Naive Years Ago

SHE COULD BARELY MAKE him out in the darkness, just sitting there swinging calmly—long legs stretched out in front of him—like he'd been expecting her to walk out of the house.

Oh crap.

"Cade. Uh, hi. Wow. You probably wonder what I'm doing here." She quickly took the towel off her head and held it awkwardly in her arms. "I mean, you may not even remember me. I'm Pey—"

"Peyton, c'mon. Of course, I remember you, Peaches."

Peaches. She closed her eyes. When they'd first started hanging out her freshman year, she'd been working on a mock documentary assignment on peaches. It had become his pet name for her.

And was not at all the reason why she'd found some peach-scented shampoo and still used it even now when she hadn't seen Cade in nearly three years.

She never dreamed he'd remember the nickname.

"I wasn't breaking in. I uh…actually knew this was your house and was hoping it was okay to hang out here for a couple hours. My car conked out."

"I know."

She didn't move from the doorway. "Know I was aware that your family owned this house or that my car broke down?"

He studied her with those ridiculously blue eyes of his. "Both, actually. You used to sit out in the woods and watch the parties I had here."

Oh God. What was she supposed to say to that? He had to think she was some sort of a stalker.

"I—" The urge to flee into those woods now to end this conversation was almost overwhelming. Could this be any more cringey? She cleared her throat. "How did you know I was there?"

Now Cade looked away like *he* was the one who had something to be embarrassed about. "You left a Cheerwine soda cap, and I found it. You're the only one I know who has even heard of that drink, much less buys it. After that, I spotted you a couple of times."

He'd spotted her a *couple times*? This kept getting worse and worse. "Cade, I'm so sorry. I wasn't stalking you when I was out here. I just…"

Desperately wanted to be a part?

Felt included even though she'd been outside and not actually involved in what was happening?

Got to watch Cade, see him laugh, and feel like she was part of his inner circle?

Yeah, she was definitely going to need to run into the woods any second now to escape this conversation.

"Hey." He reached out a hand slowly toward her as if he didn't want to spook her—which was scarily intuitive.

"It's okay. Then. Now. You're always welcome here, Peyton, whether I'm here or not. This is a safe place for you. Always."

That definitely wasn't what she'd been expecting. But before she could figure out how to respond, he continued. "I saw your car on the side of Kingston Road. I took a peek under the hood. Looks like your plug wires came loose. Easy fix. I didn't have the keys to try, but it should start now."

"Oh. How did you know what to look for?"

Why did the air feel so different now that he'd moved closer? She couldn't stop drinking him in...all of his six-foot, leanly-muscled self. He was wet, she realized. Had gotten that way fixing her car.

"You don't spend years with Baby Bollinger as your best friend without picking up a few details about engines."

Right. Of course. Baby—Blake, although no one had ever called him that—was the area's top mechanic and an absolute whiz with all things mechanical.

Cade tilted his head to the side. "Mind if I borrow that towel?"

She handed him the towel, doing her best not to stare as he took it and dried off his hair, then rubbed it along his chest and shoulders. Cade dry and eighteen years old had been gorgeous with his dark brown hair and blue eyes.

Cade wet and twenty-one, made her heart stutter in her chest.

"Is that crack in your windshield from today also?" He ran the towel back up over his hair again.

"No, that's from a few days ago." When Dennis had gotten mad and decided to use a baseball bat on it.

Cade slid over on the swing and dried off the spot beside him before patting it and motioning in her direction. Peyton could no more stop herself from sitting down beside him than she could've stopped herself from breathing.

"And this?" He reached over and touched her cheekbone gently as she sat. "Is this from a few days ago too?"

Crap. The rain would've washed away all her carefully applied makeup. She felt sort of naked without it. She pulled her knees up to her chest and wrapped her arms around them, deciding not to answer his question. She didn't want to talk about Dennis, not when he was almost in her rearview mirror.

"I'm really sorry about your dad, Cade."

He set the swing gently into motion.

"Thanks. I don't know what I'm going to do without him. You may have been the one who first encouraged me with my music, but if he hadn't insisted I take a couple of semesters off from college and see what I could make happen in Nashville, I don't know that I ever would've taken the leap. I wouldn't have had the guts to try."

He stopped the swing and looked away. "That sounds stupid, doesn't it? Poor rich boy stuff. It didn't matter if I made it in Nashville because I was already independently wealthy."

She unwrapped her arms from her legs and touched his elbow. "No. The desire to create...I completely understand that."

"You still doing all your film stuff?" He smiled at her and resumed swinging. "You had such an eye for it, Peaches. A true gift."

"Yeah. I got a full ride to the London Film Centre. I leave in October."

He whistled through his teeth. "I'm not surprised. I remember what you could do as a freshman. I'm sure you've only gotten better since then."

Had he just shifted a little closer? She couldn't resist

relaxing into his warmth—even wet, his big body gave off heat.

"Maybe after film school, you can lower yourself and do a music video for me some day. Although, I guess having one song on the radio doesn't mean I'll have a long-term career in the industry."

"But you're going to stay in Nashville and try?" She turned a little so she could see him. Then he slipped an arm around the back of the swing making it easier.

"Yeah." He shrugged; she shifted closer. His arm slid down onto her shoulders. "Aunt Cecelia isn't as supportive as Dad was. And she now has controlling power over my inheritance until I'm twenty-five."

"Will that be a problem?"

"No, it doesn't bother me, and she and I came to an agreement. There was something I really wanted to invest in, and she said yes if I agreed not to fight her on other stuff."

"What did you want to invest in?" As soon as the words were out of her mouth, she wanted to take them back. They'd been friends once, but she didn't have the right to ask that now. "Sorry. I shouldn't ask."

He smiled and pulled her closer. "No. It's okay. You know how Baby's brother Finn and Zac Mackay just got out of the army? They're using the skills they learned in the Special Forces to start a survival and self-defense training facility. They're going to call it Linear Tactical."

"Wow." She didn't know Zac or Finn personally, but everyone from around here knew *of* them.

Heroes.

"I know I wasn't in the military like them, but those guys taught Baby and me damn near everything we know about fighting, the wilderness, tactical awareness. When we were growing up, we used to follow them around like puppies. This Linear Tactical thing they're starting—teaching survival skills to people? It's important. I can be a silent partner and help them get started."

"That's amazing," she whispered. "All of it."

He was quiet for a long minute. "Dad loved those guys too. He would've wanted me to do this."

She shifted so she was facing him, pulling one leg up onto the swing. The sadness pouring from Cade over losing his father was almost a tangible thing. "I'm glad you could make your aunt understand that."

"It's not about the money."

"Your dad loved *you*. He would've wanted you to be part of something you felt was important." She wrapped an arm around his broad shoulders, rubbing gently, wishing she could massage his pain away.

He leaned his forehead against hers. "You always understood, Peaches. Even when you were that quiet freshman kid, those big brown eyes took in way too much."

She gave a half smile. "Observation is one of those skills that will hopefully make me a better filmmaker. And with you, it was always easy to…listen."

Especially since she'd hung on his every word.

He shook his head. "Watching you watch me out of the corner of your eye made me feel like such a pervert."

"*What?*"

"For wanting to do this when you were barely fifteen years old."

Before she could process what his words meant, his lips were on hers.

She'd had a couple of boyfriends in high school—Sublette County, not Oak Creek—but this was different.

This was *Cade*.

This was so far out of what she'd ever thought would

be in the realm of possibility that she'd never even let herself fantasize about kissing him.

But if she had, it would've been exactly like this.

Kissing her like he couldn't get enough of her. Like she was the only thing in his world.

He touched her cheek again, this time with his thumbs as his fingers slid into her hair at her scalp, tilting her head so he could have better access to her mouth. Her hand came up to his shoulder and pulled him closer.

She couldn't stop the little needy whimper that escaped her. It was all she could do not to crawl into his lap.

But at the sound he stopped, dropping his hands from her head as if she'd burned him.

Where there'd been heat…was now only cold.

Chapter 3

Five Young & Stupid Years Ago

HE WAS the worst kind of bastard.

Cade held his hands up beside his head like he was being robbed at gunpoint, not touching Peyton at all. But the fact was, there was no bad guy here but *him*.

She'd just whimpered for God's sake. Had he scared her?

He leaned back so he could look in to her eyes, praying he wouldn't find tears. Fear. Praying he hadn't done some sort of damage.

"Peyton. I'm sorry." He ran a hand through his hair, wanting to pull it. "What the hell am I doing?"

Why couldn't he have kept it together? Kept everything gentle and light. Not leapt on her like he was some sort of a Neanderthal.

This month had been the best and worst of his life. He'd gotten a miraculous career break. One he'd thought might never happen.

But had also lost his dad—his best friend. The grief threatened to pull him under every time he thought about it.

He'd needed to get away from everything and everyone in Oak Creek. Even his aunt and all the people who'd meant well at the funeral. Just needed to be alone.

Or so he'd thought.

Until he'd seen Peyton's broken-down POS car on the side of the road. Peyton certainly wasn't the only one in Sublette County to drive an older Buick, but as soon as he'd gotten a closer look, he'd known it was hers.

She was back in these woods, like that summer after he'd graduated and thrown all the parties where she'd used to watch.

And he'd watched *her*.

She'd been so damn beautiful, so still and quiet— unnatural for someone her age. He'd wanted to scoop her up, sit her in his lap, and hold her. Watch the party with her. Let her know she wasn't alone.

She'd always been so goddamn alone.

And here she was again. Older, but still alone.

Talking to her the last couple of hours had soothed his soul. She'd always done that for him.

He should've kept everything friendly and conversational. Kept his hands to himself. She may be a legal adult, but she was still too young for him.

He definitely should not have brought up how much he'd wanted her even back when she was a freshman. How he'd known she'd had a little crush on him then—had seen those brown eyes watching him.

Once he'd started thinking about that, not touching her had been impossible. And that kiss.

One relatively tame kiss had nearly blown his damned

mind. His fingers itched to reach for her again, but stopped at her whispered words.

"I'm sorry."

She was sorry? He was the asshole here. "What are *you* sorry for? I scared the hell out of you because of my lack of control."

"What?" Her beautiful face scrunched up.

"I didn't mean to scare you, Peaches." He tried to smile. Wanted to make her understand what that kiss had been about. "I would never expect or demand something from you. I...I have always wanted to kiss you. Even back in that editing suite."

"*What?*" she repeated.

Yep, that's right sweetheart. You're sitting next to pervy-perv.

Could he be any bigger of a screwup? He normally was pretty good with people.

"I know. I'm sorry. We were friends, and I shouldn't have felt that way. You were too young." He shook his head.

But she'd always seemed so mature, even on that first day he'd stumbled across her in the editing suite. He'd been looking for a place to take his current love interest for some...chemistry lessons. He'd thought the editing room would be the perfect place.

Instead, he'd found a quiet little freshman with the biggest brown eyes he'd ever seen. The love interest had been promptly dismissed and forgotten.

The more time he spent with Peyton, the more he genuinely liked her. She didn't care who he was, how much money he had, or what sports team he might lead to the state championship.

But she'd cared about his music. When she'd heard him strumming his guitar one day, then found out he was humming a song he'd written himself... From that day on, she'd been on him to do more with his music. Write more. Sing more. Practice more.

Because of her, a seed had been planted. His music had grown, developed, morphed into more than a hobby. It had become his passion.

When he'd discovered the truth—that she kept a low profile because she wasn't zoned to attend Oak Creek High, he knew he had to keep her secret.

He also knew he had to keep away from her, despite the way he caught her looking at him some times. Dating him? That would have brought more attention than she'd wanted. Otherwise, make no doubt about it, he would definitely have dated her—respectfully and chastely, of course —until she was older.

But he'd forced himself to stay away.

"You wanted to kiss me even back then?"

Shit. It sounded even worse when she said it. He propped his elbows on his knees, stopping the swing. "I know. I'm sorry. You've always brought out this protective instinct in me. And passion. Evidently, being away from you for three years didn't curb that." God. He was making this worse. "I'm sorry I scared you."

"You didn't scare me."

Right. He rolled his eyes. "I pounced on you."

"It was unexpected, but I promise I wasn't scared."

He studied her, trying to decipher if she was fully telling the truth. Her eyes met his without any touch of fear. But...

"You're still too young." An adult, legally, but still too young.

She laughed, but there was nothing humorous about the sound. "I'm not young. I'm not sure I've ever been young."

She was right—she'd never been flighty or silly like

other young girls. She'd always been so solid. Focused. He looked at the bruise marring her delicate cheekbone and tucked a strand of hair behind her ear. "An old soul."

He needed to leave. Old soul or not, mature or not, he needed to stay away from her. He was about to stand when she reached out and grasped his hand.

"I'm not afraid of you, Cade. And I'm not a child." She blinked like she couldn't quite find the words. "I want this. I want *you*."

He couldn't stop staring at her lips. She was telling him she *wanted* him.

He had to get out of here.

She slid her fingers into his hair, her thumb touching the top of his ear so impossibly gently. A shudder ran through him. "Stay with me here tonight."

He closed his eyes. Like he'd always known, fighting himself was hard enough. There was no way he could fight them both.

He moved his hands to her waist and had her draped over his lap a second later, her chest flush with his.

"I could no more turn down that invitation than I could stop my next heartbeat." He kissed her softly, gently nipping at her bottom lip. "I have to be back in Nashville tomorrow."

Shit. He didn't mean that as cold as it might have come across. But he felt her smile against his lips. "I have to be in London in a few weeks. We both know this isn't permanent."

"At least not right now." Maybe not yet. This wasn't their permanent time, but it could still be special. Everything about it would be special. He'd make sure of it.

He kissed her, taking his time at first—nibbling along her lips, trailing his fingers through her thick mane of brown hair. But it wasn't long before he was deepening the kiss, pulling her up more fully against him.

When his fingers touched the cool skin of her taut belly, they both sucked in a breath. He watched her eyes, making sure this wasn't moving too fast for her, as his hands slid up to cup her breasts. He couldn't hold back the groan at the feel of her nipples against his palms.

He kissed along her neck, reaching for the buttons of her shirt. She slid it back from her shoulders as soon as it was loose, and he unhooked her bra, freeing her completely to his eyes.

He just stared. At her face, her breasts, the way her chest and shoulders rose and fell with each little breath.

"You're so damn beautiful, Peaches."

He had to be closer. When she gripped his hair and pulled him toward her, his lips zoomed in on her throat once more. He reached for her shoulders and leaned her back—those breasts a perfect offering for his mouth.

And he feasted.

Every time she sighed, he wanted to take her higher. Those little moans were about to drive him crazy.

But when she started grinding against him, head thrown back, eyes closed, his control nearly snapped. He moved his leg, setting the swing into motion, bringing her down harder on him.

She rewarded him with a stuttering gasp he didn't even think she was aware of. He moved his mouth back down to her breasts, nipping and sucking and devouring, but making sure he thrust up against her with his hips every time the swing reached the right position.

God, he wasn't going to make it inside of her at this rate. But he wasn't sure he cared.

He grabbed her shoulders and pulled her down hard against him as the swing thrust their hips even closer.

"Cade." Her voice was hoarse. Sexy. "I—I…"

She was close, the movement of her hips becoming wilder. He wanted her to let go. Wanted to see her face as she lost control.

"Yes, Peaches. Don't hold back."

He placed his leg down hard on the ground, stopping the swing and pulling her down harder to grind against him. He slid his fingers into her hair and covered her mouth with his as she cried out over and over, riding him.

He decided right then and there he wanted to hear that sound as often as possible—wanted to see her lose control as often as he could.

Maybe now wasn't their permanent time. But damn it, there would be. However long he had to wait. However often he had to fly to London.

It might not be right now, but they would be together.

He rubbed her back gently as she lay slumped against his chest.

He knew the exact moment the post-orgasmic haze started to fade. Tension crept into every muscle and she began to ease herself back.

"Cade. I'm so sorry that I…" she faded off, not looking at him.

He never stopped rubbing her back gently. "That you came on my lap and it was the sexiest thing I've ever seen? I hope that's what you're about to say."

She peeked up at him. "But what about you?"

"Well, one, don't you dare think that wasn't super-hot for me too, because it was. And if that's all you want to do tonight, that's more than fine."

He would survive. Somehow. But there was no way in hell he was going to pressure her.

"What if that's not all I want to do tonight?"

Then he would get on his knees and thank his lucky

stars. "Then I'd say to put your arms around my shoulders and hold on tight."

She immediately did just that and he couldn't stop his smile. Thunder crashed overhead. He stood up, her slight weight barely registering as she locked her legs around his waist, and he walked them towards the door. "How about we make our own storm that lasts all night?"

He growled, hands tightening on her hips as she reached over and nibbled on his earlobe then whispered, "There's nothing I could want more."

Chapter 4

Present

CADE STARED at himself in the hallway mirror.

Bloodshot eyes. Three days' worth of beard. A disheveled mop of hair that badly needed cutting. Every part of his body hurt like hell. He hardly recognized the haggard face looking back at him.

His stomach took that moment to growl loudly enough to actually startle him.

Everett Templeton handed him a cup of coffee and a plate with a sandwich on it. He'd been one of the first people Cade had met on the Nashville scene five years ago when his debut song released. Over the years, Everett had become Cade's writing partner, opening act, and close friend.

"You're a god among men, Ev." Cade took a sip of the brew, ignoring the fact that it was almost too hot to tolerate.

Everett shook his head. "You look like you're coming off a bender."

"Apt enough, I guess." Although this bender hadn't involved alcohol. Cade scrubbed a hand through his hair and glanced at the mirror again before quickly looking away.

"Get what you needed?"

Cade sat on the couch and took a bite of his sandwich. "Four solid songs. Good ones."

God knew it had been a while since that had happened.

A couple of years.

Everett sat in the overstuffed chair across from the couch and put his feet up on the coffee table. What would Aunt Cecelia say if she could see boots on the antique mahogany table?

Thankfully, she wasn't here. She was back in Oak Creek.

"Songs are good," Everett said. "But what about you, C? Did you get what *you* needed? Forget the music."

Cade put the sandwich down, his appetite gone. "Does it matter if I got what I needed? Doug ended up in the hospital."

He'd gotten hit in the head when a small lighting rig collapsed as he was walking backstage at a potential tour site.

"That very well could've been an accident."

"Maybe. But we both know it should've been me back there and Doug out front." If it hadn't been for a last-minute phone call from the label, that's how it would've happened—the rig would've collapsed on Cade.

Both of them looked up as Mark Outlawson, Cade's head of security, walked into the room.

"Mark, tell Cade the lighting rig situation with Doug was an accident. That would make my life so much easier."

Mark shrugged one of his linebacker-sized shoulders. "It's possible."

"But not likely." Cade ran a hand over his face. He definitely needed a shave.

"I looked over the rigging myself. It's *possible* it was an accident. But given the incidents we've been dealing with and the fact that you should've been the one who got hurt, I would say this looks like an escalation."

Incidents like a broken window at Cade's house, graffiti on the front gate, the shrubbery and trees along his property being poisoned and dying.

All had seemed like random or accidental acts. But Mark was looking deep—especially now that someone had gotten hurt.

The quiet, burly man had been with Cade for six months as head of his personal security. Cade had always needed security during big concerts and tours, but he'd sure as hell never thought he'd need security during his downtime. Mark had come highly recommended from the people he trusted most: his friends at Linear Tactical.

Cade rubbed his eyes. "So you think all this stuff is some sort of threat?"

The big man leaned up against the wall. "Absolutely a threat. To what degree, I'm not sure. Except for what happened to Doug, which honestly could have been unintentional, it doesn't look like the perp actually means harm."

Everett leaned forward, resting his elbows on his knees. "Are we talking some sort of stalker here?"

Mark shrugged. "There haven't been any letters or any identifying patterns, so if it is a stalker, it's not one who's seeking attention. We're not to the point where I would suggest getting law enforcement involved, but we could bring on some extra security guys if you want."

Cade leaned back onto the couch and forced himself to grab the sandwich and take a bite. "I really don't want. I like having as few people living in my personal space as possible."

Mark nodded. "I don't think added security is necessary. Right now, we're probably dealing with a run-of-the-mill disturbed person. Or hell, it could be a couple of teenagers just trying to make trouble for one of the local celebrities. But all that can change, so we need to keep our guards up."

Cade took another bite of his sandwich. "Roger that."

"You're sure we don't need more security?" Everett asked.

"Cade's a lot better than most of my clients. He's aware of what's going on around him and doesn't have his head up his ass like a lot of singers do."

Everett chuckled. Cade just took another bite of the sandwich. He wasn't offended. Being told by a former Navy SEAL that he didn't have his head up his ass was high praise indeed.

"I learned survival skills and situational awareness from some of the best in the business. I don't spend all my time strumming a guitar."

Mark nodded. "The Linear guys are definitely the best when it comes to those types of skills."

"Those are your Oak Creek people, right?" Everett asked.

"Yeah. My family."

Although the one he'd wanted most to be close to wasn't there. She'd taken off to London nearly five years ago and had completely ghosted him.

That still stung. After that night at the lake house with

her, he'd been all but ready to propose. He'd forced himself to leave while Peyton was still sleeping so that he wouldn't do something stupid like ask her to go to a film school in the US.

Or pull up roots himself and try to build his career in London.

He'd left her a note with damn near every telephone number he had. His email address. All his social media handles.

And he'd never heard one fucking word from her.

He would've thought he'd learned his lesson, but even now he still scoured through independent film trade magazines and websites—anything coming out of London—to look for her name.

Damn it, if she was going to throw away what they could've had, he wanted it to be because her passion for film had overwhelmed her.

Because anything else was unbearable to think about. Hell, it was all unbearable to think about.

"If it's okay, I'd like to dig a little deeper into everyone who's on your payroll." Mark's words dragged Cade out of the foggy Peyton past. "Whoever's doing this, even if we're dealing more with mischief and less with hostile intent, has a little bit too much access to you. Granted, you're not exactly stealthy about your schedule and activities, but I'd like to poke around a little bit."

Cade nodded. His inner circle was pretty small. Trusted friends like Everett, Mark, Mrs. Hollister, his housekeeper, and Lance, his record company liaison/personal assistant. Cade could vouch for all of them, and wouldn't hesitate to do so, but the other dozens of people he employed on a full- or part-time basis? Some of them Cade wouldn't recognize if he met them on the street.

Everett let out a sigh. "Why couldn't you get yourself a

nice, average twenty-year-old college girl stalker who mailed you her panties every week? I heard that's what happened to Lowell Thaxton."

"I have it on good authority that Thaxton is in big trouble with his girlfriend about those panties!" Lance's voice called out from the kitchen.

"I'd still take that over dead plants and head injuries," Cade shot back.

"Don't blame you!" Lance was generally excited about everything. "You know the label will pay for extra security if you don't want to pay for it."

It wasn't a matter of who would pay for it. Cade had more money than he was ever going to spend in this lifetime. "We'll deal with that if we get to that point."

Mark nodded. "Hopefully, it's not going to come to that."

"Do you think this is some sort of weird attempt to get us to call off or postpone the tour?" Everett asked.

It was a reasonable question, and it affected Everett too. Not only was Everett Cade's occasional writing partner, he would also be the co-act for the untraditional tour they were conceptualizing for next spring and summer. Everett was putting it all together. He was the details man. Everyone called him that.

Smaller venues. More intimate shows. Like what Cade used to play when he was first starting out. Cade missed that. Missed the music. The intimacy.

Cade shook his head. "No. I won't be dictated to. I'm not going to be scared off the tour."

Mark pushed off from the wall. "I agree, if only on sheer principle. We've got a few months. I'll make sure the security for the tour is sound. Meanwhile, I'm going to start my search."

With a brisk nod, Mark was gone.

"That dude is scary focused," Everett said.

Cade finished off the sandwich. "Scary focused is what you want as long as he's on our side."

Everett grinned. "True that."

"I need to shower. And a break from inside my head. Then maybe we can go over those songs I scratched out while I was in the writing cave."

The angst over Doug's accident had been good fodder for writing. Angst always was.

Everett stood up. "Deal. Also, you got an email from someone in Oak Creek. Lance and I went through your email, trying to keep you unburied when you resurfaced."

For just a second, Cade's heart leapt at the thought of an email from Oak Creek. He immediately tamped that down. If Peyton was going to contact him, she would've done it long before now. And if she did, it wouldn't be from Oak Creek.

"Baby?" He and Baby Bollinger still kept in touch regularly, although Baby tended to call.

"No, one of your Linear Tactical people. Something about a company picnic this weekend. They wanted to make sure you knew you were invited."

Cade nodded and headed toward the shower as Everett turned to the kitchen.

Maybe he should go to the picnic. Get away from all of this for awhile. He loved Nashville, the literal hustle of the city. Everyone here had a plan: one day, one month, five year. It had an energy and desperation that he hadn't experienced anywhere else except maybe Los Angeles. Cade's creative energy had thrived on it at first.

But now...except for the past couple of days, where anger and fear had fueled his writing process, his creative energy hadn't been much of anything lately.

He turned on the hot water in his walk-in shower and

peeled off the clothes he'd been wearing for the past seventy-two hours straight. He stepped in, not even attempting to hold back his moan as the water cascaded down on him.

He needed a change. Maybe long term. He couldn't always wait for something bad to happen in order to spark his creative instincts.

Maybe being outside in the crisp Wyoming air, around people he'd known his whole life, would give him the refresher he needed. And it wasn't like he'd have to worry about a stalker there—his best friends were some of the most highly trained former soldiers in the world.

For five years, he'd only gone back to Oak Creek on rare occasions. He'd tried to tell himself it was because his career had taken off and he needed to be close to where the action was.

But he couldn't lie to himself. Part of the reason he hadn't spent much time there was because the memories of Peyton still haunted him.

She'd left him behind without a word and taken his heart with her.

But it was beyond time to face that. The Linear picnic would give him as good an excuse as any to go.

It would be good to be around people without an agenda. People whose handshakes were nothing more than a friendly gesture, not the start of a proposition.

Cade needed time. Needed wide-open spaces. Needed friends.

Cade needed to go home.

Chapter 5

Peyton shot out the back door of Fancy Pants bakery and dashed for her car.

Mother fracker. Son of a biscuit.

She was going to be late again.

Even worse, she was using her there's-a-four-year-old-with-big-ears-and-a-bigger-mouth-living-with-me language even *inside* her own head.

But *shit*. She was going to be late and have to listen to another lecture from Cecelia O'Conner on the importance of punctuality and diligence in one's work.

As if it made such a huge difference whether Peyton cleaned the O'Conner house bathrooms at 3:30 or 3:37.

And all because she'd gotten caught up in capturing her friends Violet and Jordan developing a new recipe in the bakery's kitchen. The two had been having such a good time trying different flavors and textures in the pastry even though Jordan owned her own technology company now and no longer worked at Fancy Pants. Peyton hadn't been able to stop herself from grabbing her phone, regardless of it being an older smartphone model she'd bought used, and recorded as many clips as she could. She'd cut them together later and a mini-documentary.

Sigh.

Peyton refused to focus on that jagged little wound in her heart that never quite healed.

The what-ifs. The what-could-have-beens.

She had a house to clean. Job number three.

Peyton would've told Cecelia where she could stick her job and her lectures—would've stayed far, far away from anything having to do with the O'Conner family—but the pay was fantastic.

She was almost to the point where she was out from under her debt and able to make the exorbitant payments for Jess's school each month without having to buy the reduced-price meat at the supermarket.

Multiple part-time jobs: janitor for Linear Tactical, shop help at Fancy Pants, and housecleaner for the O'Conner family, as well as occasional waitress at the local bar, kept Peyton pretty busy. Plus, her most important and *full-time* job: mom to the best kid on the planet.

She loved that job but needed the other three pretty badly. Including cleaning the O'Conner mansion.

Peyton had history with the O'Conner family, including the nondisclosure agreement she'd signed five years ago involving Cecelia's nephew. If it was weird that Cecelia had hired her now, Peyton had decided not to look the gift horse too hard in the mouth.

Maybe Cecelia didn't know who she was. God knew, she and the older woman didn't tend to run in the same circles.

It was only by sheer happenstance that they'd even come face to face when Cecelia had picked up an order from Fancy Pants. Peyton had been working, Jess coloring at one of the nearby tables.

For a few minutes, Peyton hadn't even realized who Cecelia was, and once she had, she'd forced herself not to panic and do what she wanted to.

Take her daughter and run away as quickly as possible.

But she needn't have worried. Cecelia hadn't recognized Peyton either.

Peyton didn't know if that made it better or worse.

She only knew Cecelia had seen her cleaning service advertisement and offered her a job cleaning that giant house of hers a couple of weeks later. Offered too much for Peyton to dismiss it out of hand.

The money from working relatively few hours a week was paying for Brearley Academy, Jess's private school—one of the most sought-after and rigorous programs in the country. Peyton had been amazed when Jess had received an invitation to apply, even more so when she'd been accepted.

Of course, Jess was basically a four-year-old genius, so Peyton shouldn't have been surprised.

She pulled up to the O'Conner estate, a few miles out of Oak Creek proper, and used her security code—which only worked on certain days at certain times—to let herself in, dragging her cleaning supplies with her.

No sign of Cecelia. That was good. Get in, get out, move on.

Peyton hoisted her bag of supplies over one shoulder and made her way upstairs into one of the many bedrooms. There were six bedrooms, and seven baths, but since Cecelia lived in the house alone, there was mostly only basic cleaning to be done each week. That still took several hours.

And she still spent almost all of that time specifically *not* thinking about the fact that Cade had grown up in this house.

Not thinking about Cade at all. Which was what she should be doing right now.

She turned to the work at hand, digging out her dust cloth and furniture polish and wiping down the formal, expensive furniture, shelves and molding. Peyton could never live here. Jess would destroy the place in minutes with just her grubby fingerprints.

She'd only made it to the third bedroom when Cecelia's shrill soprano rang out from behind her. "I see you finally decided to arrive, Peyton."

Peyton took a breath before she turned around to face the older woman, reminding herself how much this job paid. "Hi, Cecelia. Yes, I was a few minutes late, but I'm already working, so there's nothing to worry about."

"Need I remind you how many people are willing to take your place if you cannot take this job seriously?"

Peyton could barely resist the urge to roll her eyes. "No. No need to remind me of anything. I will make sure to work all the hours you are paying me for and make sure your house is as clean as possible."

"Yes, well, you'll need to hurry. I have guests coming around five o'clock today, and you'll have to be gone by then."

"Sure, that's no problem."

"Well, then…" Cecelia flicked her wrist toward the bedroom, and turned sharply to leave.

Peyton didn't stick her tongue out at the other woman. That was pretty much the most that could be expected of her.

The hours slid by quickly as she went from room to room, first dusting, then vacuuming. She ignored the way her stomach tightened as she came to Cade's old room. She just did what she had done every week: straightened her shoulders and trudged on.

Hell, she'd done that ever since she'd watched that airplane leave without her five years ago.

Eventually, she worked her way through the bedrooms and baths upstairs and headed downstairs. She made her way through the formal sitting room and dining room and into the kitchen. It had its own staff, so it didn't need much.

Working out the kinks in her back, she walked into the far back den. This was the last room. Her favorite room. The only room that had escaped Cecelia's uber-formal decorating tastes.

The room Cade had hung out in with his dad to watch sports. The only room in the house Peyton had ever been in before she'd started cleaning. Instead of formal, the furniture in here was relaxed, homey, with overstuffed chairs and a comfortable couch facing the fireplace. There was a large flat-screen TV that took up nearly one whole wall.

Cade had brought her here because he'd said he wanted to be the first person to screen a Peyton Ward original movie—in this case, the peaches project she'd finished her freshman year.

Her heart had been in her throat the entire time, both from watching her hard work come to life on a relatively large screen and because Cade had been the one to watch it with her.

She loved this room. It held such a good memory. One that remained despite everything else.

She plopped down on the couch. She'd worked at Fancy Pants for hours this morning and then had come straight here. Cecelia never set foot in this room, so it was probably safe to take five minutes.

She melted into the leather sofa, stretching her legs in front of her. She wanted to sit for a second and rest. Not think about anything

She laid her head back and closed her eyes. Just a five minu—

"Peyton?"

Her eyes flew open—this was not Cecelia's nail-scratching-chalkboard soprano coming from behind her. It was a deep, masculine voice.

One she hadn't heard in more than five years.

"Cade?" She shot off the couch and turned.

He was here. Peyton's eyes ran over him, taking in the changes since she'd last seen him at the cabin. She'd seen him on television and in music videos, of course. No one could live in this area and escape talk of *the* Cade Conner.

She'd learned how to harden herself against seeing him on the screen. Distancing herself.

But in person, all those carefully-built defenses collapsed.

He took a step forward into the room, and she took a step back. She blinked a couple of times to make sure she wasn't dreaming.

Those blue eyes—oh God, those blue eyes that were so unbelievably familiar—narrowed in confusion. "Are you here to see me? Did you know I was coming?"

Was she here to see him?

Like she was going to show up now and casually wait for him on his couch?

She shook her head wildly. "Uh, no. No, I didn't know you were coming home today." As he circled the couch toward her, she moved in the opposite direction, keeping her distance.

His eyes narrowed further. "Okay. Are you here to see Cecelia?"

"Um, something like that." She glanced down at the dusting rag in her hands, and quickly hid it behind her back.

"Okay. Do you want me to get her?"

Peyton swallowed a bark of hysterical laughter. "No! No, I mean, it's okay. I'm fine."

He eyed her now as if she was some crazed animal who needed calming. They continued circling the couch: Cade approaching, Peyton retreating.

"Do you want to sit back down? I'm getting a little dizzy."

Did she want to *sit down*? And what, talk about old times?

She could feel the walls starting to close in around her. Her own breath sounded loud in her ears. She had to get out of there while she still could. She started backing toward the door.

"I'm sorry. I have to go," she mumbled.

She was going to throw up all over the place.

And the only thing she could think was that Cecelia would make her clean it up and Cade…would watch.

As she cleaned vomit.

In his house.

"Peaches?"

Oh no.

Oh no, no, no, no, no!

He took a step closer, hand outstretched.

"No! Don't touch me!" The words were way too loud, way too emphatic.

But if he touched her now, she would crumble. Forget cleaning vomit. Someone would have to clean *her* off the floor.

"I have to go. I'm sorry. I have to go." The last part came out as a sob. She turned and ran from the room.

In the hallway, she briefly remembered that her cleaning supplies were still in the back hallway. She didn't care.

Escape was the only thing that mattered.

Chapter 6

From her bed, Peyton heard the pattering of little feet and knew that there were only moments of peace left. She looked over at her clock—six thirty, not too bad, even though it was Saturday—then closed her eyes again as she heard her bedroom door creak open.

"Mommy!" The sweetest voice in the world. When Jess wanted to be. "Mommy, wake up!"

Peyton would never tire of hearing her daughter's rambunctious, loud voice. The child had absolutely no concept of quiet. Only loud and louder.

And laughing. The kid loved to flat-out belly laugh. You couldn't be around her for long without being caught up in it.

There'd been a while at first, when Jess's cries had been so pitiful and soft—when they'd come at all. Watching her as a premature infant struggle to breathe, struggle to *live*... Peyton would never get tired of hearing her now—even if it was at ear-bleeding volumes.

Peyton rolled toward Jess but didn't open her eyes. She let out a big snore. Jess giggled—loudly.

This was their morning routine, and it was Peyton's favorite part of the day. It wouldn't be long before Jess outgrew it.

"Mommy! Wake up lazy bones!" More giggling.

Peyton moaned like she was about to wake up but then snored again, even louder. Jess's laugh rang out, and she started poking Peyton on the shoulder.

"Lazy bones. Lazy bones. Wake up!"

Peyton kept her eyes closed as she scooted closer to the edge of the bed where Jess stood. She puckered her lips for a kiss. Jess kissed her sweetly, and Peyton's eyes opened.

"Morning, Mommy." Her face was right up next to Peyton's. All Peyton could see were bright blue eyes.

The same eyes she'd seen last night.

Peyton wrapped Jess in her arms and swung her up into the bed.

"Morning to you, baby girl."

Jess rolled her eyes. "Mom. Not a baby. I'm already in school, remember?"

"I know, kid. I'm pretty sure you'll be starting high school next week."

"Nah." Jess grinned at her. "Got to become empress of the elementary school first."

Empress of the elementary school? Where did she come up with this stuff? All Peyton could do was stare at her clever daughter and tuck a strand of hair behind her ear.

To be honest, there had been times she'd second-guessed her decision to raise Jess by herself. But she had no doubt that Jess was the single greatest thing that had ever happened—or ever would happen—to Peyton.

And if Cade didn't want her—or Peyton—then he could shove his guitar right up his...

"Let's go have pancakes!" Jess wiggled free and slid down the side of the bed. "Aunt Riley's here."

Peyton sighed. She had hoped for a few more minutes of snuggling. And honestly, a few more minutes of not having to face the real world and the literal and figurative mess she'd left yesterday.

But she got up and dressed in her normal house-cleaning attire of khakis and a T-shirt. The last thing she wanted to do was go over to the O'Conner estate, even to pick up the supplies she'd left there. Cecelia probably already had a lecture planned out.

And the thought of seeing Cade again...

Peyton would rather just stay in bed for the rest of her life.

It had caught her so off guard. When she'd first started working there, she'd been terrified Cade might show up. But he never had.

And then yesterday he'd had the nerve to ask if she wanted to *sit down and talk*? After everything that had happened between them?

Peyton had never been someone to get angry. She'd always been quiet—had learned from an early age that keeping her head down and her opinions to herself was the least painful way to survive. She'd learned how to express herself in a different way. Through film.

For as much good as that had done her. Once London had been taken away, there hadn't been many choices for a film career for someone with a great aesthetic eye but without training or contacts in the business. Especially not in the heart of Wyoming.

She glanced at her reflection in the bathroom mirror as she brushed her teeth. No, she didn't have a career in the field she'd planned. She didn't really have a career at all.

But she had a fantastic daughter—one who at not quite

five years old wasn't afraid to speak her mind. Who never lived in fear. Who was happy and healthy and loved. *That* was the biggest win, and more important than any job or career.

And hell, maybe Peyton would just get a late start. Go to film school in her thirties or forties.

So what if that seemed far away and ate a little at her soul each day?

Damn it, she wasn't pathetic.

She turned away from her reflection and headed out to the kitchen. She wasn't surprised to find eight-year-old Ethan Bollinger at the stove next to Jess. That kid was here more often than he wasn't, not that Peyton minded. He had saved Jess's life four months ago, or they'd saved each other's lives, or something.

All Peyton knew for sure was that they'd been trapped out in the woods with a killer. Ethan had ended up with a compound leg fracture protecting Jess. But at least they'd come back alive.

So yeah, Ethan could come around whenever he wanted. Not that Jess would allow it to be any other way. Not with *her* Ethan.

Peyton walked to the coffee maker and poured herself a cup. "Ethan, has your new brother made it into the world yet?"

He glanced over his shoulder, grinning, looking so much like his dad, Finn, and uncle, Baby, she couldn't help but smile herself. "Nope. Charlie says he wants to make the most dramatic entrance possible—just like Dad did when he saved her that one time."

Peyton was glad Ethan could smile about it. Then again, he'd been sheltered from the worst of what had happened to Charlie. Finn had indeed made a dramatic entrance to save her.

And now they were married and Charlie was about to give birth any day now.

"Charlie also says that if anyone mentions a whale anywhere around her, she can't be held responsible for her actions." Ethan turned back to the stovetop.

"Or hippo," Jess chimed in. "Uncle Finn said, 'What about hippos?' and Aunt Charlie threw a frying pan at him."

Ethan shook his head. "Then Dad was stupid enough to say, 'I didn't even know you knew how to use a frying pan.' Then he ran."

Jess and Ethan looked at each other and laughed—that big belly laugh Peyton loved so much. She was glad they found it funnier than Charlie obviously *didn't*.

"Stay out of the line of fire, you two." Peyton sat down at the table next to Riley Wilde. Her friend was still in her nursing scrubs. "Aren't you supposed to be supervising the pancake-making?"

Riley looked up from whatever she was checking on her phone and grinned. "Why? We both know those two can out-cook us any day. We went over basic stove top safety, and I told them that just because I was still in uniform didn't mean I wanted to perform any medical care."

Peyton looked over at the kids. They were having a good time. "Thanks for coming by and pretending to supervise."

"Speaking of medical care, I didn't almost kill myself on your cleaning stuff trying to get through the mud room."

"Yeah, I left it at a client's. I have to swing back by there today." Peyton took a long sip of her coffee, hoping Riley would take the statement at face value.

Riley got up to grab the first round of pancakes, and Peyton thought she might be safe.

No such luck. Riley slid a plate in front of Peyton as she sat back down then poured enough syrup on her own pancakes to put herself into a diabetic coma. "You left your stuff over at Linear?"

"No. The O'Conner house."

Riley's eyebrow raised over her fork. "You wanted a little extra time with Cecelia O'Conner today? Didn't get enough of that fun sauce yesterday?"

Peyton concentrated on cutting her pancake into a perfect square with her fork. "I, uh, got flustered and ran out."

Riley slammed her fork down. "God dam—" She cut herself off when both children spun around to catch the bad word. "I mean, gosh dang it." Her volume dropped to a whisper. "Did Cecelia say something to upset you? We can go over there together right now and give her a piece of our mind."

"Cecelia wasn't the problem."

Riley rolled her eyes. "Cecelia is *always* the problem. I know she pays you well, but she has no right to say anything about *anything*. Especially not now, years later. What did she do?"

Peyton cut another piece of pancake with deliberate care. "Honestly, it wasn't anything Cecelia did."

She finally glanced up from her plate. "Cade showed up."

Riley stared at her hard for a moment, then pushed her plate away and stood, walking to the kids. "You guys have enough pancakes? Time to turn off the stove. Your mom and I need to go outside and talk."

"Okay," Jess said. "We have six for both of us, so that might be enough."

Riley got the kids settled at the table, then grabbed Peyton's hand and pulled her out back onto the tiny patio, closing the door with a resounding thump.

"Are you okay?"

Riley was the only person Peyton had ever told the whole story about Cade and Jess. And she shouldn't have —*legally*—done that.

"I—I could've handled it better. I wasn't expecting to see him."

"Did you stab him in the eye with the nearest sharp object?"

Peyton let out an exasperated breath. "No, I refrained."

"Then I think you handled the situation just fine."

"The man was just visiting his childhood home. It hardly called for violence."

Riley crossed her arms over her chest. "You forget that I was at the hospital, Peyton, both times. I was there when we almost lost you, and I was there when we almost lost that little mini-you in there."

Riley had been one of Peyton's nurses, then had become a close friend. Peyton walked over and grabbed her shoulders. "I know you were. You were there when nobody else was. When I was invisible to everybody else. You've looked out for Jess and me, and you know I love you to death."

Riley unfolded her arms and pulled Peyton in for a hug. "What Cade did to you was wrong. He may not have put you in the hospital, but he should've been there to help out. Maybe not with the Dennis incident, but at least for when you had Jess."

"I signed the—"

"I don't care what you signed. The O'Conner family was one of the richest in the state before Cade went off and made millions in Nashville. Fucking hell, he should've

47

at least paid for the hospital bills even if he was dick enough to knock you up and then refuse to have anything to do with you."

"What happened with Dennis wasn't Cade's responsibility."

And neither was Jess once Peyton had signed the paperwork Cade had sent her when she'd notified him she was pregnant. An agreement to terminate the pregnancy and sign a nondisclosure agreement never to talk about anything that had happened with Cade.

In exchange, Peyton had gotten a check for ten thousand dollars and his word not to drag her into a nasty court battle.

She'd needed the money, so she'd taken the check. But she hadn't terminated the pregnancy as agreed.

She didn't know exactly where that left her legally, but she wasn't going to risk anything by demanding child support now.

Peyton hugged Riley tightly then stepped back. "This is an old argument. And it doesn't change the facts."

Peyton could see her friend visibly swallow her words. She wanted Peyton to go before a judge, require a paternity test, and force Cade to take responsibility for Jess.

Peyton wasn't going to do it. She wasn't going to drag her daughter's very existence through the mud for everyone to see and gossip about. Jess was too smart, too sensitive not to be affected.

Jess was hers. That was enough.

Riley sighed. "Okay. We won't talk about it today. But are you alright? Obviously, if you ran out without your stuff, you were pretty shook. What did you and Cade say to each other?"

Peyton rubbed her eyes. "I think he was just as

surprised to see me. He thought I was visiting Cecelia. . .or him."

Riley shook her head in disbelief. "Like you heard he was coming into town and decided to stop by his house five years later? After everything?"

"Yeah. Pretty much exactly like that."

Riley leaned back against the porch railing. "You know, I knew Cade when we were growing up. He was younger than me, ran in different circles, and his whole family was rich as God, but he was never an asshole. If I hadn't seen what he'd done with my own eyes, I would've never believed him capable of something like this."

"Listen," Peyton said. "I've been fortunate. I know Cade has been back a couple of times, and I was able to avoid seeing him. I don't know how long he's back this time, but the fact of the matter is Oak Creek is his hometown. The Linear guys are his guys too."

"If the Linear guys knew——"

Peyton shook her head, cutting Riley off. "But they don't. And they're never going to."

Riley let out a sigh and crossed her arms over her chest again. "All I'm saying is they would kick his ass. Hell, Boy Riley has taught me some moves. *I'll* kick Cade's ass."

Riley's long-term boyfriend, also named Riley, was an extreme sport YouTube sensation. He wasn't in Oak Creek very often, but Peyton had no doubt he'd taught his girlfriend a few moves.

"Nobody is kicking anybody's ass. Hell, it was so long ago, Cade probably wouldn't even know why some midget nurse was attacking him."

"I prefer ninja midget nurse, if you don't mind," Riley huffed out.

"Alright, ninja midget. I need you to be cool. You can't

let anyone know I've talked to you about this, especially Cade, or I'm in big legal trouble. Let's just get through however long he's here. Keep everything as easy as possible."

"What can I do to help?"

"Watch the kids while I go get my stuff."

Chapter 7

Mark hadn't been thrilled about Cade going out for a run on his own.

But since Cade was more than capable of protecting himself, and wasn't the damn president, he'd gone anyway. He wasn't going to change his life or his routine because of a stalker he may or may not have in a completely different state. Here he had home turf advantage.

Neither Mark nor Everett were going to be thrilled when they got his text that he wasn't coming back to his house. He'd had one built a few years ago, much farther from town, when it had become evident that way too many people knew where he lived if he stayed at Cecelia's house.

There hadn't been any real problems at Cecelia's house over the years when he'd come to visit, but no privacy either. The new place allowed him a lot more freedom since it was farther away from town.

But right now, what Cade wanted wasn't at his new home; it was back at his aunt Cecelia's.

He wanted to know why Peyton had been sitting on the

couch in the den yesterday as if she'd visited the house dozens of times before.

And he sure as hell wanted to know why she'd completely lost her shit at seeing him again. He couldn't lie, he'd thought about what it would be like to see her again. He'd imagined her laughing nervously and apologizing for not responding to any of his texts or emails.

Or maybe she wasn't sorry at all for ghosting him. She'd had a life trajectory planned out before they'd spent that night together, and Cade hadn't been part of it. Honestly, he could respect refusing to let anything derail her.

But yesterday, seeing her look at him with something akin to fear in her eyes? That he couldn't stomach.

He slowed down to a jog as he finished five miles and started up the driveway to his aunt's house.

Maybe Peyton was just a little nervous about his celebrity status. It wasn't something he thought about a lot, but he knew it could affect people. He would hate it if that was true, but he would deal with it.

But it hadn't seemed like that at all. It wasn't a sort of starstruck or even embarrassed discomfort.

It had been a *get the hell out of here as fast as possible* discomfort.

Cade was going to have answers, there was no doubt about that. He'd start with his aunt. Maybe figuring out the relationship between Aunt Cecelia and Peyton would provide some insight.

He pushed for speed the rest of the way up the long driveway, then decided to go into the back rather than the front.

That's when he saw the vehicle.

Peyton was still driving that POS Buick? He could

hardly believe that thing still ran. It had been on its last legs five years ago.

One more question.

He was about to have answers.

He let himself in the backdoor, grabbing a dishtowel to wipe off the worst of the sweat. He didn't want to be smelly and disgusting when he faced Peyton again.

"I-I had an emergency and had to leave. I'm sorry."

Cade stopped in the middle of the kitchen at the sound of Peyton's voice in the front formal living room.

"You should be sorry," Cecelia shot back. "Not finishing your duties then leaving your supplies all over the house where I had to pick them up is unacceptable. I thought I was paying you to clean, not vice versa."

"With all due respect, Cecelia, I finished all but one room and only left the supplies in one area, not all over the house. I can finish cleaning today if you want."

Cade stood there trying to make sense of what he was hearing. Peyton was *cleaning* his aunt's house? His house? That couldn't be right.

"No, that isn't necessary. I finished it myself. I placed your supplies in the first garage. Please just get your things and return next week. I'll allow you to continue since we've never had any issue like this since you've started working here. Don't make it a habit."

Peyton muttered something he couldn't hear. A few seconds later, the back door opened and then shut. Cade stood frozen in the middle of the kitchen holding the dishtowel in front of him, sweat dripping on the ground.

What the hell was going on?

Peyton was gone, but that was probably for the best anyway. He needed to know what he was dealing with before talking to her.

He finally forced his legs to work, walking toward the living room, wiping sweat as he went.

"Aunt Cecelia, was that Peyton Ward you were just talking to?" As if he had any doubt.

Cecelia turned around, hand at her heart, strained smile on her face. "Cade! I didn't realize you were coming back here today. Aren't you planning to stay at your house? Of course, this is your house too, I don't mean to imply otherwise. You're always welcome here."

"I was out for a run and decided to stop by and talk with you. That was Peyton, right?"

Her smile became more strained. "Why, yes dear. Do you remember her?"

"We were…friends in high school." He took another step into the room. "Does she clean the house for you?"

Her lips pressed together. "Yes, that's right. She comes in once a week and does basic cleaning."

He reached up and wrapped the towel around his neck, trying to figure out exactly what was happening.

"Peyton Ward comes in once a week and cleans the house? How long has this been going on?"

Cecelia cleared her throat and glanced at the front door. "About a year. Is that a problem?"

Was it a problem? How had Peyton cleaned their house every week for the past year if she had been in London? Had she finished early? And even if so, why would she be back in Oak Creek cleaning houses?

"She was supposed to be studying film in London."

Cecelia's nose crinkled as she glanced away. "If I'm not mistaken, Miss Ward never left this area. And certainly didn't go to London."

"What?"

She gave a one-shouldered shrug. "Cade, not everyone is like you. Some people aren't cut out to succeed."

He opened his mouth to say something then closed it again when the words wouldn't come.

"Nothing was more important to Peyton Ward than going to film school," he finally got out.

Cecelia tilted her head and gave him a sad smile. "She was from Pinedale, right? Before she moved to Oak Creek? Worked at a gas station? I had her checked out before I hired her."

"Yes, all that's true but she had plans…"

"Her stepfather, Dennis Redman, is in prison. Did you know that?"

Cade shook his head numbly. No, he hadn't known that.

Cecelia walked over to him and patted him on the arm. "I didn't hold that against her. I still hired her since she had no criminal record of her own. But like I said, dear, some people aren't meant to be successful. It sounds like Peyton's family might be one of those."

"Peyton isn't like that. She was so driven…"

Cecelia shrugged again. "Well, she didn't go to college, and she makes a living cleaning. Perhaps the apple didn't fall as far from the tree as you might have hoped."

He shook his head, still trying to make sense of it all.

"It's best to leave it alone, don't you think?" she continued. "After all, you're only in town for a few days, right? I'm sure you're not going to run into her in that time. Or if you do, you should be very careful. She might try to take advantage of your celebrity status."

Cade stared as his aunt patted him on the arm then walked out of the room.

He had so many more questions. But he wasn't going to get the answers here.

CADE HAD Everett on the phone as soon as his aunt was fully out of the room.

"Dude." Everett let out an exasperated sigh. "Where are you? I thought we were going to go over the new songs you wrote. Not to mention Mark's about to send out a search party."

"I went out for a run. I need you to send a car for me over at my aunt's."

Everett's voice dropped. "You okay? I'll come get you myself."

"No. I need you to research an address for me. Send someone else with a car that I can take alone."

There was a noticeable pause. "Okay. I'll send Lance and have someone follow to bring him back. You planning to run away to join the circus?"

Cade couldn't even muster a laugh. "I need you to pinpoint the address of a Dennis Redman in Pinedale. And Renee, I think." He knew roughly where Peyton's parents lived, but she'd never actually invited him to her house, so he wasn't certain.

"Is this going to be hard info to obtain?"

"Probably not."

Everett paused again. "Is there a reason you need Redman's address?"

"I need some questions answered."

Everett let out a sigh. "Maybe we should try Google first."

"Do it, Ev. It's important. I need it now."

"Fine. Lance is on his way over with a car. Call me when he gets there."

Cade showered quickly, changed into some clothes he found in his old room, and was waiting when the car arrived.

"Everything okay, boss?" Lance asked. "Everett said you're going to get in a rumble or something."

Cade rolled his eyes. "No. Just need to find some answers."

Lance's eyes narrowed. "Sure you don't want some help? Does this have something to do with the stalker?"

"No. Nothing at all to do with that. Just an old friend I want to see."

Cade thanked his friend and got into the car Lance had brought, calling Everett as he pulled down the driveway.

"You didn't tell me you were going to visit a convicted criminal," Everett said without greeting.

Cade wasn't surprised Everett had already found that out. Everett knew people who could get the answers he wanted if he couldn't find them himself. "Is Redman out of jail?"

"No, he's still in. For assault and battery."

Shit. "And Renee?"

"Looks like she still lives in Pinedale." Everett gave him an address.

"That sounds right."

"You going to tell me what's going on, man?"

"I have some questions I need answers to." Cade disconnected the call before Everett could ask more questions of his own. His friend would forgive him.

Pinedale was like Oak Creek's poorer relation. The cousin who couldn't quite measure up: school system, medical care, general employment, everything.

Everybody in both counties knew it, but it had never been as evident to Cade as it was now as he drove to Peyton's parents' house.

He wasn't even sure *house* was the correct word for

these buildings. He was surprised some of them would make it through a Wyoming winter.

He pulled up at the correct address, one near the end of the street, this one not any worse—or better—than the others. Taking a breath, he got out of the car and walked up to tap on the door.

The door cracked open slightly. "Yeah?"

Definitely not Peyton. "Hi. I'm looking for Peyton Ward. I'm a friend of hers." Not entirely accurate, but close enough.

The door opened a little wider, enough for him to see a woman probably in her late forties staring out at him with narrowed eyes.

Deep, brown eyes. And that wasn't the only resemblance she had to Peyton—same slight build, same brown hair. "Peyton doesn't live here no more."

"I know she still lives in this area. I ran into her yesterday. Would you mind telling me where she lives?"

"She moved in with Riley Wilde after...after she left here. Then got her own place. But I can't be just giving out her address."

"No. I understand." Damn it, now he was going to have to hunt down Peyton's address himself. Asking Everett would lead to questions he didn't want to answer. But getting her address himself was going to take longer, and Cade was damn near going out of his mind already.

While he had Mrs. Redman, he had to ask the question that had been burning in his mind. "Did Peyton really not go to film school in London?"

He prayed Cecelia was wrong. The rumor mill didn't always get information right.

Renee's eyes narrowed. "Aren't you that singer from the country music channel? The one everyone's always talking about? You're Cecelia O'Conner's kid."

"Actually, I'm her nephew." He let out a sigh. "And right now, I'm just someone looking for a friend, nothing more."

"If you want to leave your number, I'll tell Peyton you were looking for her." She stepped back from the door and a few moments later came back with a pen and pad of paper. That's when he could smell the alcohol on her breath. It was pretty early on a Saturday morning for that, but Cade didn't comment. He wrote his personal direct line on the pad, well aware Renee might sell it and never give it to Peyton at all, leading to him having to change his number yet again.

"If you would make sure she gets this, I would truly appreciate it."

She nodded. "Will do."

Somehow that didn't reassure him.

"Will you at least tell me if she went to film school?"

Renee backed farther into her house, closing the door so it was only open a crack again. "No. She never did."

He closed his eyes, trying to process it

"Why?"

"That's something only Peyton can answer."

The door closed with a resounding click.

Cade walked slowly back to his car.

Peyton hadn't gone to film school. She'd had such a fundamental talent, and she hadn't gone. Why?

He hadn't even been in his car for ten seconds when his phone rang. Everett again.

"What do you want?" Cade bit out.

Shit. He shouldn't take his foul mood out on his friend.

Everett wasn't fazed. "This little wild goose chase doesn't happen to have anything to do with a Peyton Ward does it?"

Cade let out a curse under his breath. "Why do you ask?"

"You know I wasn't about to leave this alone. I wanted to know what we were dealing with here."

Peyton wasn't something he wanted to discuss publicly. "We're not dealing with anything. I'm merely trying to touch base with someone I went to high school with."

Everett was uncharacteristically quiet.

"What?" Cade finally asked.

"Nothing, man. Your business is your business. Just, according to her address at the time, she should've gone to Pinedale High School, in Sublette County."

"It was complicated. Look, it's not a big deal, and doesn't involve anything with my music, I have a few questions for her; that's all."

"Did you get your answers?"

"No. She doesn't live at home anymore, of course. Let's just drop the whole thing."

Cade wouldn't be dropping the whole thing, but Everett didn't need to know that.

"Sure. No problem. Like I said, your business is your business."

Cade felt like a jerk. Everett had been one of his best friends for years, and Cade was being a secretive asshole. "Everett. . ."

"Cade, it's okay. Whatever reason you have for wanting to keep this private, it's okay. But I want to say one thing, and maybe save us all a bunch time."

"Yeah, what's that?"

Everett let out a sigh. "If you're still looking for Peyton Ward you might want to try her current employer."

"My aunt Cecelia?"

"No. *You.* Peyton Ward works part-time for Linear Tactical."

Chapter 8

Cade made it to the Linear picnic much earlier than he'd originally expected to. His first inclination was to storm around until he found Peyton and got his answers, but he forced himself to pause.

He'd learned patience in the very same woods surrounding him right now, with some of the same men currently milling around or manning the grill. It was with them he'd learned that tactical advantage usually came to whoever was willing to best plan for it. Sometimes, planning included waiting. Gathering as much data as possible.

He wouldn't necessarily call Peyton his prey, but he was definitely on the hunt. He hadn't seen her yet and didn't want to draw attention to the fact that he was looking for her. But he was going to find her, no matter what it took.

"Is Nashville that bad?" Baby clasped him on the shoulder before sitting down on top of the picnic table next to him. "You vaguely resemble a soldier on the lookout for the enemy."

That was part of the problem, wasn't it? Cade wasn't

sure exactly what Peyton was in this situation. Friend? Enemy? She was an unknown entity.

He forced himself to relax and give an easy smile to his best friend since childhood. "Occupational hazard, I guess. You get used to people always trying to use you for stuff. Although, I know I don't have to worry about that here."

Baby chuckled. "You got that straight. Most of the people here are more likely to remember the time we toilet papered Mr. and Mrs. Mazille's house than remember whatever your best-selling album was."

And that's why this was home. Because no one here was going to ask him for his autograph, but they damn sure might ask him to help move a couch or take the trash out to the dumpster. Cade relaxed a little bit more.

Hell, most of the people here were much more concerned and excited about Dorian and Ray's presence than they were Cade's.

It was good for him. Reminded him who he really was. Living in the limelight made it too easy to get caught up in all that. To start believing his own press. Home grounded you.

But he still needed answers.

He chatted with Baby and a couple of the other Linear guys for a few minutes, forcing himself not to make any inquiries about Peyton, until he saw Riley walking in from the parking lot. He quickly moved in her direction.

He wasn't sure how or why Peyton and Riley had ended up living together after Peyton moved out of her parents' house.

He was finding out there wasn't much of anything he knew about Peyton.

He quickened his steps to get over to Riley before she got too far from the driveway. He'd prefer to have this conversation where no one else could hear.

He knew the exact second Riley saw and recognized him. Her look actually stopped him in his tracks.

Celebrity status was part of his job. Cade had never sought it out, and a lot of times it was a pain in the ass. But he was pretty used to it now and tried to take it in stride.

People reacted to him in a myriad of ways. Some were giddy with excitement. Some seemed to have a crush without even knowing him. Some, usually men, felt threatened, like they had something to prove.

But no one had ever looked at him with downright hatred in their eyes like Riley Wilde was looking at him now.

He racked his brain for something he might have said or done to her to justify any feelings that intense toward him. He couldn't remember talking to her at all. He'd never slept with her. Despite what the tabloids sometimes wanted to report, Cade had been selective about who he spent his time with romantically. Honestly, he just hadn't had much interest.

With a breath, he forced himself to start walking forward again. He was imagining things. Riley had no reason to dislike him.

But her scowl grew darker as he got closer. He put on his best smile, the one he normally reserved for talk show appearances, as he reached her side.

"Hi, Riley." She didn't look like there was a snowball's chance in hell that she would shake his hand if he extended it, so he left both hands at his side. "I'm Cade—"

"Oh, I know exactly who you are."

Oookay.

"Well, I was hoping I could ask you a couple of questions."

"Oh yeah? About what, exactly? If you need medical advice, you should ask Annie Griffin. She's an MD."

"No, I don't have medical questions." He wouldn't ask her even if he did. She seemed more likely to kill him than heal him.

"That's probably wise," she muttered.

"I actually have a question about Peyton Ward. I understand you guys were roommates?"

He watched as the anger slid completely from Riley's face, a blank mask replacing it.

"Yes. We were a few years ago."

Her tone was as emotionless as her face. The fact that she'd been so heated a couple moments before made it conspicuous.

And weird.

Jesus, what the heck was going on today?

Cade drew on every ounce of patience he had left. "Look, I don't mean her any harm. I'm just trying to figure out why she didn't go to the London Film Centre five years ago like she was supposed to."

Riley's neutral mask slipped. "Are you kidding me right now? Is this some sort of test?"

"A test?"

Her eyes narrowed. "To see what I know? What I'd say to you? After all this time?"

He ran a hand through his hair. Lance was always on him to do that more. Said it gave him a sexy, tousled look. But right now, it was the look of a man who was about to completely lose his shit.

"I have no idea what you're talking about. All I'm trying to find out is why Peyton never went to film school. Why she was cleaning my aunt's house yesterday. Why she evidently also works part-time for Linear Tactical instead of somewhere else like Hollywood."

Riley's slap across his face caught him completely by

surprise. By the look on her face she hadn't been expecting it either.

They both stood there staring at each other until she finally stepped back from him, her hands clasped into fists at her sides.

Cade forced himself not to move a muscle. He was never going to raise a hand to a woman, and especially not to one he'd grown up with. He might not know Riley well, but she didn't have a reputation as being violent or hot-headed.

So he waited for her to explain what the hell was going on.

She took a deep breath. "Why is Peyton cleaning for a living? Well, let me see. Not all of us are independently wealthy. So when Plan A doesn't work out, we have to make the best we can out of Plan B. That's what Peyton did."

Cade had no problem with that, even respected it. "Fine. But why didn't Plan A workout for her?"

Riley's eyes narrowed as she tossed her red braid over her shoulder. "This is a new level of assholery even for you, O'Conner. Are you wearing a wire?" She shook her head in disgust. "To officially answer your question: I don't know why Peyton chose not to attend film school."

Her words said one thing, but her face said the exact opposite. What wasn't she telling him?

"Damn it, Riley, I'm just trying to understand what happened. Why are you stonewalling me?"

She looked like she was going to slap him again. "Wow. The fact that you can say that with a straight face means you're more of a performer than anyone gives you credit for."

"Just tell me."

"Tell you what?" Her eyes got deliberately wider. "I

promise, Mr. O'Conner, I have no idea what you're talking about."

This was a nightmare. Obviously, there was something he didn't know. Something important. He scrubbed his hand across his face. "I don't understand. Please, I'm begging you."

She shook her head. "You really are convincing. I have to give you that. Okay, I'll bite. Peyton almost died, O'Conner. That's public record, so can't possibly be used against her."

"*What*? When?" And why would he use it against her?

"You really didn't know about that? What the hell is your end game? Five years ago, that bastard of a stepfather used her as a punching bag the wrong way. She fell down some stairs, and was unconscious for more than twenty-four hours. Nearly lost. . ." Her eyes narrowed again. "Is this a trick?"

He was about to pull his goddamn hair out "A trick? What are you talking about? She nearly lost what?"

Riley blew out a breath. "Her life. She nearly lost her life. She was in intensive care for a week. Everything changed for her, and she didn't make it to London. Okay? Are you happy with those answers? Do they meet the details of the fine print?"

He didn't know what the hell Riley was talking about. He was too busy trying to wrap his head around the fact that Peyton had nearly died, and he'd had no idea.

No fucking idea at all.

"Haven't you taken enough from her?" Riley whispered. "Just leave her alone. She doesn't deserve whatever it is you're bringing her way."

Cade nodded, only half processing whatever it was Riley had said.

Peyton had almost *died*.

"Is that why Dennis Redman is in prison? Because of what he did to Peyton?"

"Drunken bastard deserves a lot more than however many years they gave him. But at least he's out of her life." She tilted her head to the side, studying him. "You really didn't know about this, did you?"

He never would've stayed away if he had. No wonder Peyton hated him if she thought he'd known about all this and had just ignored her.

This was why she hadn't ever returned any of his emails. She hadn't been stonewalling him in London; she hadn't been there at all.

"I swear, Riley, on everything I hold holy, I didn't know."

He would've been there to support her. In the hospital, during the trial, to comfort her when the London Film Centre wouldn't hold her spot while she recovered. He could've helped fight for her. Maybe it wouldn't have made any difference.

But at the very least, she would've known she had someone by her side.

Riley shook her head. "Well, it doesn't make everything else okay, but I do believe you when you say you didn't know about this."

"I would've been there."

Riley's eyebrows rose so high, he thought she might actually hurt her face. "You're such an oxymoron, O'Conner. And a regular moron. I met Peyton because I was a nursing student at the hospital when she was there. I can't believe I didn't know her before then. She's an amazing person."

Cade had known that from day one.

He ran his hand through his hair once more. All day

he'd wanted to know what was going on. Now that he knew, it satisfied nothing in him.

He had to see Peyton. Right damn now. He itched with the need like an addict craving a fix.

"Thank you for telling me what happened."

"You leave her alone, O'Conner. You've done enough damage."

Cade nodded as Riley walked away, but it was in agreement with her second statement, not the first. Yes, he'd done damage. Not on purpose, but unintended wounds could still cut just as deep.

He wanted to make this right if he could.

And leaving Peyton alone? That was not in the cards.

Chapter 9

"Okay, Mom, play nice with the other kids."

Peyton rolled her eyes at her daughter's clever mouth. That kid.

They walked from the car to the main area where the Linear cookout was being held. Jess was about to take off. Ethan's dog, Skywalker, was already pulling her arm on his leash.

"You know the rules, squirt."

"Nothing sweet unless I ask, stay where the adults can see me, and most of all, no running off after any of the stupid dogs." Jess grinned at her over her shoulder. "Shouldn't say stupid, Mom."

Peyton shook her head. "Get out of here before I decide I'd rather go live the wild, single life out in Hawaii."

"As if you're not taking me to Hawaii with you." Jess laughed and ran off.

This was a safe place. There wasn't anything anyone here wouldn't do for Jess.

But still, just knowing Cade was in Wyoming made

Peyton want to grab her daughter and run as far away as possible.

She hadn't been sure she was even going to come today, but Cade had never shown up at any of the Linear activities, so she figured she was safe. Plus, she'd promised Jess.

They really had to work on that kid's FOMO—fear of missing out—levels. Her little social butterfly couldn't stand the thought there might be fun to have that she wasn't part of.

Just had an interesting talk with What-a-Dick O'Conner.

Peyton stared at the text from Riley, not sure whether to laugh or flee the state.

Where are you? she shot back

I'm here.

Peyton looked up and found Riley rushing toward her. A feeling of anxiety pooled in her belly and got intensified when she saw her friend's face.

"Oh my gosh, he's here, isn't he?"

Riley pulled her in for a hug. "Don't panic. We knew this was going to happen sometime. Oak Creek is too small for you to never run into each other again. You haven't done anything wrong."

Except for lie about terminating her pregnancy and not tell him he had a child.

"Right. I won't bring it up, and surely he won't ask."

Riley nodded. "Of course not. Although. . .never mind."

"What?"

Riley shrugged with a grimace. "I don't think he knew about the Dennis incident. The hospitalization. That's what I actually meant when I said I had a weird conversation with him. He wanted to know why you hadn't gone to film school."

"He asked about London?"

"Yeah. I thought it was a test to see if you had broken the terms of your NDA, so I was careful not to say anything about the pregnancy. But honestly, I don't think he knew anything about what happened with Dennis."

Peyton wasn't sure how she was supposed to feel about that news. In the greater scheme of things, did it really matter if he did or didn't know Dennis had put her in the hospital? Cade had refused to talk to her when he found out she was pregnant. Why would he have helped her in the hospital?

Peyton spent the next couple of hours trying to enjoy the picnic while avoiding Cade. Between all the Linear employees and their significant others, the gathering was like a large family reunion. Boisterous and fun, but easy to avoid someone if you were careful to keep a lookout and move in a different direction. Besides, everyone was damn near giddy about seeing Dorian and Ray again. Peyton wasn't sure of the exact details about why the couple had needed to move away from Oak Creek; all she knew was that she missed the big, quiet Dorian and owed both of them a debt she could never repay for rescuing Jess and Ethan a few months ago.

Nobody could miss the tension that permeated the entire property when a stranger showed up mid-afternoon. Gavin and Heath both obviously knew the man, and the way Ray slipped her giant headphones over her ears and began backing toward the woods at the edge of the property, Peyton guessed the couple knew him also.

Trouble was brewing.

Sometimes, the Linear guys seemed to draw trouble like a magnet. Fortunately, they had the skills and aptitude to deal with it.

Peyton didn't have the same skills and strengths as Zac

or Finn or any of the Linear guys, but she had a heightened sense of survival. She'd managed to survive for ten years with Dennis around because she'd kept her head down and knew when to get the hell out of Dodge.

She headed into the office to get more tea out of the fridge, but that might have to wait. It might be time to grab Jess and get out now.

"You look like you're about to bolt."

Peyton froze completely at the sound of Cade's voice. She'd been so busy watching the situation with the stranger unfold she'd forgotten that there was a much bigger danger to her present.

She drew in a breath and forced herself to be calm. *It's all water under the bridge now.*

She turned to face him. "Cade. Sorry I wasn't able to talk to you yesterday. Hope you've been well. I've got to go——"

He dragged her into a nearly suffocating hug, cutting off her words.

But suffocating in all of the best, most impossibly wonderful ways.

Cade.

All she could smell was him. The scent of his soap—the same one he'd used in high school—crisp and clean and strong.

All she could feel was the strength of his arms wrapped around her, holding her so tightly, they were almost doubled. His hard chest pressed up against her face. His hand as it smoothed down her hair over and over.

All she could hear was the rumble of his deep voice as he began to speak. "I didn't know. I swear, I didn't know."

Peyton knew she should pull away. If she had a single ounce of pride, she would stomp on his toes, bite him through the thin material of his T-shirt, then step back and swing at him with the best right hook she had.

But for one brief moment, she wanted to believe this. Believe all of it. His words, his body, the sound of his heart as it thundered under her ear.

Something had died in her the day she'd received that registered letter. In five years, she'd never gotten close to another man. Mostly because she'd been too busy simply surviving, but also because her heart had been broken in every possible way a heart could be broken. So just for one fracking moment, she wanted to believe this beautiful lie.

She didn't touch him herself, didn't wrap her arms around him, but she didn't pull away either. She closed her eyes and let everything flow over her.

"I could've lost you. Dennis... I'm so sorry."

With those words, the bubble burst. He *could've* lost her?

What exactly did he think he'd done when he completely cut her out of his life? Made her sign a paper so that she could never ever speak about their relationship, even to her closest friends, without fear of legal ramifications? What had he thought he'd done when he paid her thousands of dollars to abort his child and calmly told her that if she tried to contact him, he'd pursue a restraining order?

And he was concerned that he could have lost her when Dennis threw her down the stairs?

Now she stepped back, ruthlessly tamping down the part of her that grieved over the loss of contact with him.

"Don't touch me."

She kept her eyes focused on his chest as his arms slowly dropped from around her.

"Peyton. . ."

She took another step back and forced herself to look up into his eyes. God, those eyes.

She pointed out the window. "It looks like there might be some trouble brewing with that stranger who just showed up. I think I'm going to take. . ." Peyton wanted to swallow her tongue. Was she really about to say that she was going to take Jess and go home? "It's probably time for me to get going."

Cade studied the situation at the picnic tables. "It looks like Gavin and Heath have it under control. Yeah, Dorian and Ray look a little nervous, but I think you've got enough professionals here to handle any trouble that might arise. Plus, Aiden or Baby have already gotten themselves into a tactical position in case any further uninvited trouble arrives."

She looked back out at the situation and was surprised he was right. Surprised not because Aiden and Baby had planted themselves somewhere to take out potential threats, but that Cade had been aware of it. "I didn't even know you knew Heath and Dorian and Ray. I thought you were a silent financial partner."

He shrugged. "I don't teach the classes or do any of the day-to-day Linear activities, but I've spent some training time with all the guys."

There was a hard look in Cade's eye. She recognized it from working around warriors all the time—focused, alert. Deadly, if needed.

God, it was sexy.

She needed to get out of here.

"I hope you're doing well, Cade. But I really have to go."

Because her poor, tin shell of a heart couldn't bear the tiny reverberations his presence was causing.

"You have every right to hate me. I thought you were happy off in London pursuing your passion, but that wasn't the case. I should've been more diligent."

"You know what?" It wasn't as hard to force the words out as she thought it would be. "Our past is over. We don't need to talk about it, don't need to rehash things. What happened five years ago. . . It happened. Things are different now, but I'm okay."

That was so true and so very, very false. But she wasn't about to get into it with him.

"Peyton, I —"

She held out a hand, stopping him. "Water under the bridge. Things don't always turn out the way we plan, but you have to make the best of the situation."

"I heard you with Cecelia today. That you've been cleaning her house."

"That's right. I clean houses for a living. I even clean for Linear Tactical. You have a problem with that?"

She'd done it because they allowed her to bring Jess with her to work. The guys at Linear had given her a job back when she really hadn't had many options at all.

"No, I have no problem with that if it's what you want to do."

She rolled her eyes. "What I *want to do*? No, this is not exactly how I saw my life turning out back in high school."

"So you would still make films if you could."

"Of course I would, dumbass." She slapped a hand over her mouth. What was it about Cade O'Conner that had always brought out a sass in her? No one else had even come close.

He gave her a little half smile. "That's the mouth I remember from all those hours in the editing suite."

She shook her head. "That girl doesn't exist anymore."

He took a step forward, intent—*intent focused on Peyton*—clear in those blue eyes. Her cavernous tin heart shuddered again at the reaction he stirred in her. And this time her equally-as-rusty lady parts followed suit. Everything in her body was aware of him.

"You're not quiet and shy. You've trained yourself to come across that way because it garnered you the least amount of attention. But I've always known that wasn't who you really were."

He was the only one who ever had.

She had to get out of here. There was much more danger in this room than there was outside with the stranger.

"I've got to go. Take care of—"

"I want to talk to you about something."

His voice held none of the teasing lilt it had a few moments before. Her panic threatened to swallow her. Did he know about Jess?

"Cade, I—"

"I want to offer you a job."

Peyton's mouth popped open; she forced it shut. That wasn't even close to what she'd expected him to say.

"A job? Like, cleaning?"

"No, like making a music video and a mini-documentary about the song. I want you to storyboard it out and have creative control. Direct it."

She stared at him. "Did you miss the part of my past where I didn't attend film school?"

"You and I both know that when it comes to the arts, school only helps so much. You have one of the greatest film eyes I've ever seen."

"But...but I don't have any equipment. I don't know anyone in the industry who could work on a production. It takes—"

He stepped closer. "I've made a number of music videos now. I know how many people it takes. And the label has them. But I want you to take creative control of this. Your artistic eye is what I want, Peaches. You haven't lost that. Don't even try to convince me you have."

She hadn't lost it. She still looked at everything through a filmmaker's lens—it was how her brain worked. She even had her own Instagram account where she posted stuff and had a pretty large following.

But this. . .

"Cade. There's so many reasons this is a terrible idea." The biggest of whom might come running through the door and calling her Mom any second, and then this whole jig would be up.

But God, how she wanted to do it. Just one project—to use the creative muscles that had become so atrophied from nonuse.

"The label would pay well."

"The label won't want to hire me at all."

He shook his head. "That's not true. The label is always on the lookout for new talent. I've used debut directors before."

Gah! It was so hard to find good arguments when she wanted this so much. "I have responsibilities. I couldn't just drop everything and do this. I can't leave Oak Creek. Everything would have to be brought here."

It was all true. She was still going to need a source of income after Cinderella's castle up and vanished, and she couldn't leave because of Jess.

But her requests were unreasonable. She was a nobody, less than a nobody in the film industry. No one would take her requests seriously.

"Peyton." He put his hands on her shoulders lightly. "We'll work around your other needs."

"That doesn't make sense. Why would you do that? I don't understand why you're even suggesting any of this to me."

His hands dropped from her shoulders. "I've been wanting someone with a new and different eye. Someone not already jaded by working in the business. It's only three or four weeks of your time."

"I just. . ." She couldn't articulate what she was feeling.

"Don't give up this chance because it's me. Surely, we can work together for a month. It's a chance to do what you love and get paid pretty well."

If it had been anyone else, she would've already said yes.

Was she really going to do this?

"What have you got to lose?" he asked quietly.

Everything. "Nothing, I guess."

He stuck out his hand for them to shake on it. "Let's do this. It's the perfect opportunity for us both. I'll make sure you have what you need."

"Okay." She took his outstretched hand, both terrified and thrilled.

"You won't regret it."

That she wasn't so sure about.

Chapter 10

It was perhaps his greatest idea ever.

Cade hadn't gone to the picnic with the idea of asking Peyton to be the creative force behind his latest music video or the documentary the label had been clamoring for, but damned if it hadn't worked out perfectly.

Of course, nobody was going to take the news well that Cade wanted to bring on a literal unknown to helm it. Not Lance, not Everett, not the label, but that was the good thing about where Cade was in his career; he had the pull, the freedom, to make demands he hadn't been able to make when he was first starting out.

Peyton had said yes, so this was going to happen.

Because hell if Cade could escape the thought of Peyton almost *dying*. From the moment Riley had told him, it hadn't been far from his mind. Peyton had almost died, and he'd had no idea.

The thought would be keeping him awake for a lot of nights to come too.

But it was more than Peyton's injury. Everything had

changed in his mind—what he'd thought of as reality was wrong. Peyton's life was completely different than what he'd thought. For five years, he'd believed himself to be the injured party in their relationship.

He wasn't.

She'd been willing to forgive him for being MIA when she'd needed him most. He wouldn't take that for granted.

But despite her forgiveness, he'd known down to his core that if he'd let her walk away from him today at the picnic, that would be it. She would be gone for good.

And maybe he would've let her if it hadn't been for how she'd clung to him for a brief moment when he wrapped his arms around her. Nestled into him like they'd never been apart. Should never be apart.

He'd felt the same.

But then, way too soon, he'd felt her erect walls around herself, pulling herself together, remembering the truth about them.

Withdrawing.

Panic had coursed through his system like a waterfall. He would've done anything to keep her with him. To keep her from walking out of his life. He'd had no idea what that was.

All he was trying to do was give her the chance she should've rightfully had in the first place.

They hadn't discussed the details, which was probably good since he didn't have them. Then some little girl had yelled about Charlie peeing herself, and everyone had packed up the picnic and headed to the hospital where Finn and Charlie's son, Thomas, had been born.

Cade grinned. All in all, a great day. The stranger who'd showed up at the picnic causing tension hadn't posed a threat, Cade had secured a definite way to keep

Peyton in his life for a while, and he'd become an honorary uncle.

"Now that's a big smile." Lance had a beer in one hand as he walked into the kitchen with Everett by his side. "Haven't seen that for a while."

Cade's smile didn't dim. "The smile has its reasons."

Everett walked to the fridge and pulled out stuff to make sandwiches. "Have fun at the picnic? Find your girl?"

Cade caught the beer bottle Everett tossed to him. "Yes, to both."

"We've been going through that new stuff you wrote." Everett slapped mustard onto the bread before piling on ham and cheese. For as long as Cade had known him, the guy had loved his sandwiches. For someone so skinny, Everett ate like a linebacker. Sandwiches were a nightly ritual when they were on tour.

Lance nodded. "That's some of your best stuff. 'Echo' especially."

Everett glanced up from his sandwich prep. "We know what you put down was rough, and 'Echo' isn't finished, but—"

"No, I've got what I need to finish it."

Everett and Lance thought "Echo" was new, but really Cade had been trying to piece that song together for years. Only right now did he realize what had been missing from it: Peyton.

"I'm going to finish it, probably tonight," Cade continued. "And I've decided this is the song I want to do the documentary around. And I want to do it here in Oak Creek."

Lance pushed away from the counter, excitement lighting his eyes. "Finally! And given that 'Echo' is undoubtedly going to be a hit, I'm sure the label will be fine with sending a crew out here, rather than Nashville. However you want to do it, we're behind you one hundred percent of the way."

Cade took a long drag of his beer. "Glad to hear that. Because I have a pretty unorthodox plan I want to put into action."

TWO HOURS LATER, Cade was sitting out on the back porch, nursing another beer. The first one had gotten warm and eventually dumped during the debate with Lance and Everett about Peyton taking on the creative director's position for the video and documentary.

"Sure you don't want something stronger?" Mark closed the door behind him as he walked onto the porch, moving completely silently, impressive for a man of his size.

"Heard all the discussion, did you?"

Mark chuckled. "The conversation was. . .heated."

Heated was an understatement. Neither Everett nor Lance thought using Peyton for the documentary was a good idea. The stakes were too high. They didn't understand why Cade would want to bring in a literal unknown. This wasn't the time for nepotism.

Cade shrugged. "They had a lot of reasonable arguments against this."

Mark walked over so he was standing next to Cade on the railing and looked out into the night Wyoming sky. "But you don't care about their arguments, reasonable or otherwise."

Cade took a sip of his beer. "Honestly, no."

Mark chuckled again slightly. "Well, it's your choice.

Plus, I believe in giving the underdog a chance. The person with the most to lose will fight the hardest."

"Peyton has an amazing eye when it comes to film. I'm not doing myself a disservice by putting her in charge of this project. It won't take Lance and Everett long to realize it."

"Not to mention they don't have any choice about it."

Cade tipped his bottle in Mark's direction. "Exactly. The label is going to want final approval, but they would've wanted that no matter who was directing. And since I don't play the star card very often, they were willing to appease me this time. So Peyton gets to show what she can do."

He didn't doubt for one minute it would be nothing less than amazing.

Mark looked over at Cade like he had something to say, but then looked away.

"What?" Cade asked.

"Nothing. Never mind."

Mark wasn't the talkative sort, on any given day, but it wasn't like him to be coy.

"Spit it out, Outlawson. Everybody else has chimed in on the plan."

"I have no problem with the plan. You know what you're looking for and what's at stake. If she's the one who you think is best, I support that."

"But?"

Mark's lips pursed and he ran a hand through is short cropped black hair. "I need to tell you I ran a background check on Peyton Ward when I found out she was of interest to you."

"That was unnecessary."

Mark shrugged one large shoulder. "Given the situation with the possible stalker, I'm pretty much looking into everyone connected to you. It's what you pay me to do."

Cade took another long drag of his beer. "Peyton and I went to high school together."

"Yes. When did you last see her?"

"Five years ago. Right after she graduated."

Mark didn't say anything, just nodded slowly. Cade knew the man had something he wanted to say.

Cade decided he didn't want to know. Not this way.

"Look," Cade said. "Whatever it is you found out, keep it to yourself. I've already done everything wrong when it comes to Peyton. Starting a second time by invading her privacy isn't the move I want to make."

Mark sighed and turned to lean back against the railing. "Fair enough. She's a law-abiding citizen. I didn't find anything I would insist you know before working with her. Her stepdad, on the other hand, is an asshole."

Cade's hand tightened on the beer bottle. "*That* I already knew."

"Yeah. The incident with him wasn't pretty. And evidently, it wasn't a one-time thing with either Peyton or her mother."

Cade wasn't surprised. Peyton had never once talked about her home situation except for insisting that she would be putting it in her rearview mirror as quickly as possible.

Which she hadn't.

He wanted her to trust him enough to tell him about all this herself. Wanted to get to know her now as the person she'd become. He didn't care how she made a living, but he'd like to know why she'd given up on her dream. Maybe London had been out, but surely there had been other routes she could've taken.

There was so much about her he didn't know and wanted to learn.

He looked out over the Wyoming scrubland

surrounding his house, gently illuminated by the light of the moon. Despite his heated discussions with everyone tonight, he was at peace.

Because getting to know Peyton Ward was finally going to happen.

Chapter 11

What the hell was she doing?

Ten days after Cade offered her the directing job, Peyton stood at the storyboard table for the "Echo" music video and documentary.

It had been a crazy week. A few days after the picnic, Gavin's sister, Lyn, was kidnapped, and it had taken nearly all of the Linear Tactical men, not to mention help from law enforcement from all over the country, to shut down a massive criminal ring intent on perfecting mind control.

As usual, Peyton only knew the peripheral details. The Linear guys tried to shelter her as much as possible. She was just glad everyone was back safely. It had been rough and had slowed down work on the film project somewhat.

She'd been afraid it wouldn't happen at all. That someone would clarify to Cade just exactly how crazy this plan was.

But instead, the production company had people in Oak Creek two days later. They'd rented and renovated part of a warehouse on the outskirts of town. A preproduction team had been sent in to get everything started.

Real professionals. People who had been working in the business for years, some of them decades. And every single one of them was looking to Peyton for creative direction.

The temptation to turn and run out of the room had threatened to swamp her daily. But so far, she'd managed to stave it off and direct people as needed.

"You've got that I'm-in-over-my-head look." Everett Templeton—*the* Everett Templeton who'd also had songs on the radio for years—nudged her gently with his shoulder as he came to stand beside her in front of the large table they were using to map out the shots they'd need to film.

"I know there are more advanced ways to do storyboarding than this." She gestured to the color-coded notecards with various descriptions written or drawn on them.

He glanced over at her, raising an eyebrow. "Somebody has been listening to Silas Hayes again."

She tapped a card against her cheek. "It's a little hard not to." Silas had been the creative force behind a few of Cade's other videos. He hadn't liked being replaced, especially by someone with no experience like Peyton. He hadn't said anything outright but had made an art out of passive-aggressive mutterings under his breath.

"Silas is a prima donna, and pretty much everyone just tolerates him. A lot of well-respected directors still use old-school storyboarding techniques. The tactile feel of it gets the creative juices flowing."

She smiled over at him, relieved. Everett had been a pretty constant source of support all week. And honestly, except for Silas, everyone else had been pretty supportive too.

That still didn't stop Peyton from feeling like a complete fraud.

Who was she kidding? She *was* a fraud. She had

neither the education nor experience most of the people on this project had.

"Nobody else has given you a hard time, have they?"

She shrugged. "No."

"That's because they recognize your talent. Schooling doesn't mean much around here. There have been plenty of people who've come out of prestigious film programs who didn't have the natural eye you have."

"They all know I'm here because Cade specifically asked for me." She was still trying to wrap her head around that herself.

Everett chuckled. "That's something *everyone* is used to. Believe me, Nashville is all about who you know. The important thing is, Cade thinks you're able to do this. I was skeptical when he first mentioned you, I'll admit. But I'm totally on board now, Peyfilms007."

She couldn't stop the flush that stained her cheeks at the mention of her Instagram account. "Nobody knows that's me. How did you find it?"

He grinned over at her. "Mark Outlawson, Cade's security expert, can find damn near anything. But more importantly, why would you hide that? Those short films are absolutely brilliant. Plus, showing how you conceptualized them, organized them and then actually completed the camera work is pretty amazing. Nearly seven thousand followers can't be wrong."

She nodded. She'd never really planned for the account to become so large or popular. She'd started it because she'd needed an outlet for all those ideas crashing around inside her head. She'd been totally surprised when people had started following her and asking for more.

"Once word got out you were Peyfilms, I don't think anyone questioned your ability."

"Except Silas." They both said it at the same time then laughed.

Peyton relaxed slightly. "Well, I don't know who could have possibly let the crew know about that account." She nudged Everett. "But thank you."

He winked at her. "Hey, my number one priority is doing what's best for Cade's career. And granted, that's generally what's best for my career too. I'm sure his reasons for asking you to head up this project are more complex than merely your abilities, but seeing what I've seen, I think he's made the right choice. That it pisses off Silas is just a bonus."

"I haven't seen Cade around much this week." As soon as she said the words, she wished she could take them back. Cade wasn't needed for this part of the process. A regular director wouldn't be asking about him.

"He's been in his writing cave most of the week." Everett picked up one of the notecards and studied it. "None of us have seen him."

"Oh. Writing music? Does he close himself off?" She grimaced. She sounded like a fangirl. "I'd like to under-stand his creative processes."

He smiled over at her. "Cade's creative process has never been easy. He's one of those types where pain and angst fuel his creative juices."

"Oh."

"The good news is 'Echo' has the potential to be the greatest song he's written in a while. A huge hit."

She blew a strand of hair off her face. "Great. No pressure."

"Aw, is the newbie feeling overwhelmed?" Silas Hayes walked up on the other side of the table and picked up another note card, shaking his head. "Not too late to admit you might be in over your head. Let the adults handle this."

She plucked the card out of his hand. "I'll be fine." She prayed that was true.

Silas gave her a friendly smile that was decidedly lacking on the friendliness part. "If you say so."

She took in a calming breath. "I'd like for us to collaborate and make this project the best it can be. If you have ideas or see things I don't, I would be more than happy to hear them and make changes accordingly."

Silas tilted his head and studied her. "When you've been in this business longer than half an hour, you'll see that it doesn't work like that. But don't worry; I'll be around."

Waiting for her to fail. He didn't say it, but then again, he didn't have to.

"Thanks, Silas," Everett said with an eye roll. "We appreciate the camaraderie you bring to the table, as well as your altruistic spirit."

Silas shrugged. "You and I both know what's going on here, so let's not pretend. I'll do my job, and hopefully she'll be able to do hers. If not, I'll do her job too, I guess."

He turned to study the storyboarding idea cards.

Everett shook his head at Peyton and patted her hand.

They spent the next couple of hours going over the potential setup for both the music video and the documentary, Silas not helping much, but at least not hindering.

The documentary wouldn't be storyboarded, of course, but they did need to plan some of the shots they wanted to get overall.

"If I can get some of Cade writing, it would be perfect," she muttered, thinking of what that could add to the feel of the twenty-minute mini-movie. "I think his fans would really love that insight into him."

"He'll never agree to it," Silas muttered. "Believe me, we've tried for years to get footage inside the writing cave."

Everett nodded. "Silas is right. Cade's pretty maniacal when he's in the zone. He doesn't want anyone around. Most of the time, he doesn't even remember to eat, much less want to talk to anyone."

She tapped a pen against her lips. "Maybe we could set up a camera in there and let it run. We don't need a lot. Only a glimpse into who he is in there. A few seconds of what it's like as a song comes together."

"You're going to have to work within reality, Peyton." Silas grabbed the card she'd marked as *writing cave* and tapped it a few times against the table. "Documentaries are real life, but they're the real life the singers are willing to provide the public. Just because you want it, doesn't mean it's going to happen."

"Would ten minutes be enough to get you what you need?" Everyone froze at the sound of Cade's voice behind them. Peyton turned around slowly, her eyes drinking him in. "It's a small space, and Silas is right. I don't generally invite anyone in there. It's a personal place. Private."

"Um, yes, even ten minutes would be great."

"Okay," Cade said. "Done."

Silas threw up his hands and walked away without a word.

She barely noticed, too busy looking at Cade without quite meeting his eyes. He was standing next to Everett, the two friends both attractive but so different. Where Everett was handsome in a more fashionable way with his skinny jeans and careless blond hair, Cade was rugged, almost brutal, in his good looks.

A couple days' worth of beard covered his hard jaw, and her fingers itched to touch it.

Why? What was wrong with her that one look at this man made her body betray her so desperately? Touching him last week at the picnic, being so close, feeling his hard body against hers, had reignited something inside her she hadn't been able to shut back down.

It didn't help that he was looking at her like he couldn't get his fill of her either. Like he wished no one else was around.

Or was she hallucinating?

And even if she wasn't, what did it matter? There was enough water under the bridge between them to fill the Grand Canyon.

Her body might want him—*damn it*—but she'd be an absolute fool to get close to Cade again.

Then she finally met his eyes.

"Hey you," he whispered.

Those eyes, so impossibly blue, currently tired and a little bloodshot. Blue eyes that reminded her even more why she couldn't afford to get near him again.

But something about seeing him now, a little tired and worn down made her realize the truth.

She was going to have to tell Cade about his daughter.

Tell him that she hadn't had the abortion he'd insisted on five years ago. That she'd taken his money but hadn't been able to go through with it.

Which was, probably to Silas's sure delight, going to be the end of her short stint as creative director for the "Echo" project. It was the reason she'd kept her other jobs, even cleaning Cecelia's house. This job was paying ridiculous amounts of money, but she couldn't afford to be replaced in the other two in case. . .

Well, in case Cade decided that she wasn't worth the effort like he had last time.

Or, even worse, fired her and decided to take some sort of legal action against her once he found out she hadn't done what the signed paper said she would do.

"What, Peaches? What just happened to put that look in your eyes?" Cade stepped in closer.

There was no way she was getting into it in front of everyone here. Especially Silas, who watched them with narrowed eyes.

"Nothing's wrong." She forced a smile. "We were just going over potential shots for the documentary. And also, I know I haven't heard 'Echo' yet, or seen the lyrics, but I was wondering if perhaps it might work for us to integrate the documentary seamlessly into the music video and keep the same style. Deep focus and over-the-shoulder shots, remaining more true to life. Artistic, but real."

Cade and Everett looked at each other.

"I told you," Everett muttered.

She bit her lip. Told Cade what? Did they hate the idea? Yeah, she had a good creative eye, but wasn't particularly well-versed in country music videos. Her ideas may be too far outside of the box for them to even want to consider it.

"Look, if it doesn't work for you, tell me. I can come up—"

"It's perfect. Everett told me everything you've done so far has been spot on." Cade reached over and squeezed her hand, rubbing his thumb across her palm before letting go. "Keeping the video true-to-life will be an ideal fit. 'Echo' is the most real song I've written in...ever. And it's the style you're best at, so that makes it even better."

She fisted the hand he'd just touched, her fingertips

running over the place his thumb had stroked. His words, his trust, as well as Everett's, meant everything to her.

But stress pooled in her gut. She needed to tell him now, before they got in any deeper. It was only fair.

"Okay, I'm glad it'll work. But"—she glanced down at her hands, unable to meet his eyes—"I'm going to need to talk to you about something before we go any further."

She didn't look up when she heard Cade step closer. "Something about the project?"

"Yes." She made her voice as strong as she could. "Something about the project. We need to discuss it before we start primary filming."

For the first time, she understood the meaning of *deafening silence*. She could hear nothing else but the absolute lack of sound in the warehouse.

"Okay," Cade finally said. "How about we head over to the writing cave right now? We can talk about whatever you need to, and then you can get the shot you want."

She forced herself to look at him. "I'd prefer not to have a film crew in there when we talk."

He shrugged. "To be honest, I'd prefer not to have a crew in there at all. Do you know how to operate the camera yourself?"

"Yes, but—"

"My writing space is my most intimate, personal space. I'm inviting you in because...well, for a number of reasons. But I don't want a crew in there. Only you."

Now both Silas and Everett watched them intently. Hell, so was the rest of the small crew.

"Fine. We'll talk, and I'll get the shot, if. . .that's what you want."

She tried to hold on to her hope loosely, knowing there was every chance she might be talking to Cade's lawyers by the end of the day rather than him. She wanted to do this project so badly. This week, as stressful as it had been, had also been a dream come true. Working on a film project from start to finish. . . She never thought she'd have this sort of opportunity at this point in her life.

So she tried to prepare herself now. If it got taken away from her today, she didn't want to be devastated. Her life would be no worse off than it had been before Cade had breezed back into it. She still had her amazing daughter, still had a strong body to do the work that allowed Jess to have the opportunities that would enable her to excel.

Cade gestured for her to walk with him out of the warehouse, and she did so, swallowing the feeling that she was walking to her own doom.

She'd survived without Cade O'Conner for the past five years. She'd be fine without him once again.

Chapter 12

He was going to lose her.

Cade felt it as clearly now as he had last week at the picnic. If he let Peyton go now, she was going to somehow slip through his fingers.

Maybe not physically, but if she got her guard up now, she was never going to be his again.

Not that there was any guarantee of that anyway. But at least there was a chance. So he pushed for her to come to the writing cave and talk to him. He didn't want to wait.

He didn't care what it was she wanted to request that had put such a trepidatious look in her eyes: more money, more time, more help.

Whatever it was she needed; he would see she got it.

He just didn't want her to close herself off against him. He wanted to nurture that quiet but feisty side of her that came out when she was around him. Wanted to encourage her artistic eye. Wanted to hear her laugh.

He wanted Peyton—in all her parts.

He opened the door to his writing room and glanced around, wincing. Maybe he ought to pick up a little bit while she was out in the van grabbing the camera and lights she wanted to use.

This room was his sanctuary, a guitar, bass, and baby grand piano sitting in one corner—all of which he could play, but guitar best by far. Under the window on the east side of the room was a desk holding the electronic equipment he needed to actually record, including both a recording mic at the desk and one in a miniature sound booth next to the window.

The entire room was soundproofed, giving Cade the creative freedom to be as loud as he liked at any time of the day or night without having to worry about disturbing anyone else in the house. The opposite was also true. . .there would have to be a near nuclear holocaust in order for him to be able to hear it in here.

The couch opposite the window had seen more use as a bed than an actual place to sit. A shirt and pair of socks were strung over its arm. He grabbed the folded blanket off the back and placed it strategically over the clothes.

The opposite side of the room led into a bathroom and a large closet that had been converted into a kitchenette. He shut the doors to both—they were not fit to be seen by man or camera.

On the south side of the room was his desk. Actually, his dad's desk. Large and made of oak. The kind of dark, masculine wood that had gone out of style, replaced by sleeker models that allowed for charging stations and rolling keyboard drawers. But Cade loved this huge hunk of furniture. Knew it could take the beating if things weren't going right, and he needed to sit on it. Or beat it with his fist.

He could recall one day he'd actually paced back and forth on top of the desk as he worked out a tune.

It was now covered in papers—pieces of the song

"Echo" he still couldn't quite work together. He was missing something, but he didn't know what.

All he knew was that the final pieces of this song were going to come to him. And when they did, he would be ready.

"Is it okay for me to come in?"

He spun toward the doorway at the sound of Peyton's soft voice.

"Please." He rushed over to her to help her with the small lighting tree she was carrying. "Yes, come in."

He moved out of her way so she could look around, his eyes continuously falling to the small smile that lit her mouth. "Is it what you expected?"

"I guess I'm a little glad to see it's so…homey. Not formal."

"Like how Cecelia has decorated the house."

"Yes." She gave a rueful shrug of one shoulder. "Of course, I wouldn't judge if that's what you wanted in here. Someone's creative space is their own domain. No one else has the right to tell them what does or doesn't belong. But this place has a distinctive *you* feel to it. I like it."

Cade had never once cared what other people thought of this space. Everett had offered to bring in an interior decorator, add feng shui or something, but had backed down when Cade threatened to stick a boot up his ass. He liked this room the way it was. Had one almost exactly like it at his house in Nashville.

But Peyton's opinion mattered to him. Knowing she approved had him releasing a breath he hadn't realized he'd been holding.

He held up the light tree. "Where do you want these?"

She tensed immediately, turning from where she'd been studying the instruments in the corner to face him. "Anywhere is fine."

He raised an eyebrow. Even he knew the positioning of the lights made a difference in a film shot. "Anywhere?"

"Yeah. I'll set the lights up in a minute. If...you still want me to."

"Is this about the talk?"

She let out a breath. "Yes."

He set the lights down and walked toward her, not really surprised when she took a step back. "Peyton, whatever it is you need, just tell me. We can work it out. We can talk. I know I haven't been around, and I'm sorry. But we were always able to talk, right?"

She crossed her arms over her chest and looked at him like he'd kicked a puppy into oncoming traffic.

"Really? You expect me to just *chat* with you after everything?"

The venom in her voice now had him taking a step back. He held out his hands in a gesture of surrender. "I didn't know about your accident. I swear. If I had known, I would've been here. I would've done whatever I could to help you."

She shook her head in disbelief. "Believe me, I never expected you to show up after...the incident. You'd made it quite clear you wanted nothing to do with me."

What? "I don't understand. I thought you were the one who wanted nothing to do with me. That you'd decided whatever happened between us was nothing more than a one-night stand."

"Oh, I think the huge packet of legal papers said otherwise."

He froze. Something was happening here that he didn't understand. "What legal papers?"

She rolled her eyes. "Seriously? That's a little ridiculous, don't you think? I can't even talk about it with *you*?"

He took a step toward her. "You can talk about

anything with me. As a matter of fact, I wish you would. I don't understand what's going on."

"That makes two of us. None of this makes sense." She wrapped her arms around herself.

"Peaches…" He reached toward her trailing a hand down her arm.

She jumped back like he'd burned her. "No. No, don't you touch me, Cade. Don't *Peaches* me. Don't act like you didn't—"

She stopped, shaking her head.

"Like I didn't let you down five years ago?"

"*Let me down?*"

The wealth of agony in her words was almost impossible to bear. Jesus. He reached for her again but stopped when she seemed to almost shrink in on herself.

"You call a nondisclosure agreement and wanting me to have an abortion *letting me down?*"

Cade felt like every muscle in his body seized up. "What are you talking about?"

She didn't answer, just turned and walked over to look at the window to stare at the Wyoming landscape.

Nondisclosure?

Abortion?

Abortion meant…

"You got pregnant that night? You had an abortion?"

The silence stretched out so long between them, he thought he would lose his fucking mind right here in the room that had always been a sanctuary for him.

"Peyton," he finally said, his voice sounding hoarse even to his own ears. "I need to understand what happened."

She turned from the window toward him. "No."

His eyes were glued to her face. No.

No she hadn't gotten pregnant? Had he misunderstood what she'd said before? This felt like a nightmare. "No?"

"No, Cade. I didn't have an abortion as instructed."

It took a moment—an excruciatingly long moment—for the pieces to fall into place. "But you did get pregnant."

She silently shook her head as if she couldn't believe he'd even asked her that.

"Where is the baby—what happened to the baby?"

"I kept the baby. Jessica Elizabeth Ward. Jess. You might have met her at the picnic on Saturday or at least heard her announce that Charlie had peed herself when her water broke."

Curly brown hair. Running around laughing. Holding hands and whispering with Baby's nephew, Ethan, every once in a while.

Cade hadn't paid much attention to the little girl beyond thinking she was cute and vivacious.

"My daughter?" He grasped the back of his office chair as he tried to take it all in. "I have a daughter?"

"Do I need to worry about your lawyers showing up at my house since I didn't have that abortion?"

He was hearing her almost through a haze. What made her think he would've wanted her to abort his child?

He had a child. Jess. That lively little girl everyone had been talking to and smiling at.

Why hadn't he paid more attention to her? How old was she? What was her favorite food? Was she smart? What was her favorite flavor of ice cream? Did she still believe in Santa Claus?

It felt like thousands of questions circled Cade's mind. Things he wanted to know about this child. *Needed* to know.

But they were all pushed aside by the one question he couldn't ignore.

"Why, Peyton?" Before he could even think about what

he was doing, he'd moved in front of her, hands on her upper arms. "Why did you keep it from me? Why didn't you tell me you were pregnant?"

She flinched, staring at him, and he immediately let her go.

God, after what she'd been through with her stepfather, he shouldn't touch her in anger, even if he wasn't hurting her. "I'm sorry. I—"

The slap caught him across the face struck before he'd even realized she'd moved.

"How dare you say that to me." Her words were sharp enough to slice. "You can threaten me with lawyers for breach of contract, or even be angry that I said one thing and did another. But don't you *dare* accuse me of not telling you I was pregnant."

"God damn it, Peyton." He stuffed his hands in his pockets. He wasn't going to take a chance on touching her right now.

But God. Damn. It. What was she talking about?

She took a step back, and he forced himself to let her. He wasn't sure what to ask next.

All the fire seemed to leave her, and she stood there, shoulders slumped. "I'm sorry. No matter what, I shouldn't have hit you." She rubbed both hands over her face. "I knew this little dream job would be over as soon as I told you about Jess."

"You should've told me about her long before now. Why didn't you?" He still couldn't wrap his head around it.

She shook her head. "Look. I don't want anything from you. I signed the papers five years ago, and I've never talked to anyone about Jess's father. You're safe. The NDA is still in effect. I followed everything except having the abortion. If you want the money back that you paid me, I can get it to you. It'll just take a while."

With every sentence she spoke Cade felt more lead inside his chest. It was all so impossible; he didn't even know where to start.

But Jesus. Oh Jesus God, she was talking with too many specifics for this to be a simple misunderstanding. "No. No, I don't want any money. You don't have to worry about that."

She nodded sadly. "I'm going to go now. Obviously, we can't shoot anything today. And me directing isn't going to work out, things will be too awkward between us. I shouldn't have let it get this far."

"Awkward." It was all he could manage to parrot. He was going to be sick.

She nodded, staring at him with those brown eyes. "I'm going to go. Thanks for the opportunity here, and you know, for not making me pay back the money. I—I..."

She turned and ran out the door.

"Peyton—" He took a few steps after her but stopped himself.

There was so much they had to talk about. But not until he had all the facts.

Not until he knew how guilty—even if unintentionally —he was in this farce.

And he knew exactly the person to talk to.

Everett rushed toward the writing cave as Cade exited.

"Hey, what the hell happened? Peyton just ran out of here like the place was on fire."

"I can't talk about it right now, Ev. Where's Mark?"

"Back in the security office, I think. Is everything okay? Is it something with the stalker?"

Cade gave a curt shake of his head. No everything definitely wasn't okay.

"No. Nothing about the stalker. I've just got to talk to him."

Everett nodded and slapped him on the shoulder. "I'll come with you. Whatever's going on, we'll figure it out together."

Cade looked over at the man who was not only a business partner but one of his best friends. "Not this time, Ev. This is something I have to do on my own. At least for a little while."

Everett squeezed his shoulder. "Right. Okay. Well, I'm here whenever you need me."

Damn it, Cade was hurting people no matter what he did. But he couldn't worry about Everett right now. This situation with Peyton, and the shit storm Cade suspected was about to hit, had to come first. "Thanks, man."

Without waiting for a response, he jogged back to the small room Mark had set up as a security office. Cade knocked briefly before opening the door. Mark sat at the desk, which faced the door, looking over documents on an iPad.

"Boss." Mark nodded at him as Cade came in and sat in the single chair in front of the desk. "Everything okay?"

"I was wrong. Tell me everything you know about Peyton Ward."

Mark put down the iPad and picked up a folder that rested at left corner of his desk. "I see. Are you sure? Is there a certain place you'd like to start?"

"Let's start with the fact that she gave birth to my daughter a little over four years ago, and for some reason thought I wanted her to have an abortion and has signed a nondisclosure agreement stating she would never talk about me being the father of her child."

Mark pressed his lips together. The man either had an excellent poker face or had already been aware of this information.

"I'd have to agree. That's an excellent place to start."

Chapter 13

"What did you do?"

An hour after learning everything Mark knew, every instinct Cade had told him to get to Peyton as soon as possible to fall down on his knees and beg her forgiveness for what had happened five years ago.

It was so much worse than he could have imagined.

But he couldn't go, not until he talked to his aunt and tried to make some sort of sense out of all this.

"I'm afraid I'm going to need you to be a little more specific." Cecelia looked up at him from behind her rather dainty Queen Anne desk. She'd had that desk as long as Cade could remember. The gentle lines and curves of the piece of furniture were in direct odds to the shrewd and often cunning business decisions she made from her computer on top of it.

Cecelia had always been the business-minded person in their family, even when Cade's father had been alive.

"Peyton Ward."

Cecelia let out a sigh and closed the laptop, then stood slowly and deliberately. "What exactly did she tell you?"

Cade swallowed the fury that had been threatening to consume him since Mark had shown him the file. He had to work the problem. Get the answers he needed from Cecelia who was only going to respond to communication on the same level in which she operated: cold and collected.

Answers first, then he could lose his shit.

"Peyton didn't tell me anything. Or, I should say didn't tell me anything I shouldn't have already known since my signature was on the nondisclosure agreement and a check for ten thousand dollars."

Cecelia didn't even flinch.

"Technically, Peyton should be required to return that money since she didn't follow the terms she originally agreed to."

Cecelia *knew*. She knew about Jess. She knew he had a daughter, and she hadn't told him.

Cade had been wrong; he was going to lose his shit right here and now.

He slammed his hand down so hard on Cecelia's desk pens and papers flew off.

"You had no right. No fucking right."

Cecelia threw up her hands and walked over to the minibar in the corner of the room. "I had no idea you'd been involved with Peyton Ward. You never once talked about her. Never brought her home to meet us. When I looked into her, it didn't look like you had any connections whatsoever."

"You should've asked me."

She poured herself two fingers of Macallan. "I know you'd like to make it as simple as that, but it's really not."

"Peyton and I had sex when she was eighteen. She got pregnant and thinks that I told her to have an abortion and never speak about this again. It's a little difficult to understand what's not simple about that. Jesus, Aunt Cecelia, it's hard to understand what's not *horrible* about that."

She took a sip of her expensive whiskey. "I was trying to protect you. Protect the family. It was a tumultuous time. Oliver had just died. Your career was skyrocketing. I was trying to protect us from anyone who might take advantage."

"And little eighteen-year-old Peyton Ward was one of the big baddies at the gate?"

Cecelia threw back the rest of what was in her glass. "The Ward family has been around a lot longer than you might think. Peyton does not come from the best of stock."

He didn't even try to stop his eyes from rolling. "Regardless of Peyton's pedigree, you should've told me she was pregnant. I know you had power of attorney for me, and I was more interested in making music at that time than I was taking care of the family fortune. But you should have made sure I was aware of this."

Cecelia let out a little sigh. "I know it would be much easier for you to cast me as the villain in this little play, but before you do that, I'd like to show you something."

He followed as she set her glass down walked out of the study and up toward the attic. Cade wouldn't even have thought his aunt knew where the attic was, but she walked up the stairs and into the extended room with a purpose that spoke of distinct knowledge. She didn't stop until she was standing in front of file boxes stacked taller than Cade.

"What is that?"

"Your fan mail and items sent to you at this address."

"You've kept five years' worth of fan mail?"

Cecelia laughed. "Oh no dear, I have a service that goes through that for me now, not that I get much here anymore. This was all from the first few *months* after your first song came out. The weeks following Oliver's death."

That was a lot more than he would've expected.

Cecelia ran her fingers down some boxes, obviously looking for something specific. She found the box she wanted and slid it out of the pile. Then opened it, only to take out another, smaller, box, metal this time, with a combination lock on it.

She shook her head ruefully as she placed it on a box and unlocked it. "I don't know what I thought this tiny lock would protect us from. Believe it or not, I was doing the best I could at the time. You weren't the only one whose world was reeling."

She pulled out a group of files from the box and held them against her chest. "I'm not sure if you're aware of this, but between your music sales and the fact that you had recently inherited all of Oliver's money, you were one of the wealthiest twenty-one-year-olds in the country. And it was all new to me too, Cade. Your fame, the media. Plus, I suddenly had all the O'Conner business decisions to make. It was the reason I took over your email address—because it was linked to the business. You had a life and career in Nashville and I thought I was doing the best thing for you by running as much interference as possible."

"But why would you do something like this?"

She let out a sigh. "Within six weeks of your father's funeral, I received three letters from people claiming to be your illegitimate sibling, two from women claiming they'd already given birth to your child, and four claiming to be currently pregnant."

"Jesus." He scrubbed a hand over his face. He'd had no idea.

"I hired a private investigator. Long story short, you don't have any illegitimate siblings, none of the women who claimed to have had your children actually had, and only two of the four women claiming to be pregnant were pregnant at all."

"Peyton was one of those two."

Cecelia nodded. "Peyton Ward was one of those two. But the other, Sarah Lennon, was making a lot more noise. Threatening to go to the press, the police, the queen. Hell, everyone."

He vaguely recalled that. "I remember you asking me if I knew her. If we'd ever dated."

"You told me you hadn't, and I believed you. Our lawyers called her bluff, offered a DNA test. She made some noise about how that might harm her fetus. She took a small settlement, and we never heard from her again."

"And Peyton?"

"Miss Ward had the bad luck of sending her email so that it arrived as I was walking out the door from the Sarah Lennon settlement."

Shit.

"I was already familiar with the Ward family and the trouble they could cause," Cecelia continued. "I knew for a fact you'd never dated Peyton Ward. After what we had gone through, I decided to take a more abrupt approach with her. I offered her the lump sum to terminate the pregnancy, required a nondisclosure agreement, and asked her not to contact you again. I figured if she was legitimately pregnant with your child, we'd hear from her again. If not. . ."

If not, the O'Conner family had dodged a bullet.

And yet somehow the life of an eighteen-year-old had been completely ruined.

Cade ran a hand through his hair. Cecelia was to blame for some of this, but not all. He should've followed up. Instead of being an ass and getting his feelings hurt when she hadn't responded to his messages, he should've followed through and made sure she was okay.

The truth was, he'd wanted to believe Peyton was okay. He'd been excited and focused on his own career, so while his pride may have been pricked that she hadn't wanted to talk to him, he hadn't really worried about her. Not the way he should have.

He should've made sure.

"Cade, I swear I was doing what I thought was best. Protecting the family name the best way I knew how. Sometimes that means making ugly choices."

Cecelia looked away.

"But at some point you realized the baby was mine, didn't you?"

"Not until last year. Believe it or not, Peyton Ward and I do not run in the same circles, even in a town the size of Oak Creek. I hadn't really thought much about her. Then I saw the child."

"Jessica. Jess. My daughter's name is Jess."

"I know."

"Why didn't you do something about it then, Cecelia? Tell me and let me do something about it?"

"By what? Admitting our guilt? She could cost this family millions of dollars, not to mention your reputation in Nashville."

"I don't care about my fucking reputation, Cecelia. We ruined Peyton's life. Took away the future she'd been planning since she was old enough to know what a camera was."

"I helped out in other ways."

"By offering to let her clean the house?"

"Amongst other things. I pay her handsomely for her services."

Cade had to get out of here before he did something

he would regret for the rest of his life. He turned away. But turned back at the sound of boxes falling to the ground. Cecelia had thrown them to the ground, angrier than he'd ever seen her.

"I did what I thought was best to protect this family. I'm not perfect, I understand that. But I refuse to allow someone from the Ward family to sully the O'Conner name. Not again."

"Again?"

Cecelia shook her head. "We have no proof that the child is even yours, no matter how similar the features. Don't go admitting your guilt. She might take advantage of it. You have too much at stake."

One thing was for sure; Cecelia was right about him having too much at stake. But not in the way she meant.

Cade turned back toward the door without another word. The more time he spent here, the more time he was wasting. The only thing that mattered now was making things right with Peyton.

And if she could find it in herself to forgive and let him get to know the daughter he never knew he had.

Chapter 14

Peyton sat on her couch clutching a cup of coffee between her hands for warmth even though it was a mild September day. She glanced out her window, which was much smaller in size and didn't have nearly the view Cade's writing cave had.

But it was hers, damn it. This whole house, tiny as it was with three bedrooms and one bath, was hers. She'd never once been late on a mortgage payment, even though it had occasionally meant extra shifts at Fancy Pants.

She took a sip of her coffee, not caring that it was mid-afternoon and there were other things she should be doing. Jess wouldn't be home for another couple of hours. Riley was going to pick her up and take her by to see baby Thomas before bringing her home.

Because Peyton was supposed to have been working all day on the film.

Not anymore.

She'd have to get up and call Riley, as soon as she had the energy to go get her phone out of her purse on the kitchen table. Which may be never.

She should at least be glad that Cade didn't seem to have any intention of demanding the ten thousand dollars back. She'd spent that money on medical bills, and just surviving, long ago.

She'd slapped him. No matter what, she shouldn't have done that. But to phrase the question that way—*why didn't you tell me you were pregnant?*

Not, *why didn't you tell me you decided to go through with the pregnancy?* Or *why didn't you tell me you changed your mind?*

To imply she'd never told him about the pregnancy at all had sent a fury through her. She'd slapped him before she'd even been aware she was going to do it.

Riley would undoubtedly approve. Or maybe even berate Peyton for not using her fist rather than an open palm.

Cade hadn't gotten mad. He'd just looked confused. Or looked *more* confused.

Evidently, the thought that she might have carried the baby to term, despite instructions otherwise, had never even occurred to him. That was if he'd ever actually thought of her at all.

She didn't care. As long as he wasn't sending his lawyers after her, suing her for breach of contract, she had no reason to think about Cade O'Conner whatsoever.

A knock on the door startled her; her heart stuttered in her chest. Nobody knew she was home right now.

Except Cade.

She set down her coffee on the kitchen counter as she passed, rolling her eyes when the knocking came again, louder this time.

"Okay, O'Conner, hold your horses—" She pulled open the door and found her mother standing there.

"Mama? What are you doing here?" Peyton held the door open with her foot as her mother breezed inside. She loved the woman, but talking to her always tended to be emotionally taxing and exhausting.

"Hi, baby. Kisses. . ." Renee smiled, kissing Peyton on the cheek.

Peyton breathed in deeply to try to see if she could catch the scent of alcohol on Renee. Over the years, Renee had become a professional at hiding the smell, but Peyton had become a professional at detecting it. Right now, she could smell it, but only faintly. Which meant Renee had been drinking at some point that day, but not so much that it had taken over.

"You doing okay, Mom?"

"Oh good, sweetie, good. I don't suppose that little angel is home now, is she? I want to hug my sweetums." The gushing was just her mom, no alcohol needed. Drinking or not, Renee loved Jess.

"No, she's at school then is going to visit Charlie and baby Thomas."

"Oh, that's too bad. I love that little sweetums." Renee rubbed her arms with her hands.

Peyton narrowed her eyes, scrutinizing her mother's words and actions more closely. She hadn't smelled much alcohol, but the way her mother was flitting about and repeating herself made Peyton wonder if she'd misjudged.

"Mom, come over here and sit down. You need to tell me, have you been drinking?" They both knew the rule. Renee wasn't allowed in the house if she'd been drinking, especially not if Jess was home. The kid was way too observant not to realize something was different about her beloved Granny.

Renee sat down at the table and put her head in her hands. "I promise, I only had one drink. . ." She looked up at Peyton and immediately corrected herself, "A couple of drinks. It was earlier today, and I stopped. I promise."

Both of them knew Renee never had just *one* drink. And earlier today could mean many things too.

"How did you get here? Did you drive?"

Renee shook her head rapidly. "No. No. Kitty Wilks was coming into Oak Creek, and I caught a ride with her."

Peyton wanted to believe her mother. Renee always tried to keep her addiction to alcohol from getting the best of her, especially since what happened with Dennis, which had almost cost Peyton her life. But still, it was a daily struggle. Peyton turned back to the kitchen. "Do you want a cup of coffee or something to eat?"

"No, I'm fine. Really. But I would like for you to come down here and sit with me. I need to talk to you about something."

Peyton tightened her grip on her mug. Talking with Renee about something—particularly something that required Peyton to sit down—was hardly ever good. She refilled her coffee before walking to the table. She was going to need it.

As soon as she sat, Renee grabbed her hands. "First, tell me how things are going with you. I haven't seen you in a while. You look a little sad."

She was so not getting into this with Renee. Peyton had never shared her problems with her mother—especially since Peyton was the one who'd been more of a mother for years. Renee didn't even know Cade was Jess's father.

Even without the nondisclosure agreement, Peyton wasn't sure she would've told her mother that.

"I'm doing fine. Jess loves her new school, and it's challenging her in all the best ways. Everything's fine."

"Well good, that's good." Renee tapped her fingernails against the table until Peyton finally reached over and grabbed her hand.

"What's going on? Just tell me."

115

Renee looked bleakly at Peyton. "It's Dennis. They're giving him early parole."

Peyton let go of her hand as she jerked back from the table. "What?"

Renee reached for her, but Peyton scooted back. "I know, honey, I know. He wasn't supposed to be up for parole this early, but you know how everything is with over-crowding and everything."

Peyton sucked her breath in and out, fighting to keep her panic in check. Dennis was getting out of prison. She thought it would be another year or two before she had to deal with this.

"Honey, as part of his parole, he has to honor the restraining orders we placed against him."

Peyton flinched, the circumstances surrounding that order crystal clear in her memory. It was a miracle she hadn't miscarried.

"If he comes near you even once, he'll go right back to prison. And this time, he'll have to serve his entire sentence." Renee reached across the table to try to take Peyton's hand again, but Peyton stood. She didn't want to be touched right now.

"When does he actually get out?" She walked to the sink and poured her coffee down the drain. She didn't want it now.

"Sometime coming up. That's all I know."

Peyton gripped the counter and silently looked out the window over the sink. How much more emotional turmoil could this day hold?

"Come on, Mama, I'll drive you home. I've got to get back to work." Not exactly the truth, but true enough. She needed to call Violet at Fancy Pants and see if there were any shifts she could pick up while Jess was at school.

Since now her days were pretty empty.

"Okay. Thank you, honey."

Peyton let out a small sigh. It hadn't even occurred to Renee to have an arrangement for how she'd get back home when she'd caught a ride here. That was her mother. She lived in a world where she ignored anything requiring too much thought or effort or unpleasantness.

Or having a husband who abused both her and her daughter.

Peyton had long since given up trying to figure out how her mother's mind worked. The best she could do was to make sure she didn't ever put her own daughter in that position.

She bundled her mom into the car and got her home safely. They didn't say much on the drive, both of them preoccupied with their own thoughts.

"Even out of jail, he'll have to stay in Cheyenne," Renee muttered as Peyton walked with her inside the house. "That's what the police officer who called me said. Dennis will have to check in with the parole officer regularly."

How often was regularly? Unless it was once every few hours, Dennis would still have time to make the five-hour drive between Cheyenne and Oak Creek without the parole officer being any wiser.

And even if he did have to check in every day, how long would that last? Certainly not forever.

Peyton didn't share any of these thoughts with her mother. Renee was barely holding it together as it was.

"Mom, all we can do is take each day as it comes. Don't let this make you fall off the wagon. You're stronger than that."

"No, I'm not, but you are. You always have been. Just because you were quiet didn't mean you weren't strong.

Dennis thought you were weak, but I always knew the truth, baby."

"Thanks, Mama." Peyton leaned her forehead against Renee's. She might never have been a great mother when it came to protection, but Peyton had always known her mother loved her.

"You sure you don't want to tell me what's bothering you? I can be a good listener, you know."

For a brief moment, Peyton was tempted to let Renee be the mother just once.

But that wasn't going to solve anything.

Renee sat down on the couch and Peyton looked around, not wanting to leave her mother if she was going to struggle with the fears inside her mind and use booze to try to soothe them. Peyton didn't see any bottles lying about, which was a good sign, but didn't necessarily mean the coast was clear. As a teenager, she'd once caught her mother taping a gin bottle on the inside of the toilet box.

"Cade O'Conner came by here last week looking for you."

Peyton froze. She hadn't expected that from her mom. And she'd called him, *O'Conner*, not Conner, his stage name.

"Cade and I went to high school together for one year."

"I used to know his aunt Cecelia."

"You did? I didn't know that."

"Your dad knew her better. They went to high school together and dated a little bit. Then I moved to town, and he started dating me instead. She wasn't happy about it, but he was never serious about her."

"I had no idea." Peyton winked at her mom. "You heartbreaker."

Renee gave her a huge smile, and for a brief moment,

Peyton could see the woman her mother had been twenty-five years ago. Bright and happy with her whole life ahead of her. Before Peyton's father had died, leaving Renee with a preschooler and few skills. Before she'd married Dennis.

Not at all like the woman she normally knew as her mother—the one on which alcohol and abuse and stress had taken a heavy toll.

"Anyway, Cade asked why you never went to film school."

"And what did you tell him?"

"That he'd have to ask you that."

Peyton ran her fingers along the top of the couch. "Yeah. He knew I was supposed to go to London. Evidently, the fact I didn't go came as a shock to him."

"I know I haven't been a great mother. . ."

"Mama, don't start. You did the best with what—"

"Not like you're a great mother to Jess." Renee grabbed her hand as she walked by. "But I want you to know. . .I'm not blind. I immediately recognized the resemblance between Jess and Cade. Jess's blue eyes. It's like looking at a little mini-replica of his."

Peyton couldn't talk about this. Not today, after everything. "I've got to go, Mom."

Renee let go of her arm. "You don't have to talk to me about it. And I'm not going to say anything, not that anyone would believe me if I did."

"It's a complicated situation. And I can't talk about it."

Emotionally or legally.

"That's fine. Remember, I love you, and you're a good mother. And that Jess is yours and has never lacked for anything."

Tears filled Peyton's eyes. She kissed the top of Renee's head. "Let me know if you hear anything else about

Dennis. And be strong, Mama. Watch your shows and eat ice cream. Don't drink."

"Okay."

What a day. Peyton almost stopped by Fancy Pants to talk to Violet but decided to go straight home. Maybe she would eat some ice cream of her own.

An unfamiliar truck parked outside her house spiked her awareness. It wasn't Riley or any of the Linear guys. She had to remind herself that Dennis was still in jail, at least for the time being.

And if he showed up, he wouldn't be driving a new-looking pickup truck.

Then she saw someone sitting on her front porch step.

Cade.

Chapter 15

Shit.

Peyton wanted to grab the nearest spoon and literally carve out the part of her that was excited to see him. How stupid could she possibly be? When would she learn the man wasn't good for her?

She parked her car and took a deep breath. She could handle this. Whatever it was he wanted, she could handle it.

He stood as she approached—always the gentleman—but it didn't take more than a glance at his face to see that it was downright haggard. He'd already looked a little rougher than usual earlier today from the time he'd spent locked away writing.

But now he looked like he'd been to war. And had barely survived.

"Cade," she whispered. "Are you okay?"

She couldn't imagine anything bad enough to make him look like this.

He shook his head and gave a laugh that held no humor whatsoever. "You're asking me if *I'm* okay?"

What did that mean? "Um, yeah. You look a little upset."

He ran his fingers through his dark hair, standing it on end. "A little bit upset doesn't even begin to cover it." He reached down and picked up a folder.

Legal papers. That wasn't good.

"Did you change your mind about the money? Do you want me to pay it back?" She tried not to let the panic swallow her. Coming up with ten thousand dollars would take her months, especially if she needed to make some changes to ensure her safety if Dennis decided to return to the area.

She rubbed her hand over her eyes.

Keep it together. Talk to him. Work something out.

She wasn't sure exactly what her legal recourses were, or his. She didn't want to get sued.

She turned away to look out at the trees and give herself a chance to pull herself together. She refused to have a breakdown in front of Cade.

"Peyton."

"Look." She didn't turn back around, trying to pretend indifference. "I don't have that kind of cash lying around."

"*Peyton.*"

God damn her own traitorous body that even now— even now—reacted to the sound of his deep voice saying her name. Her brain interpreted it as being soft, gentle. Like he wanted to care for her and protect her.

When he was really here to do more damage.

You know what? God damn *him*, too.

"Just leave, Cade. I don't have the money, so have your lawyers contact me or whatever."

"Damn it, Peyton, I'm not here for the money!"

Now she spun around. "Then what are you here for?" God, her fingers itched to slap him again. What was it about this man that always brought her fire to the surface? No one else on the planet came close to doing that.

He recognized the violence in her. "You want to hit me again?"

"Maybe."

He actually took a step closer. "Could I talk you into using your fist this time?"

"*What?*"

"Maybe a good right hook from you might make both of us feel better. God knows, I deserve it. I deserve anything you want to say to me. Any punishment you could think to dole out." Those blue eyes were bleak again. Tortured.

"Why are you here, Cade?" The words were barely more than a whisper.

"I'd like to show you what's in this file." He held up his hand. "I don't ever expect you to talk to me after today. And I will never blame you for that. But I want to explain what happened. If I could have an hour of your time, I promise you never have to see me again if you don't want to. And I swear, from this day forward, you don't have to worry I'll take legal action against you, no matter what you choose to say or do, publicly or privately."

She stared at him. The words sounded promising, but maybe her mind was playing tricks on her again. She couldn't trust herself when it came to Cade O'Conner. That was the one thing she knew for certain.

"I don't understand what you want."

"All I want right now is an hour of your time."

She nodded, hoping her heart wasn't about to get battered again, and unlocked her door to go inside.

She walked in and dropped her bag on the small table by the door. He stood, hovering just inside the doorway, looking a little lost.

"Spit it out, O'Conner."

"I didn't know," he finally said.

She rolled her eyes and walked into the kitchen, getting a glass for water, needing something to do with her hands. "I figured that out already by your utter shock back in the writing cave. You thought I went through with abortion."

"No, I didn't know about *any* of it. I didn't know you were pregnant. I didn't know about the nondisclosure agreement. I didn't know about the agreement to terminate the pregnancy."

She set the glass down before it slipped through her numb fingers and turned back to him. Surely she had heard him wrong.

"What?"

He stayed where he was against the door. "I know this doesn't excuse what you've been through, but I wasn't aware any of this had happened five years ago."

She shook her head, trying to clear the cobwebs. "How can you not have been aware? That was your signature on all the paperwork. Believe me, I got it out and compared it to your signature on the senior page of the high school yearbook."

"You did?"

"I'm so pathetic, aren't I?" She sighed heavily. "I was convinced there was some grand conspiracy keeping you away from me. That you would never treat me that way. So I dragged out the yearbook and compared the signatures."

"Peyton…"

"Ends up Occam's razor was right."

"The simplest answer is usually the correct one," he whispered.

She wasn't surprised he was familiar with the principle. "Yep. And the simplest answer in this case was that you'd signed those papers. No conspiracy."

His expression was pained. "Yes. I signed the NDA, but without reading it. I signed the check too, but before it was actually made out to anyone, I'm sure. It was right after my dad died and Aunt Cecelia had power of attorney when it came to all the money, but some things I still needed to sign. I—I didn't really read them."

She stared at him, still scrambling to understand. "I tried to call you. Text you, when I first found out. You changed your number."

He flinched. "I did. There were issues with my service provider in Nashville. I had to get a new phone. I sent you an email with my updated info." Now he took a step toward her but stopped when she flinched. "I sent it to the London Film Centre email you gave me that night."

She'd never gotten it, of course, because she'd never been in London. Neither of them needed to say that.

"I'm not trying to say I'm blameless," he continued. "When I didn't hear back from you, not even a word, I thought that meant you had no interest in talking to me. That you'd moved on with your perfect film life and had left me and what we'd shared behind."

He took a step toward her and panic bubbled up inside. He couldn't touch her. Not now.

He stopped. "I thought you'd left me behind, Peaches. That I was part of your past. And if you were able to walk away so easily, I was damn well going to too. You were everything to me, and I thought you wouldn't even take the time to return an email. That you were ghosting me."

"I didn't. . ."

"Of course, you didn't. I know that, now.. I should've checked in on you. Should've had Baby swing by and see if you were alright. Should've stalked you on social media until you talked to me. But I didn't because I was too proud, and too busy proving to myself how much I wasn't thinking about you. How much I was over you."

They stood staring at each other for a long minute, neither knowing what to say. Peyton knew this should change everything for her. She'd dreamed, at least in the early days, of Cade coming to her and saying something exactly like this.

That it had all been some tragic misunderstanding. That he would never have abandoned her in that way.

But now? Now all she felt was numb.

"What do you want from me?" She finally managed to get out.

His shoulders slumped. "I want whatever you will give me. I'd like to get to know Jess…"

The numbness inside her vanished. "Jess is *mine*. You can't just waltz back in here, claim you're blameless, and expect some rights to her. I will fight you."

Right now, she meant that literally. Physically. If he said he wanted custody of Jess, she would tear him to pieces.

There was a reason mama bears were the most dangerous.

He held hands out in front of him, palms up. "No. I would never try to take Jess from you. She *is* yours. I just. . .I just want you to know that you're not in this alone anymore. I want to help you in whatever way I can. Financially, emotionally, however. Whatever way you'll allow. It's all up to you."

Tears welled in her eyes. God, she felt like she was in shock—so many different emotions barreling through her so quickly, shifting without warning.

He took a couple steps closer, and all she could do was stare at him. "You really didn't know?"

"I didn't know, but I was still at fault. Believe me, if I'd known, nothing in this world would've kept me away from you."

"I needed you." The tears finally fell. "I was so alone and we needed so much and you weren't around. You wanted nothing to do with us."

The next thing she knew, she was in his arms. "That was never true. I've always wanted you. Even when I thought you'd left me behind, I thought about you every day. *Wanted you* every day."

She sobbed against his chest, all the emotions overwhelming her. She cried for the frightened teenage girl who had watched her dreams disappear, then had almost died in the hospital. She cried for the days she'd sat alone, watching Jess in the NICU, wanting to hold her newborn and not knowing if she'd be alright.

She cried for the five years that she'd worked so hard trying to provide for herself and her daughter, thinking the man she loved wanted nothing to do with her. With them.

She cried because it was too late now to fix any of these things.

"We'll mutually terminate the NDA," he said against her hair as she quieted. "You can speak to whoever you want about our situation. Hell, you can go on the talk show circuit—tell everyone what an asshole I am. I don't care. But no matter what, you don't ever have to worry about finances again. Whatever you and Jess need, I can make it happen."

He kissed the top of her head. "I think my hour is about up."

She nodded against his chest, took a steadying breath, and moved away from him. She gathered her strength. "Thank you for coming here and explaining everything."

She took another step back.

"No, don't thank me—"

She held out a hand to stop him. "Today has been filled with a lot of surprises for you, so the fact that you came over here with the intent to make things right is admirable."

"Thank you." His voice was unsure, his eyes narrowed as he studied her.

Yes, Cade definitely had good instincts. He obviously knew something was wrong even if her words were neutral.

"You asked me what I needed from you. How you could help me."

His nod was instant. Exuberant. "Yes, anything, Peyton. Any amount of money you need, any help I can provide. All you have to do is ask, and I promise I'll give it to you."

She knew what she needed.

She nodded, then took another step back. "What I need is for you to stay out of my life and as far away from me and my daughter as possible."

Chapter 16

"Okay, Peyton, spill."

Riley picked up the box of pizza she'd brought over that they'd eaten with Jess and Ethan. The two kids were outside playing with Skywalker, their beloved dog.

Peyton had managed to keep it together for the past three days since she'd told Cade she didn't want anything to do with him.

Oh God, had she really told him she didn't want anything to do with him?

"There. That look right there." Riley stuck her finger almost at Peyton's nose. "What is going on?"

"My mom stopped by a couple days ago and let me know Dennis is getting out of jail soon. Early release."

Riley let out a curse that would make a sailor proud.

Peyton rubbed her neck. "The restraining orders are still in effect, and he'll go right back to prison if he comes near me. But still. . ."

Riley slid an arm around her shoulder. "Oh honey, I'm so sorry. But you're not alone anymore. You have all the

Linear guys. Not to mention security working for Cade has to be more robust than everyday Oak Creek."

Peyton couldn't help it, she flinched at the mention of Cade's name. She hadn't told her friend she wasn't working for him anymore.

Riley saw the flinch.

"What?" she demanded. "Something happened, didn't it? The other day when I brought Jess home. You said there was nothing wrong, but I could tell there was."

Peyton couldn't help herself. She told Riley the whole story. Her friend's eyes grew wider and wider until Peyton finished.

Riley slumped down into her chair, shaking her head. "Holy shit. He didn't know? Do you believe him?"

"Yes." It was a simple answer, but an honest one. Cade had never been a liar. And what purpose would it serve to lie about this, anyway?

"And now he wants to be a part of your life? Get to know Jess? Help you?"

"That's what he said."

"And how did you respond?"

"I told him I wanted him to stay out of my life for good."

Peyton didn't even realize she was crying until Riley's arms folded around her. She would've thought after crying all over Cade, then crying all over her pillow the past three nights, she would've been out of tears.

But evidently not.

"Mommy, do you need to change your tampon?" Jess's ridiculous question knocked Peyton out of her sobfest. She pulled away from Riley and grabbed her daughter onto her lap. Riley tried, and failed, to swallow her laughter.

"Do you know what a tampon is?"

Jess smiled angelically—never a good sign—and shook her head no. "I heard Aunt Charlie say it."

Peyton glanced over at Ethan. The little boy roughly resembled the color of a beet and looked like he'd rather be anywhere on the planet except standing in her doorway.

"Aunt Charlie talked to you about tampons?" Jess was not quite five. Surely this discussion could have waited a few more years. She wiped her eyes with the napkin Riley slid over. At least this talk was helping reset her emotional spiral.

"No, Aunt Charlie was talking to Uncle Finn about tampons. He didn't want to change baby Thomas's poopy diaper. Aunt Charlie told Uncle Finn to stop his boo-hooing, change his tampon, and deal with it."

Riley howled with laughter and Peyton couldn't stop a snicker herself. Ethan still looked like he wanted to melt into the floor.

"Well, that's probably not a phrase we should use all the time and generally tampons have nothing to do with crying."

Jess snuggled into her. "But are you okay, Mommy? Why are you sad?"

Peyton hated the thought of her daughter worrying. She tipped her back in her arm and tapped her on the nose. "I'm alright, baby. You know how it is. Sometimes you just have to cry, and that's okay."

"Yeah, that's okay."

Peyton looked down into those stunning blue eyes. *Cade's* stunning blue eyes.

And suddenly, she realized what all her emotional angst was about. Why she was *still* crying.

She couldn't do this. Couldn't cut Cade out of her life. She'd never known her own father, and her life had been emptier because of it. Jess had a chance to know her father.

He was a good man who would bring so many positives into her life.

She looked over at Riley. "I can't do it. I can't tell him to get lost outright."

Riley rolled her eyes. "Well, you can if you want to. I would support that completely."

"But I'll regret it."

Riley nodded. "Maybe."

The real question was, how did Peyton keep her heart from being trampled in the process? She wasn't sure if Cade was interested in her at all. And wasn't sure which would be more terrifying: if he was or if he wasn't.

The kids helped her clean up the rest of the mess from dinner. Riley helped too, although she was responding to so many messages on her phone, she could barely do anything productive.

"I hope you're telling Boy Riley that you're using him to get out of doing dishes."

Riley rolled her eyes. "Please. Boy Riley is somewhere in the Himalayas about to attempt some ridiculous snow-boarding stunt. He's buried deep in preparation mode. I'll hear from him once it's done."

"Then what are you doing? Pretending to text so you can get out of dishes duty?"

Riley grinned. She turned to Ethan and Jess. "Tampon Finn is on his way to get you two rug rats. You're in charge of helping out with baby Thomas this evening. You're spending the night Jess, so go grab a change of clothes and a toothbrush."

"No," Peyton interjected, hating to see how her daughter's face fell. She loved spending the night with Finn and Charlie and Ethan, but Peyton hadn't allowed it since the baby had been born. "We need to give Aunt Charlie a little more time to adjust to new life with the baby—"

Peyton stopped when Riley walked over and pointed her phone screen right in Peyton's face. It was a text message from Charlie.

I do not need more time to adjust to a new baby. Send your fucking kid over and let Riley have her way with you.

Peyton tilted her head so she could see Riley around the phone. "Something you want to tell me about?"

"Yup. We're going out."

"WHAT IN THE world are we doing?" Peyton asked three hours later.

Almost every woman she knew in Oak Creek, plus a couple she didn't know, currently inhabited in her living room.

"Pre-gaming!" everyone around her yelled, since this was the fifth time Peyton had asked the question.

Over in the corner, Jordan Reiss danced with her future sister-in-law, Violet, to some god-awful hip-hop song. Annie and Lyn were making some sort of blue cocktail in the kitchen—although a medical doctor and a PhD candidate should probably know better than to drink anything that color.

Riley and Wavy Bollinger stood over Peyton, fussing with her hair and makeup. Charlie provided extra instructions via video chat.

Peyton felt way, way out of her comfort zone. Like, light years out.

"I'm so glad they're doing it to you this time instead of me!" Annie called out.

"And count yourself lucky they're not making you wear a bustier." Violet waggled her eyebrows.

It hadn't been so long ago that Wavy and Riley were

working their magic on those two women when they'd been new in town and about to go out.

Peyton had always been invited on the girls' nights out, but she'd turned them down. Spending money on alcohol seemed like such a waste when there were so many other things she needed to pay for.

Yet tonight, no one was listening to her when she tried to be reasonable and talk them out of the planned festivities.

"Electric Smurf." Lyn grinned as she walked over, holding a glass of a bright blue liquid and handed it to Peyton. Wavy and Riley argued over eyeshadow colors.

"Are you doing this to get back at me for the time Jess almost destroyed your laptop?" Peyton whispered to Lyn. She'd lived with Peyton and Jess for a couple of weeks when she first got to Oak Creek.

"If your little monster hadn't tried to help, Heath and I never would've gotten things worked out between us, nor would we have busted up the criminal ring. A lot of good came of Jess nearly destroying my dissertation. So drink up."

Since Annie was a well-respected doctor, Peyton decided not to inquire about the wisdom of Lyn having shots so soon after a traumatic event and hospital stay. Maybe this was what the doctor had ordered.

She clinked her glass against Lyn's. "To getting answers."

"To you, my friend." They both sipped the blue liquid. Sweet, but not bad.

"Is Jenna going to be okay?"

They both looked over at the young woman in question. She was talking to Neo, someone else Peyton had only met tonight. The tiny blonde evidently was some sort of computer genius and had helped rescue Lyn and Jenna when they'd been kidnapped.

Jenna had been held against her will much longer than Lyn. She wasn't from around Oak Creek but had formed a bond with Lyn.

Lyn nodded. "Jenna will be okay. She's not drinking; all she wanted was a night of quasi-normalcy. She just needs to remember she's so much more than that person who was kidnapped and abused so long."

Suddenly, Peyton's problems seemed minuscule.

"I'm glad she's here."

Evidently Riley won the eyeshadow argument. She started to apply the golden hues, but then stopped, laughing. "What the hell? My hand isn't working right. You do it, Wavy."

Peyton laughed at Riley. "How much have you had to drink?" She took a sip of her own Electric Smurf to make the preening a little more bearable.

"Basically nothing! My body just thinks I'm drunk. That'll make getting my buzz on a lot easier." Riley, laughed, rubbing her fingers. "Damn fingers are numb. They've been doing that a lot lately."

"Are you sure you're okay?"

Riley scoffed with a wink. "My hair currently matches our drinks. Of course I'm okay."

"I don't understand why I have to get all dressy and made up just to drink here at home," Peyton finally said when Wavy, Charlie, and Riley decreed her a finished masterpiece.

She could feel every eye in the place on her at her question.

"What?" Peyton asked.

"You do understand what pre-game means, right?" Riley shook her head. "It means you start at home before you go out. We're going to the Eagle's Nest. It's time for some dancing."

Oh no. "I don't really dance."

"I didn't dance either when they first suited me up." Annie smiled. "Don't worry, the Electric Smurfs will help your sense of rhythm."

Somehow, Peyton doubted it.

"Okay, so are we ready to go?" Peyton asked, about to stand up. Maybe they could get it over with early.

"No." All the women said in unison.

"Not until nearly midnight." Wavy grabbed some of the blue concoction for herself.

Midnight? Peyton had honestly hoped to be back home and in bed before then. She had to work at Linear tomorrow.

"By the way, both Zac and Finn said if you come in tomorrow, you're fired." Riley gave her a big grin. "They said there wasn't anything that needed to be done there that couldn't wait until next week. So whatever is going through that head of yours, you can just forget it. Geez, Peyton, you're the oldest twenty-three-year-old in the history of the world. Go out and have fun for once."

Everyone cheered and someone cranked up the music. Peyton looked around. These women were here for *her*. They didn't know exactly what was going on, but they knew she needed a pick-me-up, so they were willing to support her.

The least she could do was enjoy the effort.

She wandered back into her room to get a better view of what Wavy and Riley had done to her. She studied herself in the full-length mirror behind her door.

They hadn't gone all-out crazy like she'd been afraid. She looked young. *Pretty*. Like someone twenty-three years old should look before going out to a bar. Tight jeans and heels and a pretty plum blouse that hung off one shoulder.

They'd curled parts of her long hair so it fell strategically down her back in soft waves. The long-debated eye shadow made her brown eyes seem massive in her face.

This was what she would've looked like had her life gone the way she'd originally thought it would. Not always in khaki pants and a t-shirt rushing from one job to the next.

She sat on the bed and stared at the mirror.

Someone knocked and the door creaked open. Riley stuck her head in. "You doing okay?"

"Just admiring your handiwork."

She grinned. "You look good if I do say so myself."

"I'm afraid, Ri."

Riley closed the door behind her. "Of going out tonight? We can stay here. It's already halfway to a rave in your living room anyways."

"Not only about tonight. About my life in general. About telling Cade it's okay for him to get to know Jess. I'm afraid he'll want to be near me too. And I'm afraid he *won't* want to be near me."

Riley gave her a soft smile. "And you don't know which you want more."

"Would I be a complete idiot for even thinking about being close to him again?"

"No, not at all." Riley sat next to her.

"Cade isn't the only guy I've been with, but I sort of shut down after I had Jess. There hasn't been time or energy to look for someone else."

And if she admitted it to herself, she hadn't wanted to be with anyone who wasn't Cade.

"I haven't even thought that way in a long time," Peyton continued. "But then I saw him a couple of weeks ago, and it was like a switch was turned back on in my body. For all the kissy and sex stuff. How stupid is that?"

"Not stupid at all. You're a young, healthy woman. You have needs and desires. How they got woken back up doesn't matter. The way I see it, you really only have one question you need to answer now that your switch has been flipped back on."

"Oh yeah, what's that?"

"Who do you want to be your electrician—Cade or someone else?"

Chapter 17

Cade once more looked like he'd been on a three-day bender, but this time it was because he'd actually been on a three-day bender.

The DJ at the Eagle's Nest was playing a song about getting drunk on a plane. It was a rowdy Friday night at the bar, half the town country line dancing in the middle of the floor, and the other half mulling around the bar and tables.

Cade sat in a darkened booth in the far corner, watching the revelry going on around him. He may have been pretty consistently drunk for the past seventy-two hours—although not on a plane—but he definitely wasn't going to be laughing and carrying on like everyone else.

He wasn't even sure exactly why he was here at all except for Baby sitting across from him. Cade had been quite content being miserable in his own house, drinking and barking at everyone.

Baby had showed up tonight, dumped Cade's ass in the shower, then dragged him out here.

"Remember when we had to drive all the way into

Reddington City to find a bar to use our fake IDs?" Baby sipped on a beer; Cade nursed a scotch as they looked around them.

"They never would've let us in here, that's for sure." That was the thing about a small town. It was a small town.

Cade looked over where Aiden Teague was having a drink with Gabriel Collingwood, the former Navy SEAL who now lived in the area, soon to be Aiden's brother-in-law.

"I hear Aiden bought a ring and plans to propose to Violet soon. And of course, Jordan and Gabe are all but attached at the hip." Baby shook his head.

Cade nodded. "Linear guys are falling like flies."

"Tell me about it. First my brother and Charlie. Dorian's married too. Zac and Annie have a date picked out. Now Aiden. There's something in the water around here, I'm telling you." Baby tipped back his beer.

Cade studied Aiden and Gabe. Both men looked happy. Just like at the picnic, everyone had been content.

Why? Because they hadn't fucked everything up.

"Those guys aren't stupid." Cade pinched the bridge of his nose. "They found the right women and did the right thing. They didn't blow their chance by having their heads up their asses and only being concerned about their career and their own life in Nashville."

Baby laughed and leaned back in the booth. "Whoa there, drunk boy, I somehow get the feeling we're not talking about the Linear guys anymore."

"I don't want to talk about it." He folded his arms over his chest.

Talking about it wasn't going to change anything.

Stay out of my life and as far away from me and my daughter as possible.

Peyton's words were all he'd been able to hear in his mind for the past three days.

Cade wasn't so drunk that he didn't notice when Baby signaled the bartender and traded out Cade's scotch for water. He didn't argue. That was probably better anyway.

Drinking wasn't helping. Could sober be any worse?

Baby spent the next couple hours talking to him about nothing in particular, letting Cade sober up a little. Cade really wasn't prone to drinking the way he had been over the past couple of days. He'd tried writing, but there was absolutely no music or lyrics in his head.

Alone in silence with only the realization of how badly he'd wronged Peyton with no way to make it right.

The bottle had seemed like the best option.

But sobering now, he realized the drinking was nothing but a tiny, ill-fitting bandage for a gaping wound.

Baby was a good friend, distracting Cade with Oak Creek stories while deftly, as only Baby Bollinger could, deflecting the multiple women who came their way. Some of them were looking to see if they could get a little intimate time with the local celebrity, but just as many checking to see if Baby was available. Somehow, he turned them all away while leaving them feeling better about themselves than when they'd walked over.

"You have a skill, you know that?" Cade took another sip of his water, feeling almost human for the first time in three days.

Baby sat back down from hugging a girl who'd come over, tucking a strand of hair behind her ear, and sending her on her way with a smile on her face. "I assume we're not talking about mechanics right now?"

"With women. They respond to you. They love you."

Baby shrugged. "And I love them. What's not to love?"

Cade smiled, a little surprised his body remembered

how. That was Baby in a nutshell. From anybody else, Baby's actions would be those of a player, someone using his good looks and charm to manipulate women into giving him what he wanted.

But Baby had always been authentic in his love for women. He genuinely cared about them and wanted to spend time with them. Actually, he was sort of like that with men too. People responded to Baby.

Cade almost pointed out that Baby could get a job in Hollywood or Nashville and make a lot of money doing exactly what came so naturally to him—influencing other people. But his friend would never be happy manipulating others no matter how much it might pay.

Cade leaned his head back against the top of the booth. "You ever think about getting out of this town, Baby?"

"Naw. High school dropout? Mechanic? Where am I going to go that's better than here?"

Cade shook his head. "We both know you got your GED a few years ago. You're a damn fine mechanic but could be a shit ton more than that." Like a *NASA engineer* more than that.

"How about we talk about what's put you on this massive bender rather than my boring career trajectory? It's been a long time since I've had to talk you down from the ledge."

Maybe talking about this would help. It couldn't possibly make matters worse.

"I screwed something up." Cade wrapped both hands around his water glass. "Something important."

Baby stretched his arm out across the back of the seat. "Then unscrew it up. You've got money, connections, fame. It's hard to think of a situation that you couldn't unscrew-up."

"How about one where I find out I'm a father and in essence have made the mother of my child's life a living hell for the past five years? Unknowingly, but still at fault."

Baby's eyebrows raised so high, Cade thought they might find a permanent place in his hairline. "So a *literal* screw up."

"Yeah, I guess you could say that."

"Did this woman contact you? Does she want money? Is she threatening to go to the press?"

"All she wants is for me to stay out of her life."

Baby shrugged. "Are you sure that's a bad thing? Obviously, you don't really know this woman if you didn't know about your child for five years. What kind of person keeps that a secret?"

"Peyton Ward."

Baby went completely still. "You're Jess's dad. Holy shit." His hands balled into fists. "I think I'm going to kick your ass right now."

"I wouldn't stop you. I deserve it."

"You have more money than freaking God, and Peyton has been working her ass off for years cleaning houses. Hell, she's the freaking janitor for Linear."

Every word was like a slice across Cade's skin. He wanted to order another drink, but that wasn't going to change anything.

"I know. Believe me, if I had known about the baby, if I had known Peyton was still in the area at all, I would have done something about it long before now. I thought she moved to London to go to film school."

"Peyton went to film school?"

"She would've. She never actually made it." Thanks to him.

Baby shook his head like he was trying to clear it. "How do you even know her at all?"

"She actually went to Oak Creek, even though she lived in Sublette County. You'd already dropped out. It was my senior year. She lied about her address so she could do the special arts program. She's incredibly gifted when it comes to film."

"I had no idea," Baby murmured.

"She kept it a secret. Had a full ride to the London Film Centre. I thought she'd gone and didn't want to have any contact with me. Ends up she tried to contact me and was told to terminate the pregnancy and sign a nondisclosure agreement."

Baby stared.

To his credit, he didn't reach over the table and start pounding Cade's face in. He stayed calm, only the tiniest twitch in his jaw giving away his tension. "You're going to tell me right fucking now that you weren't the one who sent her that. Please, Cade. I don't want two decades of friendship to be over."

Cade wished he could be offended, but he had no right. "Aunt Cecelia sent it, not me."

Baby relaxed slightly. "Shitty thing to do."

"In her defense, she really was doing what she thought was best. A lot of stuff went down that summer, between my career, Dad's death, and the changes in the company. She thought Peyton was a freeloader."

"Peyton is the least freeloading person I've ever known. She works damned hard to give Jess what she needs. And Jess. . ."

Even hearing her named gutted him. Cade had no idea what he was going to do about his daughter if Peyton refused to have anything to do with him personally.

"Jess is absolutely amazing," Baby continued. "She and Ethan are inseparable. Ethan has already informed Finn that he plans to marry her when they get older. And the way he's been so protective of her because she didn't have a. . ." Baby trailed off.

But what he was going to say was obvious. "Ethan's protective of Jess because she hasn't had a father around."

Baby shrugged. "Well, you know Charlie isn't Ethan's biological mom. He can still remember the time with his birth mother—and it wasn't pretty; that bitch screwed him up pretty badly, even tried to sell him—before Finn found him. So not having a father around to protect you is a big thing to my nephew."

"So you're saying an eight-year-old might kick my ass."

"I'm pretty sure Ethan might have to get in line behind a number of the Linear guys when they find out you're Jess's dad. Everyone assumed he was some deadbeat somewhere."

"It's nothing more than I deserve. Believe me, if I could kick my own ass, I absolutely would. Peyton wants nothing to do with me. Wants me to stay completely out of her life."

"So that's the reason for the drinking binge? Not because you found out you're a dad?"

"Hell no. I wish I had known about Jess from the very beginning. Believe me, things would've been much different." Different like he would've married Peyton. Would've made sure every single day she and the baby were safe and secure and cared for. "But now she's basically told me to get lost."

"So what are you going to do about it?"

"What can I do about it? Nothing."

Baby folded his arms over his chest and shook his head. "Really, asshole? You're just going to give up? That's it—walk away?"

"I can't make Peyton include me in their lives."

"But you could show her you're willing to fight for her.

145

To woo her. To put it all out there on the line. To make *yourself* vulnerable for once rather than her. And if she still decides to tell you to fuck off, that's her choice."

Baby was right. "But it won't be because I haven't tried everything in my power to get her to say yes."

"Exactly."

"You know, for someone who decided to drop out of school, you're pretty damned smart."

Baby shifted uncomfortably. "Listen, about school, I need to tell you something."

"What?"

"I decided a few months ago to. . ." He caught a look at something over Cade's shoulder and shook his head. "Oh shit."

"What?"

"Were you serious about fighting for Peyton? Showing her you want her?"

Cade nodded. "Yeah. Why?"

"Because she and her posse just walked through the door."

Chapter 18

The women drew a lot of attention inside the bar. Cade wasn't surprised when half the Linear team showed up thirty minutes later. Not that they needed to worry about anyone from town causing problems for their women. There was too much respect, and a healthy dose of fear, for the guys.

Besides, these women didn't need men to fight their battles for them. They were more than capable of holding their own ground.

Some of them had lived through the worst the world had to offer—kidnapping, attacks, human trafficking—and had survived. They may be in high heels and drinking blue concoctions, but they were warriors. All of them mentally and emotionally, some of them physically as well.

As soon as they came in, Cade gave up his back corner booth. He didn't care now about anonymity and not being bothered.

He wanted to be bothered by one person in particular who was currently dancing with her friends. He sat at the bar, facing the dance floor, along with the Linear guys. The chatter was lighthearted and jovial. The men knew their women might be cutting loose, but they were all safe and would be coming home to them when the night was all said and done.

God, that's exactly what Cade wanted.

When Gavin Zimmerman, acting sheriff of Oak Creek, joined them at the bar, they made room for him.

"Heard the ladies were out in full steam tonight, so thought I better stop by."

"Don't worry." Zac took a sip of his beer. "No fights with any of us, so they're not on any man-hating-sisterhood rampage. Just having fun."

Nobody but Baby threw a sidelong glance in Cade's direction, so he knew Peyton hadn't broken the nondisclosure agreement. Damn it, he was going to destroy that fucking document as soon as possible.

Not that he worried Peyton would say much anyway, although in some ways he wished she would at least tell her friends. Even knowing that once word got out, the Linear guys would kick his ass. Still, he wished she could do it.

"I'm glad to see Jenna joined them." Heath Cavanaugh adjusted the strap of the bag he carried with him everywhere. Cade didn't know Heath well but knew the man-purse—*murse*—everyone teased him about held a portable defibrillator. He was keeping a close eye on Lyn, as was her brother Gavin. Cade couldn't blame them; they'd almost lost her not long ago.

"Who's that tiny blonde?" Cade asked. He hadn't seen her around before.

"Neoma," Kendrick said. He was Linear's computer specialist, but Cade didn't know him very well. "She goes by the name Neo."

And Kendrick obviously had eyes for Neo.

"Honestly, I'm most happy to see Peyton out with them," Gavin said. "She needs it."

Almost everyone murmured their agreement.

"It looks like her drink is empty." Gavin shook his head. "It's not going to take long for someone to remedy that. I think almost all of the men in town have been waiting for some sort of sign of encouragement from Peyton. She won't have to wait long if she wants company."

Cade looked around. There was no doubt the men in the bar were interested, just biding their time.

Oh, hell no. There was no way he was letting someone else move in on Peyton.

He ordered one of those crazy blue drinks they'd all been sipping on and walked toward the dance floor. He could hear people murmuring behind him but didn't care. So what if he made a point to never single out one woman while in Oak Creek, or anywhere for that matter.

He was singling one out now.

And hopefully, would be singling her out for a long time to come.

He walked toward Peyton, drink in hand, careful not to bump into the many gyrating bodies all around her. The line dancing had ended a while ago, and the mood was much more relaxed as the night had worn on. They'd be making last call soon.

He wasn't even sure Peyton knew he was here.

Her back was to him when he reached her. Some of her friends could see him, including Riley, but nobody made any move to block him from talking to her.

He held the drink over her shoulder so it was right in front of her face.

"You guys? Come on," she said without turning

around. "You know I'm not trying to get stupid drunk. I'm already making a fool out of myself as I am."

He bent down close to her ear so she could hear him without him having to yell. "You are very definitely not making a fool out of yourself. I can promise you that."

She spun so fast, her drink spilled on his shirt. "Oh my gosh. I spilled my drink on you."

"It'll be fine. Dance with me."

Her eyes grew big as she stood there staring at him. "I don't know if I should."

Another woman, not one of Peyton's friends, sidled up to him. "I'll dance with you, Cade."

"Why don't you dance with me, sugar?" Baby swooped in and steered the woman away. "I think Cade's got his hands full."

Baby Bollinger was the best anti-wingman ever.

"Dance?" He asked Peyton again. "Or if you'd rather sling the rest of your drink directly into my face, that works too."

All of her friends had stopped dancing and were staring at them, but Cade didn't care. If admitting what had happened and that he was a scumbag to her friends would get Peyton back in his life, he would do it in a heartbeat.

"How about if I hold that and you dance with the man." Riley took the drink out of Peyton's hand. "You can see if he might be the electrician you're looking for."

Peyton stared at her friend for a moment, then finally nodded. Riley faded away and he wrapped an arm around Peyton's slender waist and captured her other hand in his, holding it against his chest.

"I have to warn you I'm not much of an electrician. But if you need one, I'll help you find one."

A mischievous smile covered Peyton's face. "No, I can find whatever I need."

The beat from the song the DJ was playing was too fast for the type of dancing they were doing, but he didn't care. She was in his arms. That was all that mattered.

But he didn't know how long he had. She might come to her senses at any minute and storm out.

"I'm not giving up, Peaches. I want that to be clear." He pulled her a little more closely against him. "However much time you need is fine. I won't rush you. But I'm not giving up. If friends is all we can ever be, that's fine. But like it or not, Peyton Ward, you're the mother of my child. That's a responsibility I take seriously, and I'm going to do my damnedest to convince you to let me be in as many parts of your and Jess's life as possible."

She swayed with him, staring up at him as one song ended and another one began, this one thankfully slower.

"I want to know Jess." He felt her tense, so rushed on. "Not take her from you. I would never do that. I want to know her because she's my daughter, yes, but I want to know her because she's *your* daughter. I would want to get to know her even if she wasn't biologically mine, okay? Because she's a part of you."

As he looked down at her, he realized he was saying nothing more than the absolute truth.

She nodded. Then a troubled look entered her eyes.

"What? What worries you? We can talk through it."

"I'm drunk. I'm afraid I won't remember what you said tomorrow."

He brought her hand up to his lips. "Then I'll gladly say it all again tomorrow. And the day after that and the day after that. Every single day until it's the first thing you think of when you wake up in the morning."

He pulled her against him and held her as they danced.

The DJ took pity on him and played a slow song next, which had all the Linear guys out on the floor dancing with their women.

They were halfway through that song when camera flashes erupted around him.

Shit. This was why he'd stayed in a back booth most of the night. Paparazzi didn't tend to follow him around all the time, probably because he didn't give them much fodder, but him dancing multiple songs this close to Peyton? That was something the gossip rags would want to hear about.

He immediately turned so he was shielding her face from the cameras and walked her off the floor with an arm around her shoulder, keeping her pressed against his chest.

The exuberant cameraman followed, but Cade had learned long ago that the best way to deal with them was keep your cool and get out of their sight.

His friends had his back, stepping into the guy's way, making it difficult for him to follow Cade off the dance floor. But Cade had to leave. Now that word was out that he was here, more paparazzi would arrive.

Mark and Everett met them as they cut back toward the bar. Everett looked pissed, but Mark was already working the problem.

"I've got a car ready out back," Mark said.

Cade nodded. "I'm going to take Peyton home. I just need a couple-minutes head start."

"You got it, boss," Mark said already turning behind them.

"You okay?" he asked Peyton, kissing the top of her head.

She stumbled slightly. "I think so. Are the police after you?"

He chuckled. "No. The press. Generally, a lot more annoying."

He steered her around the bar and out the back door. A nondescript older SUV was waiting in the nearest parking spot. He ushered Peyton over to it, then opened the passenger door and bundled her inside. He jogged around the vehicle, grabbed the key from under the driver's side tire rim—always the agreed upon place for them to leave the key in a getaway vehicle—and jumped inside.

He pulled safely but quickly out of the parking lot, thankful now he'd stopped drinking hours before. Mark would've never let him get behind the wheel otherwise.

"Do you have to do this a lot? Make a run for it?"

Life in the public eye could be crazy. He didn't want to freak her out so early in their relationship. "Not too often. Usually my team and I are able to plan so it doesn't get this bad."

She laid her head back against the headrest, her eyes drooping. At least he didn't need to worry that she was becoming nervous about all this. He wasn't even sure she was going to remember it at all. "It must be nice to have a team."

"It is very nice to have a team. I'd like to be part of your team, if you'll let me."

"I've never had a team."

He kept his eyes on the road but reached out to run his fingers down her cheek. "I know you haven't, Peaches. I want to change that."

"How? What are you going to do?" Her words were a little sharp, but she was rubbing her cheek against his fingers—did she even realize that?

"First and foremost, I'd like you to come back and finish the job as the director for the documentary and music video. One, because you're talented, but also because that's going to give you the financial stability that will make your life easier, you know?"

"Okay."

He rubbed his thumb down her soft skin. "Okay, you understand, or okay, you'll do it?"

"Okay, I'll do it."

"Good. You're too talented not to be behind a camera. And as for the rest of the changes. . . all I want is to get to know you. To spend time with you. To know Jess—without explaining details to her, of course. I just want to have a chance."

She was quiet for a minute. "The lightbulb has to be the right wattage or else it can blow a circuit."

He wasn't sure exactly what they were talking about. "Still thinking about your electrical problem?"

She let out a sigh that turned into an adorable little raspberry with her lips. "I feel like my electrical problem is the only thing I've been thinking about since you came back to town."

Now he *really* didn't know what they were talking about. "I'll help with it, if I can."

"I think that would be nice." Her cheek rested more heavily against his hand.

He stroked his thumb down her cheek again before returning his hand to the wheel. She let out a big yawn.

"Text Riley or someone to let them know I'm taking you home."

She took out her phone and typed something, then slipped it back in her purse. "Riley said hi."

"Is that what she really said?" He doubted it.

"She said it's okay for me to. . .let loose if I want."

With her hesitation, he doubted those were the exact words Riley used either. He pulled up in front of her small house and put the SUV in park. "It is okay for you to let loose. But it's also okay for you to sleep off those Electric Smurfs and decide how much you want to let loose on a different day."

She nodded, and he got out of the SUV, walking around quickly to open her door and help her out. He managed not to groan as her body slid slowly down his before her feet reached the ground.

He offered an elbow out to her. "Can I walk you to your door, Ms. Ward?"

She smiled—so soft and sweet—all he wanted to do was stare at her in the moonlight. "Yes. Thank you."

He took the steps toward her house slowly, wanting to take her inebriated state into account, but more because he wanted this evening to last as long as possible.

They made it to the door, and she got out her keys. He laughingly shifted her out of the way when she struggled to get the key in the lock. "Mind if I try?"

"Thanks. I'm not sure what's wrong with my fingers."

He got it on the first try and opened the door for her. "It's the blue drinks. They're a killer. Be sure to take two aspirin and drink a full glass of water before you go to bed. Then if you have a queasy stomach in the morning, eat some yogurt. That will help, trust me."

She stood framed in the doorway, nodding solemnly. "Aspirin, water, yogurt. Check."

He tapped her on the nose. "Good girl."

She stared at him for a long moment, eyes becoming more narrowed. Was she about to yell at him again? Tell him to get lost?

"Cade O'Conner."

He braced himself for the emotional blow. "Yes, ma'am."

He wasn't expecting her to step closer to him and grab

his shirt by the center. "Riley said it was okay to be loose. Is that what you want, for me to be loose?"

Oh, sweet lord, he could actually feel her fingers rubbing against his chest. "I think she actually said *let* loose."

She waved the other hand around. "Let loose, be loose, whatever. The question is, do you want me, Cade O'Conner? Do you want to kiss me?"

Did he want to kiss her?

He didn't even honor a question so ridiculous with a response. For someone who made a living with words, he knew that sometimes words couldn't do a situation justice.

Only actions could.

He backed her against the door frame and swooped his lips down on hers. He wanted to be gentle, take his time, seduce her slowly.

Peyton didn't seem too interested in that. She wrapped her arms around his neck, plastered her body to his and pulled him closer. The second her tongue licked against his lips, he lost the battle for slow and gentle. He slid his fingers into her hair at the nape of her neck and tilted her head to give him better access.

Complete access.

How many times had he dreamed of doing exactly this —kissing her until neither of them could breathe? Yes, he wanted to do all the rest, but kissing her had been what had haunted his dreams for the past five years.

Their mouths fused together, her tongue danced with his, advancing then retreating, daring him to do more. He loved it, but also knew it was out of character for her.

He loved the language he was reading in her actions but knew it was the alcohol writing the script.

There was nothing he wanted more than for her to let loose *and* be loose with him. But not tonight. He wanted to make sure she chose those things when she had all her wits about her.

He wanted to be her team. That started right here and now by making sure she made it into bed safely. Alone.

He forced himself to slow the kiss way down, easing his lips back so he could nip at hers, tease her, kissing her gently and softly.

He ran his tongue along the seam of her lips, forcing himself not to think of other places he'd love to run his tongue, but withdrew when she tried once again to deepen the kiss.

"I want you. I want to be the one you let loose with." He whispered the words against her mouth, sucking and nipping gently and between words. "But not tonight. Tonight, all I want to do is kiss you."

And he did. He kissed her for the five years that he'd missed. He kissed her for that night at the lake house when kissing her was probably all he should've done. He kissed her for every single dream he'd had about her over the years.

The kisses moved from sweet and tender to passionate to desperate then back to gentle once more.

Cade only stopped when Peyton finally yawned.

"I'm sorry." Her eyes burst open, and she grabbed his shirt, pulling him to her. "I'm not bored, I promise. I just haven't gotten much sleep the past three days."

He leaned his forehead against hers and chuckled. "Me neither. Let's get you inside and tucked into bed."

"But I like kissing you." She gave him the most adorable pouting look. He groaned and had to take a step back. That look was going to get her so much more than kissed if he didn't get himself under control.

"How about you go to bed now, and I promise you can

have kisses whenever you want them." He tapped her gently on lips already swollen from his.

She swayed gently into him. "We'll be each other's kissing team. And light bulb changing team too."

"I'll be on every team you want. As long as I can be on it with you."

Chapter 19

Cade wandered from his room down to the kitchen at four o'clock in the morning to make himself a sandwich.

Sleep was done for the night, like it had been every night by this time since he'd talked Peyton into giving him a chance. He'd spent the past three weeks trying to keep all the pieces of his life together. . .and separate.

The label execs were, as always, anxious to get going on the next album. They were excited about what they'd seen so far of Peyton's documentary and wanted to be able to capitalize on its success when it released.

Then there was the upcoming tour to think about and the songs that needed to be written or finalized before that. Everett was on him nearly every day.

Writing music and the tour were important to his friends. Cade understood that. As a co-act, Everett depended on it somewhat for his livelihood. Hell, they all did. But nobody was going to starve if Cade didn't go out on the road for a couple of years. Right now, he had more important things to consider.

Like Peyton and Jess.

He'd finally met his daughter for the first time. Baby had told him how amazing she was, but Cade hadn't really understood.

He understood now.

He and Peyton had agreed that him meeting Jess on neutral ground was probably best. That ended up being on a Saturday at the Linear property. Peyton was no longer working there—Cade had had a direct talk with Zac and Finn himself, letting them know how many hours she was working per week on the video and that she shouldn't be trying to work more for them. They were now getting a cleaning service to come in weekly, but Peyton had offered to help until the new staff was in place.

She took pride in her work, even janitorial stuff. Cade found he respected the shit out of that.

It was also how he found himself emptying trash one Saturday afternoon at the same company he'd helped build five years ago. A set of little hands helped.

Jess had wanted to go out and play, but Peyton had insisted that if Jess wanted to have money to buy an extra ice cream with her lunch this week, she could do a few minutes' work. Show Cade the ropes.

"Do you need money too?" Jess whispered as she picked up one of the small wastebaskets in the Linear office and dumped it into the bag Cade held open.

"Not so much," he responded, keeping his grin to himself. "But it never hurts, right?"

Jess shook her head. "Then you must be in trouble with Mom."

"Daughter." Peyton shook her head from the other side of the office where she was dusting. "Just because you have to work when you're in trouble with me doesn't mean everyone has to."

Jess shot him a side-eye look, like she couldn't decide if he actually was in trouble or not.

"I am a little bit in trouble with your mom," he whispered.

That certainly piqued the little girl's interest. She gestured for him to follow as she walked to the next trashcan. "What did you do?"

"Jess. Manners." Exasperation was clear in Peyton's tone.

"I don't mind answering, if it's okay with you."

Peyton turned around to look at him. They'd already agreed they'd wait until the time was right to tell Jess he was her father. Peyton said it was because she wanted to ease her daughter into the idea—which was probably true. But he suspected she also wanted to make sure he planned to stick around.

There was no way to prove that except to do it.

He gave Peyton a nod. He wasn't about to let her down by blurting out the truth to Jess. He wanted what was best for Jess too.

"I'm a little bit in trouble with your mom because I've been a bad friend."

Jess's blue eyes grew wide. This was obviously something the little girl understood and took seriously. "Why?" she whispered.

"I made some bad choices."

Jess made a grim face and glanced over at her mom. This was something she obviously understood also.

Peyton nodded at both of them like a wise monarch overseeing her subjects.

"Sometimes I make bad choices too." Now her face scrunched up. "Sometimes I have to sit in timeout. Or sometimes I can't play with Ethan for the whole day."

Her little eyes filled with tears. This was obviously a cruel and unusual punishment.

"Is Ethan your best friend?"

"Yes." There was no hesitation in her answer.

"You want to hear something cool? Do you know Ethan's uncle?"

"Uncle Baby?"

He held the bag out so she could dump another small can. "Yup. He's my best friend. We went to school together."

Jess broke out in a big grin, all sign of tears gone.

"Uncle Baby is the most fun. He lets Ethan and me. . ." She looked over at her mom, then her voice dropped to a whisper. "He lets us sit in his lap and help drive the tractor."

"Sounds like Uncle Baby's going to be doing some work for me also," Peyton said from across the room.

Cade stared at Jess, and they both opened their eyes wide. Jess burst into giggles.

He'd bonded with his daughter for the first time at the idea of his best friend getting into trouble. There was a beautiful symmetry to that.

When Ethan had arrived a few minutes later, Peyton excused Jess to go play.

Jess had given him a hug and fist bump—he tried to give her a high-five, but she looked at him like he was the biggest nerd on the planet—before running out. All he could do was stare.

Peyton walked over to him. "That was Jess."

"She's amazing." He stared at the door she'd just run out of.

"Yeah, she is pretty great."

"You've done a terrific job with her. Of course, I'm not surprised."

Peyton shrugged. "She's the best thing that ever happened to me."

He turned to look at her. "Do you really mean that? Do you resent what you had to give up in order to have her? Did you ever think about having the abortion?"

She turned back to her cleaning, and he thought for a minute she might not answer.

"When Dennis hit me and knocked me down the stairs, I had just found out I was pregnant. I hadn't tried to contact you yet. One of the first things they told me at the hospital was that after the trauma, it would take a miracle for the pregnancy to go full-term. But Jess was a fighter."

"Jess's mom is a fighter too. A survivor."

"After surviving all that, I just couldn't even think about terminating the pregnancy. I never considered it again, even after watching that plane take off for London without me. Even after signing papers to you saying I would have an abortion."

"I'm so glad you didn't. I know that's a day late and a million dollars short, but I'm so glad you didn't."

She reached over and grabbed his hand, squeezing his fingers. "So am I."

He'd seen both Peyton and Jess almost every day since then. Jess had so many of the Linear Tactical guys in her life that one more was no big deal. She was friendly and vivacious and everything Cade could've hoped for in a child. They were becoming closer by the day.

Peyton, on the other hand, wasn't quite as easy a nut to crack.

There hadn't been any more make-out sessions, but he'd been able to steal as many pecks on the cheek as he possibly could.

And that was perfectly fine. He'd continue his slow and steady onslaught for as long as it took. Until the day Peyton told him she only wanted to be friends, he was never going to let up.

He had to face the fact that she might say that to him. He'd been loath to actually bring it up because she might tell him that he would be permanently parked in the friend zone. If so, that would suck, but—

The power went out.

"Fuck."

He gave his eyes a couple moments to adjust, then made his way along the kitchen island to the junk drawer near the side door, wishing he hadn't left his phone on his bedside table.

He froze when he glanced out the window and saw someone outside near the small barn a few dozen yards from his property. The person eased around a corner— caught by a patch of moonlight as the moon came out from behind the clouds for a second.

Who would be out there at this time of night? A little suspicious, given that the power had just gone off. He knew for a fact it wasn't because the bill hadn't been paid.

Cade grabbed the flashlight from the drawer but didn't turn it on, not wanting to tip off whoever was out there that he'd seen him. He moved quickly into the pantry, accessing the gun box on the top shelf.

He was a country music singer, but that was because he was a country boy at heart—and this country boy always tried to be ready if trouble came his way. He didn't ever want to be dependent on someone else to defend him, no matter if he was living in Nashville or here.

Of course, he hadn't planned to need protection literally in his own backyard.

The Glock 9mm was comfortable in his hand as he kept it low to his side and made his way back to the door. He silently eased it open and stepped out into the darkness.

He kept to the shadows, aware he was not in good tactical position if someone was watching for him.

He might not be the only person out here who had a gun.

Then again, it might just be one of the guys—Everett or Lance or one of the security team. For what purpose, Cade didn't know—they would've joined him in the kitchen for a sandwich. He'd never known any of the other men to turn down a sandwich.

He moved south, staying behind trees so he could get a look at the barn's far side.

There. He spotted the person again—definitely a man —coming out from the far end of the barn, walking toward the house with some sort of box in his arms.

Cade stilled and silently pivoted on the balls of his feet, changing direction. Going back toward the house wouldn't provide him much tree coverage, but Cade would be damned if he was going to let the perp near the house with whatever was in that box. He moved silently toward the man, keeping the gun loose in his hand, ready if needed.

Cade stepped out from behind the coverage of the last tree, crouching low and sprinting to the side of the house to stay in the shadows the house provided from the moon's light. He kept as silent as possible, but something tipped off the guy. Cade froze as the guy looked in Cade's direction.

Evidently, he didn't like what he saw because he took off running.

Shit.

"Hey! Stop!" Cade left the shadows and ran full speed after the guy. The guy dropped the box and sprinted toward the woods. Bastard was quick. He still had a substantial lead when they hit the main tree line.

But this fucker would be hard-pressed to outrun Cade

in these woods. He'd been running around here his whole life.

He moved as fast as he could until he was nearly twenty yards inside the forest area.

Then he stopped and listened. This was what he'd been trained to do. He may not have been in the military, but that didn't mean Cade didn't know how to fight an enemy.

He focused his senses, slowing his breathing so he could hear everything around him more clearly.

There. To the southeast, broken branches from footsteps.

He bolted toward the sound.

He wasn't silent, it was impossible to move silently that fast through this much forest, but he was quiet enough that he was close to the perp before he heard Cade. Cade could tell the exact moment the guy realized how close Cade really was. He stopped all pretense of keeping quiet himself and made a dash for it.

You can run, you bastard, but you can't hide.

Cade was going to catch him.

The guy headed farther south, making a loop back toward the house. Good. That would make it easier for Cade to call Gavin and have the guy arrested once Cade took him down.

He ignored the discomfort of pushing his body hard. His body could wait. This had to be the stalker who'd been plaguing him for weeks. Had put Doug in the hospital.

It would end tonight.

Cade caught sight of the guy up ahead and took a sharp turn so he could cross the small stream between them and pick him off on the other side. He forced another burst of speed from his body as he leapt over the water, careful to clear it so he didn't splash and give away his exact location.

He darted around some large boulders—*yeah, buddy, keep heading back toward the house*—then cut, ready to make his tackle.

Instead, he found himself being tackled and thrown back onto the ground.

Shit, had the guy known where he was all along?

Cade grunted and threw up an arm to block the fist flying in his direction. He shifted his weight to his side, bringing up his knee and catching the guy in the waist. It wasn't a great hit but was enough to get him off of Cade. Cade shifted his weight to get back onto his feet, keeping his torso low. This perp was much bigger than he'd originally thought and would go for a blow to the head.

He did but followed it up with a combo punch to the ribs that Cade hadn't seen coming.

"Fuck…" The word blew out of him with his breath. He waited for another fist, but it didn't come.

"Cade?"

What the fuck?

"Mark? What the hell are you doing running away from me like that?"

Both of them were breathing heavily as they stared each other down. "I saw that guy take off into the woods and ran after him. I heard you yell for him, but it looked like you weren't going in the right direction, and I thought I could cut him off."

"I was basically trying to do the same thing, but from the other direction."

"Sorry about the punch, boss."

Cade shrugged. "Sorry about the knee."

They both looked around.

Cade bit off a curse. "Guy would have to be a freaking

167

idiot not to have used this distraction to his advantage to get away. He's gone. I can do some tracking, but probably not fast enough to be very effective."

Mark looked as frustrated as Cade felt. "Yeah, urban jungle is more my speed, not actual forests. We need to get back to the house. I've already called Sheriff Zimmerman. He's on his way out."

"For trespassing? Gavin might give us a hard time about that."

"He won't when he sees what's in the box."

Oh shit. "What's in the box?"

Chapter 20

"There was a fucking dead cat in the box. Dead. Cat." Everett paced back and forth, running his hands through his hair.

It was one of the few times Cade had seen his friend looking like anything less than a GQ model. Everett was like a lot of Nashville—very concerned about fashion without looking like he was concerned about fashion. His skinny jeans and Henley shirt looked a lot more rumpled than usual.

"And something similar happening at the house in Nashville a couple days ago? This shit is getting weird, Cade. Cut up cats. That's right up there with boiling bunnies."

Cade raised an eyebrow at Mark and gestured that he had the floor to speak.

It was four o'clock, and the all-hands meeting was in full swing. Everyone had already had a full day searching the forest for any sign of the perp while Gavin had gone over the box—treating it as a crime scene.

Cade had paid extra, including a signed CD and photo

op, in order to get an electrician out to his house at the crack of dawn to get power restored.

They were all shook up. Mark's news that something similar had happened two days before at the Nashville house had not helped the situation.

The big man crossed his arms over his chest. "Yes, almost exactly the same in Nashville. Someone cut the power to your house and left the box. Freaked out Daniels when he came by as his normal routine."

Everett threw his hands up in the air. "Don't you think that's something you should've told us, Outlawson?"

Mark's eyes narrowed. "You've been writing, Everett. I haven't seen you for two days since you made it abundantly clear you didn't want to be disturbed. Not to mention, I don't work for you, I work for Cade."

Everett blew out an exasperated breath and went back to pacing. Mark looked over at Cade. "You've got your hands full here too. No one in Nashville was hurt—"

"Except for the cat," Everett muttered.

Now Mark let out a sigh. "Okay, granted, that seemed pretty sick. I had one of my men take the cat to a vet. It was cut up like this one, but the vet was positive the cat was dead before it was butchered. It was an old cat that had been euthanized."

"Great, so we've got a card-carrying PETA member psycho." Everett shook his head, glaring at Mark. "I feel so much better. This is bullshit."

"Ev," Cade said. "We're all on the same side here. Mark would've told us as soon as he had something concrete to say."

Cade hoped.

Then stopped. No, of course Mark would've told him right away if there was danger. Mark was one of the most highly-respected security team leaders in the business.

"There was no message, no fingerprints, nothing concrete." Mark shrugged. "And yes, you would've been getting this information in the weekly security update. I would've preferred to have given you all the facts once we had actual facts to give."

Everett was about to lose it again. Cade held out a hand to stop the eruption.

"Mark, from now on with anything weird like this, please go ahead and provide immediate updates. Don't wait for the security briefing. No matter how busy I am."

Everett cleared his throat.

"And keep Everett in the loop too," Cade said.

Mark nodded. "Understood. You'll both be the first to know from now on."

Lance finally spoke up. "I can talk to the label and have more security brought in to assist Mark and his team. Nothing's more important to the label than your safety, Cade."

Cade looked over at Mark. "Want them?"

Mark shook his head. "No, I'd prefer to keep a close team. but I will take them up on the offer if I feel it's needed."

Cade didn't want to tell Mark how to do his job, and honestly, he didn't want more strangers around the house. "I'd prefer to keep the security team small also. There hasn't been a direct threat yet."

Everett scoffed but didn't say anything. Everyone ignored him.

"You've got people here too, Cade. You're one of us, don't forget that," Baby said.

Gavin had left after inspecting the scene this morning, but had come back to get the full info from Mark when he'd found out about the other incident in Nashville. Baby had come with him.

Cade nodded at his friends. "Thanks, guys. Hopefully, it's not going to come to that."

"But it is something we want to take seriously," Mark said. "This is the next level of escalation with the stalker. This may sound uncaring, but I'm less concerned about the animal in the box and more concerned about how this person found your house out here so quickly. I made sure that info was not readily available."

"He's right, Cade," Gavin said. "This person knew where your house was, how to cut the power, and how to come at it from the woods. We're talking about some extended planning or some knowledge he shouldn't have."

Baby nodded. "Oak Creek isn't like Nashville, though. I'll talk to Finn, make sure all the Linear guys are keeping a lookout for anyone around town who might be suspicious."

"The stalker's probably not going to be wearing a T-shirt announcing his identity," Lance said.

Gavin slipped on his hat and headed toward the door. "The Linear guys are much better trained than your average civilian," he explained. "They know who belongs around here and who doesn't. Moreover, they'll be able to spot the difference between someone acting casual and someone truly being casual. I've got to get back in town."

With that, the meeting unofficially adjourned.

Baby clapped him on the shoulder and gave him a nod on his way out. They would talk more later. Lance was already on the phone, probably with the label, and Mark walked with Gavin to the door, still talking details.

Cade and Everett walked out of the living room together.

"You okay, man?" he asked Everett as they stepped into the hall.

Everett scrubbed a hand down his face. "Yeah. It all

kind of caught me off guard. Fucking dead cat. Next we'll be finding a horse head in your bed."

Cade winced and chuckled. "I don't think we've quite reached *Godfather* status yet."

"Just give it a little time," Everett muttered.

Now it was Cade raking a hand over his face. This, on top of everything else? Dammit, he'd been so close to catching the guy this morning.

Everett squeezed his shoulder. "Are *you* okay? What are your plans?"

Everett turned back toward the offices and music rooms, but Cade shook his head, pointing to the front door. "I'm going to see Peyton and Jess. Have dinner with them. I need a break from all this anyway."

He'd had dinner with them every night for the past three weeks and didn't plan on breaking the pattern now.

Everett was obviously caught off guard by that news. "Oh. Thought you might want to write, or completely get away. Use the angst like you normally do—to create."

Part of Cade wanted to lock himself back in the writing cave and use all this frustration and anger and, yes, *fear*, to create compelling music and lyrics. A way to direct all this primal energy flowing through him.

Everett nodded. "I'm feeling it too, brother. We should use the circumstances to get as much fodder as possible. Even if not to write, to go on the road. We're not going to let this guy beat us, right? Let's get the tour up and going, maybe even earlier than this spring."

Cade rubbed his chest. Everett wasn't going to like this. "I can't. I can't just up and leave for an extended period right now."

Everett let out sigh. "Look, I like Peyton too. But she's just a woman. She'll be here after the tour. It's something she's going to have to learn to live with if she's going to be part of your life."

"Maybe. But not right now. This isn't the right time."

"No offense, Cade. But aren't you giving up an awful lot for a woman who hasn't been part of your life for all that long? You don't owe her anything."

It was time to come clean. "Jess is my daughter."

Everett's eyes grew wide. "Oh, shit."

"Yeah. And I haven't been there for her or Peyton for years. So I can't leave right now."

"Wow." Everett rubbed the back of his neck. "Listen, Peyton's doing a really good job heading up the video and documentary. And like I said, I really like her."

"But?" Nothing said before the *but* ever really mattered.

"But. . .you've got your career to think of. *'Echo'* is going to be a hit, I'm sure, but you've been out of the limelight for a little bit. You know how fickle audiences can be."

Cade waited for the pressure that normally built in his chest when he thought about this. Longevity in the music business was difficult and rare.

But the pressure didn't come.

"I don't care." He realized it was the absolute truth. "My career has come first for the past five years because I wasn't aware there was something more important needing my attention. Now that I am aware? My fans will just have to wait. They'll either be there for me or they won't."

"I get that. I really do—"

Whatever Everett was about to say was lost as Peyton came rushing down the hallway and threw herself into Cade's arms.

"Are you okay? Mark let me in. I heard someone left pieces of a dead cat scattered all over your house? And there was a gunfight?"

Rumors in a small town spread quickly but not always correctly.

He cupped both sides of Peyton's head and tilted her face up so he could kiss her forehead. Her eyes were big pools of brown in her face. "No gunfight, I promise. Unfortunately, yes, a dead cat, but not all over the house, just in a box. It seems like I've got myself a stalker."

She blanched. "There's something I've got to tell you. I should've told you before now, but I didn't think it would affect you. Dennis, my stepfather, got out of prison three days ago. Do you think he did this?"

"No. This doesn't have anything to do with you, Peaches."

"How do you know? We have no idea what Dennis is capable of, and he could very well have done something like—"

Cade put a finger over her lips. "It didn't just happen here. It happened at my house in Nashville too. Okay? I'll have Mark look into Dennis, but I don't think it's something you need to worry about."

Everett gave him a little wave and disappeared softly down the hallway, giving them some privacy. Peyton didn't look very reassured. "I promise, everything is going to be okay. I've got myself a friendly neighborhood stalker. It happens sometimes."

Not exactly like this usually, but everything was still going to be okay.

She looked a little less frantic with his words. "I heard about this and kind of freaked out. Coming so close after Dennis's release, it seemed too close to be a coincidence."

He tapped her on the nose. "You should've told me Dennis was out. I noticed you've been distracted the past couple of days, but I thought it was because of work."

"I didn't want to drag you into this. This Dennis thing

is my problem, not something you should have to worry about."

"Hey, when it comes to your safety and Jess's, there is no *my* problem or *your* problem, there's only *our* problem."

"You're right." She sighed. "It's hard to change my mindset. Plus, for years I haven't had to worry about Dennis at all. That was nice."

He tilted her chin up with a finger. "You're not gonna have to worry about him now either. I'm going to make sure of that."

He expected her to pull away, but instead she wrapped her arms around him and pulled him closer. "I'm glad you're okay."

He held her against him then tilted her chin up and kissed her.

"Have dinner with me tomorrow, Peaches," he murmured against her mouth.

"Of course. Jess and I were going to make you fried chicken."

"No, just you and me. Dinner. A date. See if Jess can spend the night with Ethan."

He thought she might refuse. He knew he was being forward, but it was time Peyton understood something.

He was not only in this for Jess. He loved his daughter and planned to be in her life forever. But Peyton was more than just Jess's mom to him.

"Jess is important to me, but you are too. Let me show you."

So much for not bringing up their future in case she friend zoned him. But he had to know.

"Let me show you what you mean to me."

Those big, brown eyes studied him, and he thought he was about to get his bad news.

But then she nodded. "Okay."

Chapter 21

"Breathe."

Peyton almost had to remind herself to do it, or she was afraid she might actually forget.

"Are you talking to yourself?"

She didn't even respond to Silas's snide remark from inside the room that had been set up as an editing suite for the documentary. They'd finished most of their shooting five days ago. Silas had been less than thrilled when Cade had ensured that the equipment she would need to edit was brought to Oak Creek rather than Peyton having to travel to an editing studio somewhere else.

He'd done it without her even asking. Done it before she'd even become aware that it was going to be an issue.

Because all the stuff he'd said that night about being on her team —granted, some of it she still couldn't remember because of the Electric Smurfs—had been true.

Cade O'Conner was hard to resist on any day. Cade O'Conner trying to woo you and make up for damages he felt responsible for was impossible to resist.

She just hadn't been certain he was wooing her as any

more than Jess's mom. Until yesterday when he'd made it clear he wanted to have a date with her.

An *all-night* date.

"Do I need to go seek out the people in white coats?" Silas asked.

"You sure you don't need to go back out of town?" she responded. It had been so nice for the past three days while he'd been in Nashville recording another music video.

He gave her his patently fake smile. "Oh no, I am definitely needed here. I'm just glad it didn't all go to shit without me for the past couple days."

She didn't respond. Mostly because she was glad it hadn't gone to shit without him here either. She'd been distracted since Dennis's release from prison, then yesterday that crazy cat madness at Cade's house had her leaving work early. She may not like Silas, but having him around tended to take off a little of the stress. He wasn't going to let her get too far off track—he enjoyed lording his experience over her too much.

At least she hoped he wouldn't let her. He might get smart and realize if he kept his mouth shut and she went in the wrong direction, it would become obvious how inexperienced she was.

But damn it, so far she *hadn't* gone in the wrong direction. The work she'd done, shots she'd plotted out and captured were coming together exactly like she'd envisioned.

It helped that Cade was damn near the perfect subject for a documentary. Those blue eyes pierced the screen the same way they did her heart.

She wasn't even trying to deny it any longer. At least not to herself. So when Cade had suggested the date tonight, she'd had no interest in turning him down or playing coy.

They'd had three weeks together. Three weeks working with each other almost daily and spending most evenings talking and playing. Three weeks of learning her body hadn't been wrong by wanting him all this time. He was still the Cade she'd been half in love with in high school.

And might be more than halfway in love with now.

How could she not be when she saw how much he loved Jess? He couldn't fake that. The way he looked at his daughter when he thought nobody else could see? That did more to woo Peyton's heart than any amount of flowers or jewelry or love songs ever could.

For the first time, the weight that only a single parent could understand, that fear that something might happen to you and your child would be left alone, eased from her.

Jess had two parents now. Two parents who loved her. If something happened to Peyton tomorrow, Jess would still have someone who would love her more than life itself.

"Jesus, Ward, you're not crying over there are you?"

"Shut up, Silas, I'm not crying. Just do your work and let me do mine."

"Is this about your stepfather? Security team briefed us all and told us we're supposed to run screaming into the streets if we see him anywhere around."

She grimaced. The thought of everyone knowing about Dennis made her want to crawl under the desk and live there.

But also…everyone knowing about Dennis meant he wasn't just going to be able to sneak up on her.

"Yeah, I'm fine. And Dennis hopefully isn't so stupid that he'll show his face in Oak Creek. That's an automatic straight back to jail card."

God, she hoped it was enough to keep him away.

"Look," she said, "let's call it for today. We'll meet back here tomorrow at noon and pick it back up."

Noon because she was hoping she'd be way too exhausted to get here bright and early tomorrow.

Thankfully, Silas didn't argue, and she no longer had to try to pretend to focus on editing. She went home, pampered herself with a bath, and took her time getting ready. Three hours later, Peyton stared at herself in the mirror wearing a simple sweater dress that accentuated her curves. The closest thing she had to lingerie—bra and panties of the same color—completed the outfit underneath.

"Time to change the lightbulb, kiddo," she whispered to her reflection.

She'd already taken Jess over to hang out with Riley, ignoring her friend's exaggerated eyebrow waggle when she saw Peyton's dress. Jess was excited when Riley explained she was responsible for painting Riley's finger and toenails for the night. They were arguing about colors when Peyton left. Her daughter was in good hands.

Cade had offered to come pick her up, but at the last moment she'd panicked and told him she would meet him in town. They were going to grab dinner at New Brothers pizza since she'd insisted she wanted to keep it casual for the first date.

She had no idea how to date someone as an adult. Maybe this dress was completely wrong. Too dressy. Maybe she should go home and change.

Cade hadn't made a big deal about her meeting him and agreed that New Brothers was the perfect place for a first date.

She could do this. Her dress was fine. She looked pretty.

"Just changing a light bulb."

She was running a little bit early, so she stopped to get gas at the main station on the edge of town. She waved to

Gavin at the pump ahead of hers and swiped her credit card. She was about to say hello when some giggling young women walked out of the convenience store. Peyton couldn't see them because of the pump, but she could clearly hear them.

"All I'm saying is… Peyton Ward? What kind of bull-shit is that? How could Cade Conner possibly be interested in someone like Peyton Ward?"

"I mean, she's got a kid and has never been married, so obviously she's got some questionable morals," a second woman said. "Maybe he's just going the easy route."

The first woman scoffed. "He's *Cade Conner*. Every route is the easy route. I mean obviously she's not going to be able to keep his attention for long."

"Pity fuck," a third voice chimed in. "There's no possible reason he'd be around her at all when there are so many other choices except for pity fuck."

The women couldn't see her as they walked in the other direction, but Gavin could. The set of his jaw told her he was about to say something, but she shook her head. His jaw tightened further, but he gave Peyton a brief nod.

"Whatever." Woman One again. "It's obvious to anybody who wants to see it that she has no part in his world. It won't take him long to figure that out. I just hope he sticks around here."

The rest of whatever they were saying was cut off as they got into their car.

Gavin started her way, but she held out a hand to stop him. "I'm fine, Gavin. I've never been too worried what the popular crowd thinks of me. I'm not about to start now."

"Regardless. What they said was—"

He was cut off when the radio at his waist went off. He

responded then returned it to his hip. "I've got to go. Are you sure you're alright?"

She nodded. "Yes."

Gavin was a good friend. A good *man*. He looked like he wanted to stay, but duty called. He gave her a solemn nod then got into his vehicle and drove away.

Peyton lowered her head to rest on the top of her car as she finished pumping the gas, the women's ugly words still spinning through her mind.

"Crass, aren't they?"

Peyton startled and spun at the sound of Cecelia O'Conner's voice as she stepped out from around another pump. Peyton had been so busy hiding from the other women, she hadn't seen Cecelia at all.

"What are you doing here?"

Cecelia rolled her eyes. "Contrary to popular opinion, I do know how to do certain things for myself like pump gas."

"Yeah, I guess there's not much choice around here."

"I don't blame you for hiding from them. Sometimes the best offense is a good defense—isn't that how the quote goes?"

"Were you hiding from them too?"

Cecelia shrugged one narrow shoulder. "Like you, perhaps not so much hiding as deciding whether it was a battle worth fighting. I generally find people of that caliber are not worth engaging."

"So you turn the other cheek? Walk away from the fight?"

"Oh no, dear. I use the other resources available to me to fight people like that. People who would hurt my reputation or my family's reputation. I keep myself distant and generally use my lawyers."

She realized Cecelia was talking about *her*, not those women.

"That's what you thought I was doing five years ago? Threatening your family's reputation?"

"To be honest, yes. I thought you were no better than those tramps we just heard. Someone trying to take advantage of my nephew and our money. I was not going to let that happen."

"All I wanted to do was let him know about his daughter."

"And yet you signed the paperwork and took the money agreeing to terminate the pregnancy."

"You couldn't force me to have an abortion."

"No, of course not. But I wouldn't have given you the money if I'd known you wouldn't adhere to the terms."

The pump clicked off, and Peyton snatched the nozzle out, using it to point at Cecelia. "I didn't want anything from him. Not the way you're thinking. I didn't want money or to capitalize on his success. I was eighteen and scared and alone. I wanted to let Cade know what had happened, but you made sure he didn't know about Jess. You should've given me the chance to talk to him."

Cecelia waved dismissively. "My job was to protect my nephew and the family name. Believe me, I'm aware of your roots. If I could've kept you away from Cade altogether, if I had known you were using the equipment my family had provided the arts department, I would've made sure Cade never got near you. I know exactly what type of family you come from."

Peyton shook her head, realization dawning on her. "This wasn't about me at all, was it? This was about whatever went down between you and my dad and mom. You kept Cade away from his daughter because of some twenty-five-year-old petty grudge."

Cecelia flinched, but it didn't take her long to rebound. "I did what was best for my family. I will *always* do what is best for my family. Family first. Always."

Cecelia turned her back to Peyton and opened the door to her car.

"And Jess? You can say what you want about me, but is Jess part of your family, Cecelia?"

Without answering, Cecelia got into her car and drove away.

Peyton put the nozzle back on the pump, then took a steadying breath.

This was not how she'd imagined her first date in more than five years would start.

She tried not to let the hurtful words the women or Cecelia had said get to her. Cade had never treated her with anything but respect and affection.

But she still was rubbing her chest as she drove the rest of the way into town. Damn, that had hurt.

She parked in front of Fancy Pants right across from New Brothers. She was getting out of the car as her phone buzzed. A text from Cade.

Running about ten minutes late, beautiful. Promise to make it worth your while

Beautiful. He'd called her beautiful. She shot him a text back.

I'm going to watch the sunset over Preston Bridge. I'll see you when you get here.

I'm on my way.

She walked down the street, the opposite direction of the evil gas station, toward the big old bridge. She'd spent a lot of sunsets out here in high school, usually before going to her job. She hadn't been out here for many sunsets lately. The years had been too busy and luxuries like enjoying the sunset had been few and far between.

She watched as the river cascaded over the rocks farther up and got deeper just before reaching the bridge. During the summer, kids sometimes jumped off.

She breathed in the crisp air. Autumn in Wyoming was a beautiful thing. She loved it here.

She wasn't going to let the gas station incident spoil her night. There would always be people like those women, and Cecelia, who thought Peyton wasn't good enough for Cade. If Peyton gave them any room in her mind now, she'd always be fighting what others thought about her.

Cade had never been Cade Conner, the music star, to her. He was just *Cade*. Her Cade. That's who he was always going to be.

But that didn't mean she might not like to hear one of his songs as she watched the last couple minutes of the sunset. She grabbed her headphones from her purse and a few seconds later Cade's beautiful baritone voice was filling her mind as she looked out at the river.

Pieces of You. She'd always loved this song even when she hadn't allowed herself to listen to it.

She stared out over the waters of the river, the reflection of the last bit of the sun making her smile. She closed her eyes and let the sound of Cade's voice take her away.

The pieces of you fit the pieces of me. Alone, we'd just be empty.

She listened to the whole song and was still smiling as the last of the music floated away. The next song started, but she stopped it, then spun sharply when she heard Cade yelling her name. He sprinted toward her, face frantic, waving his arms, looking past her.

She turned to see a car barreling at her.

She wasn't going to be able to get off the bridge in time to avoid it.

Chapter 22

That car was going to hit Peyton.

Cade had seen her at the bridge when he'd first pulled into town. She'd looked so beautiful standing there, he'd just had to watch for a minute, wishing he was the one with any camera expertise.

He'd already been jogging across the street when he realized the problem.

That car was coming way too fast and didn't look like it was in control. He called out to Peyton, frantic to make sure she was aware but realized she had headphones in.

Then realized the driver was going to hit her. Was *aiming* for her.

Cade sprinted across the street before he'd even finished formulating the thought.

The driver sped up.

He yelled for Peyton again. This time she heard him and turned, but she wasn't going to be able to process what was happening in time. That car was going to kill her.

Cade moved faster. It was like his football days when on rare occasion things had gone terribly wrong, and he'd been the only one left between the man with the ball and the end zone. Now, like then, he had to make the tackle to save the situation.

He hit Peyton at full speed; there was no avoiding that.

The best he could do was shift his weight mid-air, taking the brunt of the force as they cleared the bridge railing and flew over the side. Not two seconds later, the terrible sound of metal scraping against the safety rail of the bridge filled the air.

Cade wrapped his arms around her as they free fell for a long second.

And then the icy river water engulfed them.

The cold stole the breath from his lungs. He tried to hang onto Peyton, but the raging current tore them apart. He pushed to the surface and sucked in a breath.

"Peyton!" He didn't see her. Hitting the water at that speed, with so many rocks around, she could be unconscious.

He grabbed hold of a large boulder as he brushed past it, using it to hoist himself up and look around in the gathering darkness.

"Peyton!" Oh God, where was she?

"Cade!"

Thank God. He spun and saw her a little farther downstream, clinging to rock of her own. "I'm slipping!"

"Don't let go!"

If she did, the water would carry her, tossing her around, possibly pulling her—and keeping her—under. It was the reason adults told the kids not to jump off this bridge. The river was unforgiving.

He let go of the safety of his own rock, jettisoning himself toward her.

Her panicked cry as her grip gave away pumped more adrenaline into his already overloaded system. Desperate to reach her, he swam with the current—using every ounce of patience his Linear training had taught him—until she was within range. Blind instinct took over. Almost of its own volition, his nearly frozen hand shot out in her direction, catching her slick, icy wrist before the river could claim her. She threw her other hand up to latch onto his wrist, and he drew her closer, gritting his teeth as he strained against the force of the water.

Once they were both safely on a rock, he wrapped an arm around her and pulled her more securely up onto it. They both lay there for a few moments, trying to catch their breath.

"Are you okay?" he panted.

Violent shivers wracked her body, her teeth clattering so badly she couldn't answer, only nod. He didn't see any blood or signs of trauma.

"We're going to have to work our way to the edge. One big rock at a time. Are you ready for a piggyback ride, Peaches? Wrap yourself around me and hold on. We can do this. We're a team."

She managed another nod.

Steadily, he dragged them toward the riverbank. Too slow and hypothermia would claim them. Too fast and he risked losing his grasp. That was not an option, not with Peyton latched on to him—recovery would be difficult, if not impossible. But it meant longer in the frigid water.

Peyton's grip around his chest grew weaker.

"Hang in there, Peaches."

The last section to the shore would be the hardest—no rocks for him to grab and fast-flowing, deeper water. The darkness hid the bank.

"Y-you should l-leave me and c-come back with a rop-pe."

"No way." She was right, that was probably the surest

way to get them to safety. But there was no way he was leaving her in this icy water alone. "We're a team, right?"

"T-team."

"You hold on to me. I'll get us there. Trust me."

She hugged him closer. "T-trust you."

Battling against the current, he eased himself forward. Fuck, this wasn't going to be pretty. But he wasn't going to let her down.

He slid forward in the water, one foot at a time, until it became too deep. "Okay, here we go, Peyton. I'm going to have to swim. Hang on."

He was about to push off when lights from the river-bank nearly blinded him. Headlights from a vehicle.

"Cade!" Gavin gestured wildly, rope in hand. Thank God. Cade waved an arm, his voice too hoarse to shout.

Within seconds, Cade's numb fingers wrapped the rope around his wrist and just held on, counting on his friend and partner to pull them both to safety.

On the bank, half the town hovered around them, getting into the cold water themselves to drag them out, toweling them dry and wrapping them in blankets. Tiny lights from dozens of cameras faded in and out of focus. Damn, he'd never been so happy to see the paparazzi in his life.

The indistinct hum of a dozen voices blended into the sweetest harmony he'd ever heard. He pulled Peyton closer and kissed the top of her chilled head as the adrenaline rush faded. When they could finally talk without their teeth chattering, he gently lifted her chin to meet until their eyes met. "Are you okay?"

She nodded. "I think so. I don't understand what happened. Was it a drunk driver?"

"I'm not exactly sure what happened." That wasn't

completely true, but he didn't want to worry Peyton until after he'd talked to Gavin.

That driver had been gunning for Peyton.

After finally warming up, Peyton borrowed Gavin's cell phone so she could call Riley and assure her they were alright before Riley heard the news through the grapevine. In a town this small, it wouldn't take long.

Gavin came over to talk to Cade while Peyton was making the call.

"I'm going to have to start calling this Bad Luck Bridge," Gavin said. "This was where Sheriff Nelson went over the edge when he had his stroke."

Gavin was still acting as sheriff until Nelson decided he was ready to come back. If Dorian and Ray hadn't been around the night he'd crashed, coming back wouldn't have been an option at all.

"This wasn't bad luck, Gav. Someone targeted Peyton."

"Adam DiMuzio and one of his friends saw the whole thing. They pretty much concur. Said if you hadn't gotten to her in time, we would've had a hit-and-run on our hands."

"Probably would've had a *vehicular homicide* on your hands at the speed that guy was going."

Jesus, if he'd been thirty seconds later, Peyton might be dead right now. His hands shook again, but not from cold.

Gavin nodded. "He scraped the safety rail pretty hard, so that might give us something to go on. Pretty interesting timing given what happened at your house yesterday."

"This was a damn sight more than a dead cat in a box."

"Now that we've got an official crime, I'm going to get all of Mark's files and see what we can put together."

Cade nodded. He'd known Gavin for a long time. He may only be a temporary sheriff, but there was no one

Cade would rather have on this. Gavin was thorough, focused, and had a sixth sense—saw things in situations many others missed.

"Use Mark for whatever you need. He's got access to all my resources. There's nothing–and I mean *nothing*–more important to me than Peyton's safety. It was one thing when this was some asshole picking a fight with me. He's pushed this way beyond an acceptable level."

Gavin gave him a brief nod. "Listen, something else you should know. Dennis Redman missed his appointment with his probation officer today. There's a warrant out for his arrest."

"Shit." Cade did the math in his head. "He could've made it here from Cheyenne. Would he do something like this?"

Gavin shrugged. "Not as far as I know. He was an abusive drunk but didn't seem like the type to deliberately set out to kill someone. Either way, that's something I'm keeping an eye on."

Peyton walked back over. She still looked shook up, but at least wasn't shivering. "Riley refuses to let me have my daughter back, at least not until tomorrow morning. She said if we let something as little as almost dying get in the way of us spending the night together then we are a couple of...*pansies*. Um, although she didn't use that actual word." Peyton looked over at Gavin. "Sorry, Sheriff. Overshare."

Gavin winked at them. "I think I actually agree with Girl Riley in this case. Why don't you two go. . .get warmed up. If there's anything you need to know, I'll make sure you get word."

Gavin started moving the gawkers back off the river-bank, leaving them alone.

Cade wasn't going to lie to himself. There was nothing in the world he wanted to do more than get Peyton to the nearest bed as quickly as possible. And keep her there as long as possible.

God, he'd almost lost her.

He'd been taking it so slow and easy, not wanting to rush anything. He'd wanted to allow the trust between them to build naturally. And he still wanted to do that.

But the past hour had shown that none of them was guaranteed any amount of time. He wanted to bind her to him in every possible way he could. The instinct was almost primal.

He tried to tamp it down. Forced himself not to touch her. Because if he did, he wasn't sure he'd be able to let her go.

"Do you want me to take you to get Jess? You know Riley will understand." He forced the words out, forced them to sound light and easy. "And if not, I'll distract her while you run in and kidnap Jess."

Peyton stared up at him, those brown eyes huge in her face. "Is that what you want? Do we need to reschedule for another time?"

He stepped closer but still didn't touch her. He didn't trust himself. "This is one of those times where I want to be on your team. Whatever you need right now, I'm here. Just tell me."

She didn't hesitate. "You. I need you, Cade."

THE WORDS WERE BARELY OUT of her mouth before Cade took hold of her hand and led her back up the incline, over the bridge, and to his car.

He didn't say a word. People milled around town, obviously talking about what had happened. A few of them looked as if they might make their way over, but Cade didn't even slow down.

He firmly gripped her hand, his thumb continuously drawing a lazy pattern over the back of her hand.

He wanted her. He wanted her with the same intensity she wanted him. She wasn't going to let herself begin to doubt it for even a single minute.

He bundled her into his car and drove out of town. She thought he was taking her back to his house—not optimal given that Mark, Lance, and Everett were staying there too. She didn't want to be around a house full of people and was about to suggest her house instead. Then she realized he wasn't heading in the direction of either of their houses.

A few minutes later, she realized where they were going.

He was taking her back to the lake house.

"That's why I was late." He glanced over at her when they reached the turn off where she would obviously know where there was they were going. "I wanted to bring you out here but wasn't sure of the condition of the house. It's been a while."

"This is perfect," she whispered. Neither of them said much, but he didn't let go of her hand until they pulled up at the house.

He led her up the front steps, and she saw a swing, obviously brand new, hanging in the same spot as the old one.

"And had to have that." His smile was almost breathtaking in its beauty. "The old swing was falling apart. I owe that thing more than I can ever repay. But I hope you'll let us make new, even better, memories on this one."

"If memory serves, we had some pretty R-rated memories on that swing."

Now his smile turned downright decadent. "Then we'll have to aim for X-rated this time."

Everything in her entire body clenched.

"How about less talking, Mr. Singer-songwriter. More action."

He threw his head back and laughed. "Damned if you getting sassy with me isn't the sexiest thing I've ever heard. We'll get to your X-rated swing moves, Miss Ward. First, shower."

She couldn't argue with that, and especially wasn't arguing a few minutes later when Cade used both hands first to wash and condition her hair, then to clean her body very, very thoroughly.

"You must think my breasts are filthy. You've already washed them twice," she said with a moan, as his fingers pinched at her nipples—she sucked in a breath at the tiny burst of pleasured pain.

"You can never be too careful."

He spun her around and pressed her face-first up against the shower wall, stretching her arms out beside her head and cuffing her wrists with his fingers. She left her hands there even after his fingers slid down to her elbows then across her shoulders. He moved her hair out of the way, giving him access to her neck.

"Let's see if I can remember all the places you're most sensitive."

He nipped at the side of her neck, chuckling at the shudder that coursed through her body. "Seems like I found at least one."

His lips moved down until he found that spot where her neck met her shoulder.

And bit gently.

She couldn't control the moan that escaped her as she

raised up on her toes and pushed her body fully back against his.

Now he groaned. "I love that sound coming out of you, Peaches." His hand slid down her body, over her belly, slipping lower until his fingers pushed inside her. "Dreamed of it."

He continued his onslaught, one hand on her breasts, one driving her higher with his fingers. And his lips and teeth driving her insane on her neck.

"Do you know how many times I've thought of you exactly like this? Falling to pieces in my arms? Every damn day."

His massaged her clit exactly where she needed it, driving her back up on her toes again. She could feel him pressing against her back. Wanted to reach back to touch him, but then his fingers thrust more deeply inside her and it was all she could do to just keep breathing.

"That's it. I want to feel you come apart."

"Cade." His name over and over on a shuddery sigh was all she could manage. "Cade."

"Yes. Say it again. I want to know I'm the one doing this to you."

He continued to drive her up and up until she called his name one last time as the building tension finally broke around her. She fell heavily against the shower wall.

His fingers eased out of her and he helped her turn so her back was against the wall. She smiled up at him. "That was amazing."

He tucked a strand of hair behind her ear. "Oh, we're not done yet."

He sank to his knees in front of her.

"Cade. . .You don't have to. . ."

"Oh, I definitely have to. There is nothing in this world right now that could keep me from wanting to taste you."

She glanced down, captivated by the sight of him on his knees staring at her body like she was the most delicious thing he'd ever laid eyes on. Water ran down over his strong shoulders and back, and she traced it with her fingers.

"I have to taste you." He kissed down her belly before grabbing one of her legs behind the knee and easing it over his shoulder, opening her to him.

"Have to." He kissed up her thigh, then licked her in one long stroke, fingers clamping around her thighs as he did.

"Cade. Oh God." Her head fell back against the shower wall as he did it again.

And again.

He showed no mercy, and all she could do was slide her fingers into his thick hair and hold on as he drove her higher and higher again with his talented mouth. He didn't just taste, he *feasted*. Like he was a starving man and the only thing that would satisfy him was her.

Lights danced behind her closed eyes as her body melted in pleasure. She sobbed his name, collapsing back against the wall, her whole body shaking as the orgasm completely overtook her.

Cade kissed down her thigh again, easing her leg off his shoulder, then kissing his way up her body as he stood. He rinsed them both one last time—having to pull her physically off the wall—then shut off the water.

She was almost drunk with this feeling. He smiled at her as he toweled himself off, then gently set to drying her.

"That was amazing." She knew she'd already said that once, but it was all she seemed to be able to manage.

He kissed her more tenderly than he ever had.

"We're just getting started."

Chapter 23

"Cade. You've got drool on your pillow again."

As far as whispers went, this one was pretty loud and directly into his ear. But given Jess's normal volume, it wasn't too bad.

"That's because I was sleeping, knucklehead. People are supposed to drool when they sleep."

"Only mouth-breathers."

"You're four. What do you know about mouth-breathers?" He forced one eye open.

"I'm almost five. And I hear things. Uncle Baby was talking about *Stranger Things*."

"You've seen *Stranger Things*?"

She shrugged. "No, we're not allowed to watch it until we're twelve."

He was falling in love with this child and her amazing brain as quickly as he was falling in love with her mother. The thought should terrify him, yet here he was sleeping on a couch a foot and a half too short for him.

Cade groaned as he sat up. Five nights on that lumpy piece of. . .furniture was leaving him sore all over, but he didn't care. Until they had this stalker captured, he was stuck to these ladies like glue.

Even if it meant the couch.

There had been no other incidents like the dead cat or the car for the past five days, but neither had there been any progress on figuring out who was behind it. Dennis Redman had missed his appointment with his parole officer the day Peyton had almost been hit by the car. But it was because he'd been at a job fair—something his parole officer had approved.

But nearly impossible to confirm Dennis had actually been there.

Until this was sorted out, Cade had a team around Peyton and Jess when he couldn't be with them himself. That hadn't been too often.

He understood, even respected, the need for him to sleep out here on the couch and not in the bed with Peyton. Loved that Peyton put the emotional wellbeing of their daughter above everything else.

Even if he had a crick in his back and wanted Peyton way more than the few times he'd managed to sneak into her room like they were both teenagers.

"Is your mom still sleep?"

"Yeah." Jess shrugged. "I thought I'd give her a few extra minutes."

He chuckled. "Do you know what *precocious* means?"

She raised an eyebrow. "Do you know what *are you my mom's boyfriend* means?"

He sat up. He and Peyton still hadn't decided when the best time would be to tell Jess the truth about him. Neither of them wanted it to be in the middle of this craziness. They weren't sure if there would be emotional fallout.

"I want to be your mom's boyfriend." He wanted to be

a hell of a lot more than that. "Your mom is very special to me. She always has been."

Jess nodded. "Yeah, she's the best."

"I would never try to take her away from you, you know that, right?"

She looked at him like she might pat him on the head and escort him to Special Ed classes any minute. "Yeah, I know."

But it just went to prove what an amazing job Peyton had done with her. The concept of someone being able to replace her in her mother's heart was completely foreign to Jess.

"I'd like to be a part of both of your lives."

He really would've gotten up and made a pot of coffee if he had known there were such deep talks scheduled for this morning. He rubbed his eyes, then stretched. Jess took the opportunity to plop down next to him on the couch.

"You're famous, right?

Definitely needed coffee. "I'm a singer. A musician."

This unmistakably interested her. "You play instruments?"

"Mostly guitar. A little piano. Why, are you interested in learning? I could teach you."

There was nothing he'd like more than to teach his daughter the instrument that had brought him such joy and an amazing career.

She shrugged. "Actually, I'm already good at piano. I'm also pretty good at violin and harp."

He turned to stare at her. "You play all those? Aren't you in pre-K?"

She shrugged the little shoulder again and looked so much like Peyton, Cade's heart actually stopped for second. "I go to a fancy-smancy school. They help us figure out what we're good at."

Cade knew all about the private school Jess had been invited to attend. He knew details about Brearley Academy he was pretty sure Peyton didn't know.

"Your mom didn't mention to me that you were interested in music. She only said you were really good with math."

Not to mention off-the-charts in analytical thinking, quantitative reasoning and problem solving.

She shrugged. "Instruments are math. That's why they're so easy. I like playing Beethoven best."

"You're playing Beethoven?"

"Only on the piano and violin."

Shit. Holy shit. His kid was a genius.

"I'd like to hear you play sometime. Or maybe we could play together, although I don't really play Beethoven."

She snuggled next to him, her little legs barely stretching over the couch cushion. She flexed and pointed her toes in an alternating fashion the way any four-year-old would.

"Look." Her voice became serious. "I haven't told Mom about the instrument things."

"Why?"

"It costs extra." Her little feet stopped moving. "Mom works really hard, and I think some of it is to pay for my school stuff. I don't want her to have to work harder for me."

His heart tightened in his chest.

"Well, what if I use my famous person money and help your mom out a little with all this? She would want you to have every opportunity, you know that, right? Especially if you're good at something."

"Yeah." Jess rolled her eyes. "She says that to me all the time."

"Because it's true."

She jumped up without any warning. "Okay, good talk. Glad you're my mom's boyfriend. I've got to get ready for school."

She turned toward her room, but then spun back around and ran to him, throwing herself up on him, sure he would catch her.

And he would. He would always catch her.

Her tiny arms wrapped around his neck and he pulled her close. "Thanks, Cade."

She jumped down and dashed back to her room. "Morning, Mom!" she yelled as Peyton came out of her bedroom.

"Looks like you two made friends."

He walked over to her and kissed her, tasting minty toothpaste on her breath. "Evidently little miss approves of me being your boyfriend."

"Is that right? Do I get any say in the matter?"

He stepped back and patted her on the ass. "I don't think so, no. I'm not even sure if I get any say in the matter."

"You can't keep sleeping here on the couch. We're going to have to figure something out."

He walked into the kitchen to make coffee. "We will. We've got time."

SINCE PEYTON NEEDED some more time in the editing suite, Cade took Jess to school. It was exactly what he'd expected to find: open, bright, with engaging adults, and the best equipment and facilities money could buy.

Brearley Academy was a private, progressive school for advanced students. The waiting list was extensive and attendance was by invitation only. And even then, the parents had to pay the exorbitant tuition and fees.

No wonder Peyton had been working three jobs to make ends meet.

But for a child like Jess—and yeah, he was biased but that didn't make her any less remarkable—attending a school like Brearley Academy would challenge her and allow her to learn and grow to her fullest potential.

It was perhaps the greatest gift a mother could've given a child so advanced.

Brearley was widely regarded as one of the most difficult preparatory schools to be accepted into in the country. Peyton must have been thrilled when Jess received the invitation to attend, especially when it had seemed to come out of the blue.

Cade was willing to bet Peyton had no idea Brearley was his maternal grandmother's maiden name. That his family had founded the school more than fifty years ago. And that Cecelia had sat on the Board of Trustees for years and continued to do so.

Yes, Jess belonged at Brearley Academy. But it was his aunt who had ensured that happened.

He hadn't talked to Cecelia since confronting her about what had happened with Peyton. He'd have to face her again eventually, but he wasn't ready to do it yet.

And while he appreciated Cecelia making sure his daughter had a place in the prestigious school, she should've also made sure Peyton didn't have to kill herself to pay for it.

But he would see to that himself, starting today. He already had his business manager on it.

This evening, they were shooting one of the last scenes for the "Echo" video.

The documentary film had been finished for a while.

He didn't miss having the cameras following him around, but he certainly missed Peyton being part of that crew. She was excellent at her job—making sure they got the shots they needed while trying to be as unobtrusive as possible. Sometimes coming up with new ideas off the cuff. Everyone respected her and recognized her talent.

She was so professional and hard working. And Cade. . .well, he generally wanted to throw her down on the nearest horizontal surface and lick all that professionalism right off of her.

Everett caught him as he was walking in the door of the offices they'd turned into a mini- studio.

"You looking for Peyton? She's back in the editing suite."

"No. I'll let her work. I just stopped by to pick up my Luna. We're going to use it tonight for the shoot, but I wanted to practice for a couple hours first." Maybe he could get Jess one of his favorite brand guitars too. Maybe they made a smaller version. Hell, she was barely big enough to play a ukulele.

He smiled, then winced at the pinch in his neck from that damned couch.

Everett gave him the once over. "You doing okay? You're looking a little rough."

Cade sighed. "Sore neck from Peyton's couch. But yeah, being on watch for the boogeyman all the time takes a toll."

Everett slapped him on the shoulder. "Why don't you take a little time in the writing cave? I'm sure Mark can find somebody to watch Peyton and Jess."

Cade shook his head. "Not right now, man. I don't have any words right now. I know there's a lot of stuff going on and all the angst, but the truth is, I'm happy. Happiness doesn't mix well with songwriting, I guess."

That wasn't actually true. Cade had all sorts of words floating around in his mind right now. Some of the best stuff he'd thought of in years. And for the first time, the words were coming from a place of joy rather than pain and loneliness. But he wasn't ready to share it yet. Not with Everett, definitely not with Lance and the label.

He would eventually, but not yet.

"Damn happiness. Gets in the way of everything." Everett gave a melodramatic sigh, shaking his head.

Cade would take it. "You can say that again."

"Speaking of getting in the way, I was talking to Lowell Thaxton. Evidently, some 'Echo' footage leaked online a few days ago—I'm sure we all know we can blame Lance for that—and Thaxton nearly wet himself he was so excited about what he saw."

Lowell Thaxton was a country artist. He and Cade had a friendly rivalry. Cade generally liked the guy, although he was definitely a player. Or as he liked to call himself after one of his songs, *Country Boy Casanova*.

"Figures."

"When he heard it was an unknown director, he called me wanting all the details. I knew a video for Thaxton could be a huge step in Peyton's career if she wanted to continue this work, so I told him about her."

Cade didn't like the thought of Peyton working with Nashville's most notorious playboy, but Everett was right. This could be a huge boost for the start of her career.

"Okay." Cade forced a smile. "Yeah, that's really a good idea. Thank you. When I see Peyton tonight, I'll mention it. She's too good not to be working in the business."

"Oh, you wanted to tell her about it? I'm sorry."

Cade shook his head. "Did you already tell her? That's fine."

"No, Thaxton was passing through town, so I invited him over, and I think he's talking to Peyton in the editing room right now."

"I've got to go."

Cade didn't care if he sounded like a jealous high schooler.

Because, damn it, he *felt* like a jealous high schooler.

As he got closer to the tiny office/editing suite and heard Peyton giggle, Cade wasn't sure he wasn't going to totally lose his cool like he'd tended to in high school. And Baby wasn't here to neutralize the situation this time.

He opened the cracked door as he knocked. "Everything going okay in here?"

Startled, Peyton jerked in front of the large television screen and keyboard and spun around to face Cade.

Thaxton, who had his fucking arm resting over the top of Peyton's chair, was much more collected.

"Cade, how are you? I was doing some early season skiing in Jackson Hole when I saw the new footage of your song. Had to get my ass right over here to try to rope whatever talent was responsible for that."

Cade raised an eyebrow. "Is that so?"

Thaxton may be a player, but he was also smart. He could already sniff Cade's possessiveness over Peyton. Cade hated that he was so obvious, but he couldn't have stopped those feelings if he tried.

"That's very definitely so. I never dreamed it would be a filly like Peyton. She's something to behold—been showing me a little of the documentary. I'm so glad that footage leaked." The bastard had the nerve to give Cade a little smile as he leaned in closer to Peyton. "So glad."

Peyton's eyes expanded. "I didn't leak it. I promise."

For all her talents, she had no idea how this business

really worked. "I know you didn't, Peaches. It was probably Lance or someone else with the label. Whetting appetites."

Thaxton winked at Peyton. "Mine is most definitely whetted."

It was taking all of Cade self-control to not punch the asshole in the face.

"Thaxton, why don't we go into town, and I'll buy you a beer. Peyton has work to do."

For a second, Cade thought Thaxton was going to refuse, but then he stood, offering Peyton his hand. "Miss Ward, it was a pleasure to meet you. I feel certain you're going to have a number of offers coming in once this full video goes live, but I hope you'll place mine at the top of the list."

She reached out to shake his hand, but he took it and brought her hand to his lips instead.

Cade forced himself to take three deep breaths, squashing the urge to leap over the chairs and pull them apart.

Thaxton knew exactly what he was doing and was enjoying every second of it.

"We still on for the re-shoots this evening?" Cade asked Peyton when she smiled at Thaxton. "Or are you wasting so much time we'll have to reschedule?"

They both turned to him. Peyton's eyes narrowed. Thaxton's grin grew.

Fuck.

"I'll be there on time," she bit out..

"Beer sounds awesome, Cade." Thaxton clapped him on the shoulder.

Cade ignored the tension in Peyton's shoulders as she turned back to the screen. All he could think about was getting Thaxton out of here.

Away from her.

Of course, people were going to want her to make all sorts of creative pieces for them once they realized what she could do—videos, movies. She was just getting started.

But he'd be damned if he was going to sit here and watch Lowell Thaxton hit on her right in front of him. "Yeah, a beer sounds good. Let's go"

Chapter 24

Peyton set up and tested the lighting for the reshoot they were doing tonight. There was a team that could do this, but she'd sent them all home.

No one, including Silas, had been happy about that, but the fact of the matter was Peyton had creative control over this project, and she could do whatever she wanted.

Right now, she wanted to tell Cade O'Conner that he'd better get his head out of his ass.

Being here alone in the warehouse was actually a little bit of a relief. She'd appreciated having him around and that he'd even been willing to sleep on her couch even though neither of them really wanted him out there. Had appreciated the time and effort he was putting into his daughter and the fact that he wanted to keep them safe.

But Peyton had been alone a long time, hours each evening after Jess had gone to bed, and all of a sudden, having another adult around all the time was a little stressful.

And then, what the heck had happened a couple hours ago with Lowell Thaxton? Did Cade not want her to work with his colleagues? Before today, she would've said that wasn't true, but he'd rushed Lowell out of the room as soon as they'd started talking business.

She and Cade needed to talk about a lot of things themselves. She wasn't sure exactly where she stood with him. She didn't doubt he cared about her. That was impossible to doubt given all the time they'd spent together, both with Jess and without.

Hell, some mornings she could barely move without that delicious ache in parts of her body that had been dormant for way too long. Parts Cade had awoken.

But there was more involved in a relationship than fantastic sex and companionship.

If they were going to move forward, how was this going to work, if at all? Her life, even if she did start a career in the film industry, was hugely different from Cade's. He was famous. And the women at the gas station last week might have been crass, but they were also voicing what would surely be popular opinion.

And Cecelia... Cade's only surviving family member pretty much hated her.

How could they ever hope to make a relationship work?

Cade talked about long term, but always in reference to her *and* Jess. No matter what, she and Cade were going to be connected to each other. They had a daughter. She wasn't sure he'd really thought all this through yet—that she and Jess weren't necessarily a package deal.

He could be in his daughter's life but not have to date Peyton. Right now, he was still caught up in finding out he had a daughter. But long term he might—

Peyton froze at a muffled noise coming from the back of the warehouse where they had stored some of the film equipment they were finished with.

"Hello?" Had someone decided to come help with the shoot even though she told them not to? Had somebody been here listening to her mutter to herself for the past thirty minutes? Great. Probably Silas with her luck. "Silas?"

No answer. Maybe she was a wee bit paranoid.

The warehouse was huge, and they'd been adding more and more items to the storage area as they'd finished, preparing to ship them back to the equipment rental company. Someone had probably not stacked things properly.

But when she heard another muffled sound from that same area a few minutes later, she skipped straight to panicked. It was mid-afternoon, but this warehouse was on the outskirts of town, and she in all her brilliance, had decided to come here alone.

Cade was going to throw a fit.

"Seriously, is somebody there?"

For a split second, she thought about going to check it out. But wasn't that how every too-stupid-to-live person died in a horror movie? Dennis had nearly killed her once. She'd be an idiot to provide the near perfect backdrop for him to have a second chance.

She rushed over to the shelf where she put her bag and grabbed her phone. She'd call on the way out.

She screamed as a hand grasped her shoulder. Every self-defense technique she'd ever learned flew out of her head as she spun to face the threat.

"Whoa there, Peaches. It's only me."

"*Cade*." She sucked air in, trying to calm her racing.

He pulled her against him. "Shit, I'm sorry I wasn't trying to give you a heart attack."

"No. It's just. . .I heard something in the back. I was about to call you"

Alertness fell over Cade. Instead of chastising her for deciding to come to the warehouse alone, he turned to face the potential danger, placing himself between it and her.

The muffled sound came from the back again. Cade pulled his phone from his pocket.

"Mark, we've got unidentified noises coming from the back of the warehouse."

She couldn't hear what Mark said from his end, but Cade looked over his shoulder at her. "How long have you been hearing the noises?"

"I've been here a little over thirty minutes. I first heard the sounds two or three minutes ago."

Cade relayed the info to Mark.

Mark said something else. "Roger that, I'm going to send Peyton out."

He hit the button to end the call and slipped the phone back into his pocket.

"Like hell you're sending me out," she said. "If that's Dennis, you're not going back there alone and unarmed."

"Mark is coming in through the back door, and he's armed. You need to be out of harm's way."

"Harm could just as easily be outside as in the back by now. We need to stick together."

Cade's raised eyebrow said her argument didn't fool him, but he nodded. Good. She wasn't letting him go back there alone.

He grabbed a steel lighting pole and held it ready to swing as a weapon. "Stay behind me."

That she would do, but she grabbed a prop lamp. It wasn't the best of weapons, but if this was Dennis, she wasn't going to face him empty-handed.

They walked toward the back of the warehouse, picking up speed at a scraping sound coming from the back area.

Peyton kept close to Cade. The lighting back here was dim at best with no windows to add any outdoor light.

As they reached the back, Mark met them coming from the other direction with a gun in his hand.

"Back door was propped open." Both men looked over at her.

She shook her head. "Wasn't me. But some of the crew were bringing equipment over here earlier today."

A scrape and low moan drew their attention to the storage corner. It sounded like someone was in pain.

"Stay behind us," Cade said again.

She did, barely able to see over the two big men in front of her. When they stopped, she almost ran into them.

"Oh shit," Cade muttered, then stepped to the side so Peyton could see.

There was her mother sprawled over thousands of dollars' worth of filming equipment, moaning and almost passed out.

"Mom?" She rushed to her mom with Cade at her side.

"Peyton? Is that you baby? I've been looking for you."

Renee tried to sit up and sent more equipment cascading around her.

"Mom, please hold still, okay? I'll help you."

Jesus. Peyton looked more closely. Renee had already caused thousands of dollars of damage. The film equipment was so expensive. She'd picked the worst possible place for this little drunken bender.

Mark and Cade said something, but Peyton wasn't listening as she moved gingerly around broken pieces of lighting equipment and cameras until she could crouch down to help her mom.

Immediately, the stench of alcohol assailed her. "Tied on a good one this time, didn't you, Mom?"

"Dennis," she mumbled. "Dennis is here."

Peyton looked up and met Cade's eyes.

"Where did you see Dennis, Renee?" he asked.

"In town. He was following me." She began to cry.

"Warehouse is clear." Mark put his gun away and walked toward them. "Nobody in here but the four of us. Both doors are secure, and we have a team member out front."

Cade reached down and helped Peyton assist her mom up. It was immediately obvious Renee wasn't going to be able to walk.

"Is it okay if I carry you, Renee?" he asked.

Renee nodded. "I saw Dennis. I saw him."

She sounded more like a child than a grown woman.

Cade swept her easily up into his arms and carried her all the way to the front of the warehouse and sat her in a chair.

"I'm going get you some food and coffee, Mom." Renee needed to give her bloodstream something else to feed on besides alcohol.

Peyton put the coffee on to brew while rummaging through the snack drawer to see what the crew might've left.

"Renee, when did you see Dennis?" Mark asked. "Anything you can remember might be helpful."

"I went into town to get my hair cut. I thought I saw him when I went in, but figured I was imagining things."

"Do you remember what time that was?" Cade asked.

"Noon."

Mark was already on his phone, texting someone.

"Okay, good. Is that it?" Cade crouched down in front of her mom.

"He was there when I came out."

Renee started to sob, making it even more difficult to

understand her. "I was going to get a treat at Fancy Pants, and I saw him in the alley. Then he followed me. But then when I looked, he wasn't there."

"It's okay, Mom. Here, eat these crackers and drink this water while we're waiting on the coffee."

"He was there. He was smiling at me and shaking his head like he couldn't wait to get his hands on me."

A shiver ran through Peyton at the description. The calms right before Dennis's storms were the worst.

But it was equally possible that her mom had made this all up in her mind to give herself an excuse to drink.

The thinnest of excuses was all Renee ever needed to open a bottle.

Renee looked over at Peyton. "I know I'm not supposed to drink. I called looking for you, and they said you were busy, but you'd be here later. I just wanted to have one drink, but…"

One had obviously turned into a lot more.

"I didn't drive." She looked at Peyton with expectation, like a little kid wanting a treat for doing good. "I knew I couldn't drive."

Peyton squeezed her mom's shoulder. "I'm glad you didn't drive."

"I know I'm not allowed to see Jess if I've been drinking. But I wanted to warn you about Dennis."

Renee kept talking but was making less and less sense. Peyton knew from experience it wouldn't be long before she was pretty much incoherent. Not only because of the alcohol, but because she just wouldn't want to deal with anything.

"I talked to Gavin," Mark said softly. "There's been no report that Dennis missed his parole meeting today. The parole officer has agreed to call if Dennis missed, given the circumstances."

Cade looked over at Peyton. "I'm not trying to suggest anything negative about your mom, but is it possible—"

"It's more than possible that she imagined the whole thing," she finished for him. "That it was her subconscious wanting to give her reason to drink."

Both men glanced over at Renee, then nodded.

Peyton sighed. "I should get her home."

"No." Cade touched her elbow. "Regardless of whether this was a figment of her imagination or not, we need to set up security at Renee's house."

Mark nodded. "Cade's right. If it was Dennis she saw, we'd be playing right into his hands by sending the two of you home alone. I'll take her and get a surveillance team on her house."

That was going to cost money. *More* money. The damage Renee had done here was significant enough. "I don't know. Maybe she should just stay with me."

Cade shook his head. "I know you don't want her around Jess in this state. This is what I have a security team for."

Peyton rubbed her forehead. God, she needed to deal with the damage here. "Okay. Thank you."

She helped Mark get her mom into his car, explaining to Renee as much as possible what was happening. Her mother, as usual, was glad to leave the problems for somebody else to solve.

As Cade and Mark discussed final details, Peyton went back inside to look at the extent of the damage. She'd been right. It was significant.

And Peyton was responsible.

They were supposed to have been working late tonight on the reshoot. Instead, she'd be working late cleaning up this mess. Figuring out if any of it was salvageable so she wouldn't have to pay for it.

She dug in, carefully picking up pieces of lighting trees and cameras and setting them over to the side. Her mother had done quite a bit of damage. This was going to take a while.

"I have people I can call to clean that up."

She only looked up for a second when Cade came back in.

"It's okay. I'll do it. I want to get an idea of how much damage I'm looking at."

"Peyton." He crossed his arms over his chest. "You're the director of the project. This was an accident, and yes, and it needs to be reported, but it's not your responsibility to clean it up."

She stood and turned toward him. "But what really happened is my mom got drunk and decided to make a whirlwind of destruction in the middle of a bunch of rented film equipment. And it totally *is* my responsibility—physically and financially."

He scrubbed a hand over his face. "There's no way you're paying for this, Peyton. No fucking way."

"Well, I'm damn well not going to lie about it on some insurance report. And my mom doesn't have any money."

He slammed a hand down on the desk next to him. "*I* will fucking pay for the damages. *I* will get a crew in here to clean this up. *I* will replace whatever was broken, and *we* can move on with our night."

She wasn't exactly sure how she was supposed to feel right now, but pissed was at the top of a very short list.

"You can take your money and shove it up your ass, O'Conner. You might've been able to buy me off five years ago but I'm not quite that easy now."

"Easy? You are the least easy person in the history of the world."

"Then why are you spending so much time with me?

I'll let you see your daughter. I'm not going to keep you away from her. You don't have to be with me to get to her. Our worlds are totally different. You don't belong with me."

His eyes narrowed, and he stepped toward her. She didn't back down, didn't feel even an ounce of fear. She knew she never had to worry about that with him.

"That's it, isn't it?" he said. "That's what all of this is about. You're still waiting for the new set of papers to arrive, aren't you?"

"What are you talking about?"

"You're waiting for me to tell you about the fine print. The new NDA. My next screwup when I leave you hurt and alone."

She couldn't even deny that was the truth. "Maybe."

"Well, it's not going to happen. I love you, Peyton. I want to be with you. Want to marry you. Want to live the rest of my life with you."

She threw up both hands. "I get it, Cade. You found out you have this supercool daughter. And yeah, Jess is the greatest kid on the planet, so I don't blame you for being enthralled with her. But whatever it is you think you feel for me is wrapped up in what you feel for her. You haven't given yourself time to sort through these emotions to decide if you have real feelings for me at all."

"They're real."

She shook her head. "You're an artist. You've romanticized having a family in your mind. But the truth is, our worlds are too far apart for you and me to ever make it together. You knew that five years ago, but you've forgotten it now. Everybody knows but you."

Jesus. He wasn't the only one who'd been denying his feelings. She had no idea she'd felt this way until all those words came pouring out.

But they were true.

"Listen to yourself, Peyton. I don't care what anybody else thinks. Strangers' opinions shouldn't dictate how we act."

"It's not just strangers. What about your aunt?"

"What Cecelia did five years ago was wrong, but she did it with my family's best intention at heart."

"That's my point! I'm never going to be good enough to be family to her. She let me know that, no holds barred. She doesn't even care about Jess."

"That's not true. I'll be the first one to admit that Cecelia can come across as cold and reserved, but she's done what she could to help Jess."

She rolled her eyes. "By offering me a job cleaning her house?"

He grimaced. "Point taken. Like I said, she can be cold."

"When has she ever done anything to help Jess then?"

"My grandmother's maiden name was Brearley."

Peyton set down the broken camera in her hand slowly. "Brearley, as in Jess's school."

"Founded by my family more than fifty years ago."

"Spell out what you're trying to say, Cade, because I'm not getting there quickly enough."

"Cecelia is on the Board of Directors. Cecelia's the one who made sure Jess got the invitation to attend."

"Jess belongs there. She's one of the smartest kids in her class."

Cade walked over, careful not to step on any pieces on the ground and put his hands on her shoulder. "Yes. She is, and she does belong there. Nobody's kicking her out. But Cecelia was the one who made sure she had the chance in the first place."

All the fight flew out of Peyton. "Okay, fine. Yes, that's

a big deal, and I appreciate Cecelia making sure Jess has the opportunity to attend Brearley Academy."

Cade rolled his eyes and pulled her against his chest. "She should have paid for it so you didn't have to worry about it."

She leaned her forehead against his chest, knowing she should step away. Even though Cecelia had done the right thing, it didn't change matters overall. Continuing to stay so close to each other was just going to make matters worse in the long run.

"I'm glad she did it, but that doesn't change things for us. You're enamored right now with the thought of this family, but what you feel for me isn't real. I think you've manufactured it in your mind. The fact is, you went five years without ever thinking of me. The past five weeks have only been a mirage."

She expected him to pull away, but instead he pulled her closer.

"I need to show you something. If you still feel the same after I show you that, I'll back off for a while and give you all the space you need."

"What do you need to show me?"

"I can't tell you. It's something you have to see. But it's going to require you to give me something you haven't been truly able to give me yet."

"What's that?"

"Your trust."

Chapter 25

She'd stumbled down the rabbit hole. There was no other explanation for what was happening right now.

It was nine o'clock at night, and she was on a private jet. Her first flight ever.

Four hours ago, she'd agreed.

Agreed to let Cade's people come clean up the mess. Agreed to go with him so he could show her whatever it was he thought would change her opinion on them.

Agreed to trust him.

And this was a leap of trust in all sorts of ways. Jess was over at Finn and Charlie's again with two of Cade's security team keeping an eye on the house from the outside. Not that there were many people in the world who could get the drop on Finn Bollinger, even with three kids in his house.

Cade also had two of his men watching Renee's house. There was still no evidence that Dennis had been in Oak Creek besides Renee's statement, but Cade was taking the concern seriously.

The wellbeing of the people Peyton loved the most was in his hands, and he took that responsibility seriously.

But mostly, she was trusting that whatever it was he was about to show her might change her mind.

He was taking her to Nashville. The place he'd called home for the past five years.

Did he plan to show her his house? His studio? His life there?

She was curious, she had to admit. She would like to see how he lived, how his life worked outside of Oak Creek. She knew some of his day-to-day habits after three weeks of following him around for the documentary. But seeing the parts here would help complete the picture for her.

But it wasn't going to change anything.

Wasn't going to change what she'd said to him in the warehouse.

Wasn't going to convince her this was more than his infatuation with the thought of being a family, than it was real feelings for her.

Feelings weren't a faucet she could turn off and on at will. If he'd had no feelings for her for the past five years, they weren't suddenly just there again.

She should know. She'd been in love with him all this time. During high school and after. She'd been in love with him even when she'd thought the worst of him.

She couldn't turn off that faucet even if she wanted to. Her feelings had always been there—intensified after the past few weeks together.

But one-sided feelings weren't enough. She wasn't going to let him do anything permanent based on emotions he was manufacturing in his head.

And seeing his house wasn't going to change her mind.

"I don't normally use a private jet to travel. It seems

wasteful most of the time. Although we do use one for tours."

She couldn't even imagine how much it cost to have a plane and pilot show up at the Teton County Airport ready to take you to Nashville less than four hours after you'd called. So she was glad to hear this wasn't how he traveled all the time.

They were alone on the plane except for the pilot and copilot who also served as cabin steward. Everett had met them at the airport, evidently the person who'd made all this happen. She'd thought he might join them, but he and Cade had a talk outside the airport hangar, and Everett didn't get on the plane.

Whatever Cade had said to him, Everett wasn't happy. The second Cade turned away, Everett's face clouded over in anger.

She was sure this whole situation had to be frustrating for him. But when he glanced over and saw her looking at him, he gave her a smile and little wave before walking off.

"It's a really nice plane, although I don't have much to compare to. This is my first flight."

Cade stared at her for a moment before nodding. "I guess that makes sense."

They didn't talk much after that, both of them wrapped up in their own thoughts. She watched out the window in fascination as Nashville's lights came into view a couple hours later and they landed.

She wasn't surprised when there was a car waiting for them at the airport, a late-model pickup truck that she supposed fit right in around here. Cade drove it himself— she wasn't surprised. He liked to be in control of his own situation as much as possible.

She didn't ask where they were going. She wasn't sure

if he would tell her or not and besides, she was committed now.

But when they pulled up at a rather old looking bar on the outskirts of town, Peyton was surprised. The fact that it was in a strip mall near a grocery store was even weirder.

"Red's Lounge," she read the sign, as unassuming as the bar itself, over the door.

"Yep. I got my start here. Red herself gave me a chance to play when nobody else would. She has quite the reputation for spotting talent and getting them started."

"She sounds special to you."

Cade looked up at the sign, a winsome look on his face. "She is. I owe her more than I can repay. Red is unique. Her requirement for playing here is different than most places."

Peyton tried to swallow her jealousy. "Were you... involved with her?"

Cade didn't scoff or make fun of her question. "Not in the way that some people assume. But what I did here put my career on a certain path. And coming here over the years has always helped me get my head on straight."

Peyton nodded. Again, an interesting piece of his life, but she had no idea what it could have to do with him and her.

Cade put his arm around her and pulled her close, kissing her on the temple. "This doesn't make sense to you, I know. Thank you for trusting me."

"I have to be back in Oak Creek by the time Jess gets ready for school in the morning. Until then, show me whatever it is you think will make a difference."

He led her inside. It was different than what it looked like on the outside—there was an entire lower level that wasn't visible from the parking lot. And not at all smoky or grungy like she would have thought.

Cade obviously knew his way around and guided her through the crowd, a surprising number of people for a Thursday night, to the bar along the back wall. Multiple tables filled the room; a stage took up the entire wall opposite the bar. The three-man band up there now singing about killing time sounded pretty good to Peyton. At least they kept most of the patrons' attention.

Cade slid his hand to the small of her back as he led her to the corner of the bar where the waitresses were picking up drinks to serve to customers.

"Things will probably get a little crazy, so you'll have to sit over here. But this will be the best place for you overall."

"Are you going to be with me?"

"Part of the time."

She was about to ask him for more details when a huge man leaned over the bar and pointed at Cade.

He did not look happy.

"You think just because you're famous you can do whatever you want here, Conner? The waitresses are trying to make a living, and you're blocking their way. They don't have a cushy singing gig like you."

"Cade." She reached out and touched his arm. "I don't have to sit here. I can sit anywhere."

Cade still had his eyes on the big man now working his way from around the bar and coming toward them.

Cade turned to face him, crossing his arms over his chest. "If you know who I am, then it shouldn't bother you if I leave my friend sitting here."

Peyton really did not want Cade to get into a fight with this guy. "Cade."

"Get out of my bar, Conner. You're not welcome here."

"Why don't you let me talk to the real person in charge, and maybe I'll follow your pansy-ass instructions."

Everybody around them gasped. A couple of people pulled out their phones and started recording. The big guy took a threatening step toward Cade. . .

And then pulled him in for a hug.

Both men laughed and thumped each other on the back. Peyton thought she might beat the shit out of both of them.

"Damn it, Cade you really should have told us you were coming. As soon as Red saw you, she ran in the back to call in our extra bouncers. You know how it gets around here when you stop by."

"Sorry, Benny. This really was an unplanned visit. I didn't even know I would be in the state."

Benny slapped him on the shoulder. "You're always welcome, no matter what. You know that. We'll make it work."

"Benny." Cade held an arm out toward Peyton. "I'd like you to meet my very good friend, Peyton Ward."

"The Peyton?"

The Peyton? She looked back and forth between the two men.

"The one and only."

"Well then she can sit damn near anywhere she pleases."

Then he turned to her. "It's nice to meet you."

She nodded. "You too."

The trio on stage finished their song and house lights came on. More and more people recognized Cade, but they left him alone. Probably because they couldn't get through Benny.

"Cade Conner, it's good to see your ugly face." A woman roughly half Benny's size came around the bar and stepped in between the two men. "Social media is already abuzz that you're here, so I hope you're going to play."

Cade smiled and hugged the woman. "Absolutely, Red. If you'll lend me Blueridge. I'm traveling light today."

Red stepped back. "You know if I won't, any of the dozen artists in here ogling you will." Red didn't look around, she already knew it was happening.

"Red, this is Cade's very good friend." Red glanced at Peyton but the smile she flashed didn't reach her eyes. "Is that so? Welcome."

"His very good friend, Peyton Ward," Benny said.

Red basically did the same thing Benny had: looked hard at Cade then turned to study Peyton. This time the look in her eyes was much different. "You truly *are* welcome."

"I feel like I'm at a disadvantage." Peyton looked pointedly at Cade. "I feel like you know me, but I don't know you at all."

They all turned toward a commotion at the door. Suddenly, Peyton understood what Benny and Red had been talking about when they'd said they needed more bouncers. Word had gotten out that Cade was here.

Benny caught Peyton's concerned look and winked at her. "Don't you fret. We've had a lot of years handling situations like this."

"You head on up to the stage and get ready, Cade," Red said. "I'll stay here with Peyton."

Cade nodded. "I was hoping you'd show her the questions, if you have a chance."

Red raised an eyebrow. "Is that what you want?"

"It's why we're here." He smiled, reached over and kissed Peyton on the cheek, then turned and started making his way toward the stage.

"That boy sure is excited to show you off. Or maybe show off *for* you."

Cade shook some hands on the way to the stage, posed for a couple of selfies with fans.

Peyton glanced over at Benny who was now at the door with the other bouncers.

Red squeezed her arm. "We'll have to turn people away soon. We hold strict to the fire code around here. Don't let in any more past our maximum number. Once word gets out that Cade's here, we'll reach that number by the time he's done with his first song."

"Honestly, I don't know why he brought me here. I don't know what questions he's talking about. And I don't understand why you guys have obviously heard my name before."

The older woman—at least Peyton thought she was older, but really she could've been anywhere from thirty to fifty years old—stared at her with a measured look in her eye.

"You're Peyton. For the first couple of years when Cade came here and mentioned your name, we had bets going on whether you were a real person or not."

He'd mentioned her name? "If I was a real person?"

"I believe strongly in the concept of muses. So anyone who plays for us has to provide a name for theirs. We knew Peyton was his muse, what we didn't know was if Peyton lived in flesh and blood."

"His muse?"

Red smiled. "Every artist has them, but they're not always real live people. In Cade's case, especially since he never brought any women around, we weren't sure what Peyton was. Could have been a horse or a place. But yet, here you are."

"I'm his muse?"

Red just smiled.

"Well, what are the questions he was talking about?"

Peyton was having to speak louder as it got busier—excitement was fairly vibrated in the bar. A free show by Cade Conner.

"There's only one question that matters right now." Red yelled back.

"What's that?"

"Ever tended bar?"

Chapter 26

Cade was ridiculously talented. He was a best-selling artist, so Peyton had known that to some degree, of course. But watching him work the stage, work the crowd here at Red's, the truth was undeniable.

Multiple times Peyton got so caught up in watching him that the beer she was pouring ended up overflowing onto the bar, and she'd had to start over. Which hadn't mattered much since the people waiting for the beer were just as enthralled with what was happening on stage.

Everybody in the audience felt like Cade was singing directly to them. He oozed charisma and personality.

By the time he got to the last song—the first live performance of "Echo"—Peyton had no doubt Cade was singing to her. She knew it. Everyone knew it.

Our bodies pressed together, bathed in the morning sun.

The sound of two hearts beating, drawing into one.

His blue eyes locked with hers for every moment of the entire song. He didn't even try to include anyone else in the room.

My call has always been for you, empty always empty

Until you answered softly with an echo.
Your echo. I'm full.

How could she have been working all these weeks on this song and not have realized he was talking about her? This had to be what he'd brought her here to see.

She had no idea how quiet it had gotten inside the bar until the entire place erupted in applause as Cade finished the last note. He gave her the tiniest smile before finally giving his attention back to the rest of the audience.

"Wow, honey." Red rubbed her hand up and down Peyton's back. "I think it's safe to say you're still his muse."

"He's got an amazing talent. I've never doubted that."

Cade took off his guitar and talked to some of the people who had moved toward the stage.

Peyton glanced over at Red. "The reason I'm here right now isn't because I doubt his talent or even the emotional sincerity behind the words of that song. If anything, this proves my point. Cade is caught up in a fantasy. He's not giving himself time to see if he really has lasting feelings for me. You can't not think of someone for five years and then all of a sudden she's the center of your life."

Red tilted her head and studied Peyton. "You're here because Cade wanted to see if he could prove to you that his feelings are real?"

Peyton shrugged. "I'm not trying to make him jump through hoops. I'm trying to make him recognize that I didn't mean anything to him for the past five years, so it's unlikely that these sudden feelings he has for me now are real."

Red turned her attention away from Peyton to the patrons at the bar. "Last call!" she yelled

Various moans of disappointment came from the patrons. "Red, it's only 12:30."

"Don't care," she yelled again. "Last call. Get your picture of Cade and hit the road."

When Benny saw what Red was doing he started ushering people out also. Peyton watched them both, wondering what the hell was going on.

"Aren't you going to lose a lot of money by closing up early? This place is packed." Peyton poured two more beers for customers. Already the area by the bar was thinning as people vied for time with Cade.

"Most of these guys have been coming here for years. They're used to me closing up whenever I want to. And I've got plenty of money. I don't do this because of the money."

About thirty minutes later, Red turned to the other two bartenders. "Linda, Bill, you two got the rest of this?"

They both nodded, neither of them shaken by what was going on.

Red took the towel hanging over Peyton's shoulder and put it on the bar. "You come with me." She began walking toward some of the booths on the far end of the room. "Before I moved to Nashville, I was an investigative journalist. Benny was a cop."

She stopped at a booth near the empty back corner and pointed to the framed picture on the wall. A picture of a smiling Cade, guitar in one hand, mic in the other.

"Journalism ended up not being for me. Then Benny got hurt in the line of duty, and we both decided to make a big change. Had a chance to start up this place and did so. After awhile, we got a reputation for helping upstarts. Spotting talent. That was twenty years ago."

"Cade mentioned something of the sort."

Red grinned. "Believe it or not, Cade is not the most famous person who has passed through these doors. But I always knew that boy was special." She reached over and pulled the frame down, turning it picture side down on the table. Five envelopes were taped on the back.

"I may not be a journalist anymore, but that didn't mean *curiosity* died in me. I still liked getting to the bottom of things. Finding out the whys behind stuff."

She took the envelopes off the frame. "If people wanted their shot to play here, there was a price. They had to answer my questions."

"What sort of questions?"

"My journalism questions. Not inappropriate, but definitely digging into why they were doing what they were doing. Their hopes. Dreams. Fears. Some artists refused, and that was their right. Cade never balked. I understand why now."

"Why?"

"He wanted to talk about you, but couldn't admit it even to himself." She handed the envelopes to Peyton then nudged her toward the booth. "You open these now and read them. I think you're going to find the answers you're looking for."

THERE WEREN'T many people like Red and Benny in the world. Cade had known that from the moment he'd met them nearly six years ago. When they agreed to give him a chance to play, he'd been ecstatic.

Answering Red's questions had seemed a little odd, but in the greater scheme not too high a price to pay. The questions she asked always started off the same: who do you think about the most? Why do you think about them?

For five years his answer had been Peyton.

Only in answer to Red's questions did Cade allow himself to think and communicate so freely about Peyton.

He knew Red would keep the responses in confidence, plus no one knew him or Peyton anyway.

He'd cut her out of the other parts of his life—hadn't spoken about her or written about her. But once a year when he answered the questions for Red, he'd let all the truth in his heart come bleeding out.

Red only "required" artists to answer her questions the first year. But Cade had kept answering them long after the required period ended.

It had been his chance to put all his feelings for Peyton down on paper. A way to admit them without really admitting them. He'd never dreamed they'd end up being proof of his feelings to Peyton.

Red and Benny had gotten everyone out of the bar and locked up the place about fifteen minutes ago and tossed the keys to Cade with a knowing smile. Peyton was still sitting at the booth reading the letters.

He sat down across from her. She had letters clutched in both hands. She looked up at him, her brown eyes drowning in her face.

"I don't know what to say about these."

"It was always you, Peyton. From the time you were way too young for me, it was always you. What happened that night at the lake house only cemented my feelings."

Tears leaked out of her eyes. "I never dreamed you felt like this."

"But I was coming for you, Peaches. I hadn't solidified that in my mind, but if I'm honest with myself—and here, in this place, I've always been honest with myself about you, even if I couldn't do it anywhere else—I was done waiting. I'd given you five years. To grow up, get your degree, finish your childhood. . .I was coming for you."

She nodded. "I believe you."

"I'll regret for the rest of my life that I didn't move

sooner. That I wasn't more forceful in my actions. That I lost five years that could've been with you—been with Jess —that I can't ever get back. But I swear to you, you were never out of my heart. I don't even know if my heart is capable of beating without you in it."

He grabbed her hands over the letters. "It was always you. It will always be you. I am thankful for Jess every second I spend in her company, but even without her—it's *still* you. You're it for me, Peyton. I want every single day with you. To make up for the time we lost. And create more time."

"I don't know what to say. I feel like such a bitch making you bring me all the way out here to prove this. I should've believed you."

"No. No, don't feel that way. You had every right to doubt. And if you don't feel the same, I totally understand. But don't doubt any more that I have al—"

"I love you too." The words burst out of her. "I feel the same. I don't have any five-year-old interviews to prove it, so you'll just have to believe me. You've always been it for me."

She reached over the table and grabbed his t-shirt, pulling him to her. "I need you to show me some of Nashville."

He nibbled on her lips then pulled back. "Okay. What parts? We only have a couple of hours if we want to get home before Jess goes to school."

The decadent smile that lit her face had every dirty fantasy he'd ever considered about her coming to life. "Your bed."

Chapter 27

Peyton was exhausted. But it was a good kind of exhaustion. A hopeful kind of exhaustion.

She and Cade had gotten back at six a.m. yesterday, barely in time for her to pick Jess up and deliver her to school. Then she'd spent the morning going over the damages with the representative the rental equipment company had sent out.

Cade had been right. This was what insurance was for. The damage had not been intentional, so a claim would be made.

Taking her mom to the sheriff's office to talk to Gavin had been much more difficult. There had been no sign of Dennis at all in Oak Creek. He'd kept his parole appointments each day. The parole officer had called him exemplary.

Which made Peyton vomit in her mouth a little. But she refused to let Dennis overshadow her life.

Maybe now that she wasn't having to work multiple jobs, she could spend more time with her mom. Help her more. She obviously needed it if she was seeing things.

But all Peyton wanted to do today was spend a little time with her daughter. Cade was going to meet them for dinner, and they were going to tell Jess that he was her father.

She wanted a few minutes with Jess first, so she was checking her out of school early. This was going to be the last time Peyton was a single parent. The thought didn't make her sad, but it was still a big change.

Peyton smiled at the young receptionist working the desk as she walked in and showed her ID. Nobody got into Brearley without clearance.

"Hi. I'm Peyton Ward. I'm here to pick up Jess Ward a little early. She's in K-4."

The receptionist smiled back. "Let me enter it in the system, then we'll call her class." She tapped on her computer for a few seconds, then frowned. "It looks like Jess has already been picked up today."

Peyton frowned but wasn't concerned. Riley could've picked her up, or Finn and Charlie. Hell, most of the Linear Tactical team were on the approved pickup list. "Okay. Can you tell me who? That will make it easier for me to track them down."

The woman smiled, obviously relieved that Peyton wasn't throwing a fit. "Sure. It looks like a Renee Redman picked her up a little over an hour ago."

Renee?

Renee was not on the authorized list. Until her drinking was completely under control, Peyton hadn't wanted to give her access. Plus, she'd seen Renee yesterday, and her mom hadn't mentioned plans to spend time with Jess.

Peyton forced herself to stay calm.

"Can I talk to Mrs. Pearl please?" Peyton needed to ask Jess's teacher what state Renee had been in when she'd picked Jess up. Renee was an expert at hiding her drinking when she wanted, but maybe Mrs. Pearl noticed something. "Also, I need to talk to the director. I don't think Renee Redman is on the authorized list for pick-up."

The receptionist began to look nervous. She immediately placed a call back to Mrs. Pearl and Dr. Goldman, the director of the school, asking them both to come to the front door. Peyton got out her own phone and called Renee. After one ring it went to voicemail.

Peyton rubbed her eyes. Going straight to voicemail didn't necessarily mean anything bad with Renee. She forgot to charge her phone more often than not.

Surely, she wouldn't have picked Jess up if she'd been drinking. Renee didn't make good choices sometimes, but she loved her granddaughter.

The director was the first one to make it out to the front desk area. "Hi, Ms. Ward. Lisa told me you have a concern?"

Peyton shook Dr. Goldman's hand. She had only met the woman a few times but had found her friendly and professional. "I'm not really concerned as of yet. It looks like my mother, Renee Redman, picked up my daughter a little earlier. She's not on the authorized list."

"Let me go get the file. I'll be right back." The director went back through the buzzer door just as Mrs. Pearl came out.

She smiled warmly. "Hi, Ms. Ward. Is everything okay?"

"I came to pick up Jess, but I found out my mother picked her up about an hour ago. She isn't on the authorized list for pick-up."

Mrs. Pearl frowned, and Peyton led her a little ways down the hall to the where they could have a bit more privacy. Peyton lowered her voice to barely more than a whisper. "I don't know if I've mentioned this to you, but my mother is a struggling alcoholic. She's usually fine, but sometimes... not. I can't get her on the phone and before I panic, I wanted to see if she looked okay to you when she picked up Jess. Did you see anything that suggested drinking, or smell anything?"

Mrs. Pearl patted Peyton on the arm. "Oh, no. She looked fine, dear. I couldn't smell anything at all, and she seemed perfectly normal. As a matter of fact. . ."

The director came back through the door, interrupting Mrs. Pearl.

"Here is the paperwork, Ms. Ward. I am so sorry, you're right, there has been an error. A few months ago when you authorized your mother for a one-day temporary pick-up pass for Jess, it was entered into our system as permanent authorization. That's how she was able to get Jess today. I am so sorry. I've already changed it in the system."

Okay, she and Renee were going to need to have a talk, but since Mrs. Pearl wasn't concerned about Renee's behavior, Peyton wasn't going to freak out.

Mrs. Pearl touched Peyton's arm. "Truly, Peyton. Your mother seemed fine. She wasn't acting...peculiar in any way. Jess was excited to see her, even though she didn't really know the man your mother was with."

Panic fisted around Peyton's heart. "Man? What man?"

Mrs. Pearl and the director both looked at Peyton with concern. "Well, I assumed it was her husband. It wasn't anyone I'd seen around here before. He was around her age."

Dennis. It had to be. Peyton turned to Dr. Goldman. "You have a security camera here, right? Is there any way I could look at who was with my mother? This is an emergency."

Dr. Goldman nodded as she went around the back of the desk and scooted the receptionist out of her seat. "Of course, dear. Is everything okay?"

"No. If it's who I think it is, everything is definitely not okay."

Within a minute, the director had the footage up on the computer screen. She gestured for Peyton to come around to the back of the desk. "Here it is."

Peyton knew Dennis in an instant, although he had seen the cameras and tried to avoid looking directly at them. His hold on Renee looked polite and almost protective. Peyton knew her mom would have bruises where he'd gripped her elbow.

"That is my stepfather, Dennis Redman. He's out on parole and is not supposed to be anywhere near me or my mother. We both have restraining orders out against him."

Which evidently wasn't worth the paper it was written on when it came to Dennis.

Peyton studied the footage. Renee wasn't drunk, but she was definitely terrified.

Peyton had seen enough. "You need to call Sheriff Zimmerman right away. Tell him you have proof Dennis Redman was in Oak Creek, and he has Jess and Renee."

"Where are you going?" Mrs. Pearl's face lacked all color.

"I'm going to my mother's house to see if they're there. I'll call for help on the way."

Chapter 28

Peyton ran out the door, ignoring the protests from all three women. She knew it was dangerous to head to Renee's house alone, but she didn't have any choice. Gavin's office was on the far side of the county. It would take him at least twenty minutes to get here. She was not going to leave her baby in Dennis's clutches for that long. And plus, she had no plans of going into Renee's house alone.

Jess had a father. He would fight for his daughter.

As she got in her car and sped out of the parking lot, she swallowed the fear that threatened to overwhelm her and dialed Cade.

Cade answered on the second ring. "Hey, beautiful."

Any other time, that would've made Peyton smile, but now she jumped straight into explaining the situation. "Cade, Dennis is back, and he has Jess and my mom."

"What?" He let out a low curse. "How? Where are you?"

"I went by to pick Jess up at school, and they told me Mom had already picked her up and that a man was with her. They showed me the security footage. It was definitely him, Cade." She struggled to stem the panic building inside her.

She ached with the phantom pain of every bruise or mark Dennis had ever given her.

And now he had her baby.

Peyton couldn't hold back the sob that bubbled out of her.

"Peyton, are you driving? Where are you?"

"I'm going to my mother's house. The school is calling Gavin. But I didn't know how long it will take the deputies to get there."

"How far are you from Renee's?" He didn't try to talk her out of going, thank God.

"Another fifteen minutes." Too long. Way too long.

Peyton could hear Cade's car starting. "I'm leaving my house now," he said raggedly. "I will be there a few minutes after you. Mark is out somewhere, but I'll have him send anyone he has in the vicinity."

"Okay." Peyton fought the panic again.

"Peaches, listen to me. Do not go inside that house until I get there, do you understand? I will be there."

Peyton gripped the steering wheel in one hand and her phone in the other. She concentrated on breathing in and out. "Cade, I'm scared."

"I know you are, sweetheart. I am too. I have to get off this line, but I'm right behind you, okay? I'll see you in a few minutes."

"Hurry." Peyton hit the end button but kept the phone in her hand. Every minute felt like an hour. She drove faster as she got to the dirt road leading to her mother's house, kicking up a trail of dust behind her.

She finally slowed when she saw Renee's car in front of the house. Relief washed over her. Dennis had made a mistake by coming here. He thought she and Renee were alone, like they'd always been.

They weren't. Not anymore.

The temptation to drive straight up to the house and burst in was almost overwhelming, but Peyton forced herself to park four houses down. She didn't want to tip off Dennis that help was arriving.

Her phone's loud ring startled her. She looked down to see who it was.

Oh no. "Mom?"

"Peyton? I'm so sorry, Peyton. He made me do it. I—"

Whatever Renee was saying was lost as the phone was snatched from her.

"Hello, daughter."

Peyton blanched. The sound of Dennis's voice had haunted her nightmares for years. But she wouldn't cower. "Dennis. Where are you? Where is my daughter?"

"My granddaughter? Why she's right here. Such a pretty little girl. Although just as whiney and snivelly as you were. No surprise, I guess."

Peyton could hear Jess crying in the background. Her heart shattered into a million pieces. She put the car back in drive and sped into Renee's driveway. She wasn't going to wait outside. She didn't care what it might cost her. She couldn't protect Jess from out here.

Peyton didn't hesitate. She burst out of her car and ran up to the door. All she had to do was give Dennis something else—*someone* else—to concentrate on until Cade got here.

She threw all her weight into the door with her shoulders, relieved when it gave way easily.

But there was no one in the house.

Peyton let out a sob. "Where are you, Dennis?"

He laughed in her ear. "Do you really think I'm stupid

enough to go back to that house? You taught me all about the cops, and I'm not going back to jail. Maybe I'll just take my wife and our granddaughter and run."

"Please." She was begging, but she didn't care. "Tell me where you are, and I'll come there. Jess is only a child. She has nothing to do with this."

Dennis's quiet laugh struck terror into her very core. "Sweet little Jess is part of you, so she has everything to do with this. Everything to do with the time and the wife I lost. But maybe if you come here right now, I won't hurt her."

Peyton could hear Jess cry louder. It terrified Peyton to think of what Dennis might be doing to her.

"Yes! I'll come—I'll come! Where?"

"You'll like this. I chose it just for you since you've been spending so much time here. Your filming warehouse. I've been watching you there. I'll leave the back door open, since there's nobody here but us."

Peyton closed her eyes. She'd felt like someone had been watching her sometimes while she was filming but since she'd been surrounded by a crew, she had chalked it up to paranoia. Of course, people had been watching her.

She should've listened to her instincts.

"I want to hear your car start right now, Peyton. No funny stuff. No talking to your singer boyfriend or the sheriff. If you do, we're gonna find out if your little girl bruises as easily as you did."

Bile pooled in her stomach. She ran back her car.

"I'm coming right now, Dennis. Don't you hurt her." She started the car.

"Keep this line open so I'm sure you're not contacting anyone else. You've got ten minutes to get to the warehouse, or the fun will start without you."

Damn this phone. With it on, she couldn't get a

message to anyone. She could hear Dennis taunting Renee occasionally as she drove. She hated it for her mother, but at least he seemed to be leaving Jess alone.

Peyton drove through Oak Creek as fast as possible, for once wishing there was a cop who would notice, but of course there wasn't. Just a couple of angry drivers who honked when she cut them off.

Peyton didn't even slow down.

She arrived at the warehouse with barely seconds left of the ten minutes. As promised, Dennis had left the back door ajar.

Peyton looked back at Oak Creek before she walked in. She was so close—so many people would help her, but she couldn't reach them. And now Cade wouldn't be coming either.

She was on her own, but that didn't stop her for a second.

She opened the door and ran inside. "Jess? Where are you, sweetheart? Mommy's here."

She could hear crying from over in the back corner near the stairs. Jess may be brilliant and precocious, but at the end of the day, she was only four years old. Peyton started off in that direction when she heard the door slam behind her.

"So glad you made it on time."

Startled, Peyton spun toward Dennis's voice.

The nearly five years he'd been in prison hadn't been kind to him. He looked thinner. Meaner.

The knife in his hand looked thin and mean also. And he had a gun tucked in his pants.

Peyton backed away as he stepped closer. "Where are Jess and Mom?"

Dennis rolled his eyes. "Can't you hear that brat of yours? She never shuts up." He grabbed her cell phone and crushed it under his booted foot. "Just in case you had any ideas about calling for help."

He grabbed her arm and dragged her toward the crying. As they rounded one of the large crates, she could see where Dennis had tied her mom and Jess to the stair railings. Peyton yanked herself from his grasp and ran over to them.

"Mommy!" Jess squealed, her crying quieting.

"Hey, kiddo." Peyton hugged Jess the best she could with her small arms tied to the pole. "Don't cry. It's going to be okay."

"I'm scared," Jess whispered like she didn't want Dennis to hear.

"I know. Be brave." Peyton looked over at her mother. "You okay, Mom?"

Peyton could see the bruises forming on her mother's face.

"I'm so sorry, Peyton." Renee whispered. "He made me get Jess from school. He told me he would kill me if I didn't. I never thought they would let me take her. But I was on the list. I'm so sorry."

"Mom, it's okay. Let's just concentrate on now."

Peyton crouched down to untie the knot keeping Jess attached to the stairs.

Dennis walked over and pushed Peyton with his booted foot. "What are you doing?"

"Dennis, she's four-years-old. There's no need to tie her up. She's scared. If you want her to stop crying, then I need to untie her."

Jess glanced at Peyton, then started crying louder.
Deliberately.

It was all Peyton could do not to smile. God, this kid. She was so smart. So impossibly smart—realizing the situation and trying to play it to her advantage.

"Fine," he growled. "Just shut her up. We're all going on a trip together, and if she can't be quiet I'll gag her."

Peyton couldn't let that happen. If Dennis got them out of town, there'd be nothing stopping him from hurting all of them, or worse.

Untying Jess was the most important thing. She was Peyton's utmost priority. If there was some way she could get Jess out of the building—and out of Dennis's reach— she would do it. No matter what happened to her.

But how? Nobody knew they were here.

A high-pitched voice from the front of the warehouse rang out. "Peyton Ward, I know you are here. Don't you ignore me."

Cecelia?

Dennis shoved Peyton with his boot again, harder this time. "Who did you tell we were here? I will fucking kill you!"

"I didn't. How could I? You were on the phone with me the whole time," Peyton whispered. "That's Cecelia O'Conner—her family owns the building. She probably thinks I'm working. She doesn't know anything about you."

Peyton didn't mention that there was no reason in hell Cecelia would come looking for her.

Dennis yanked Peyton up by the hair. "Get rid of her now. And bring her close enough so I can hear what you're saying. You have one minute before I start hurting the girl."

Peyton pulled Jess to her. "I'll be right back, okay? Stay here with Granny for a minute."

Jess nodded and dried her tears. Peyton knew they weren't all fake. "Okay. Please come back."

"I will, sweetie. I just need to talk to Miss Cecelia. But be very quiet, okay?"

Peyton got up and stepped around the corner. Dennis

grabbed her arm as she walked by and squeezed it in warning. She'd have bruises there.

She'd be lucky if those were the only ones.

"I'm back here, Cecelia."

Peyton had no idea why Cecelia was here or why she wanted to talk to her. Except for their discussion at the gas station, she hadn't talked to the woman at all. Cecelia would be the last ally she'd choose.

But Peyton didn't have the luxury of choosing. Cecelia was here and a source of help—if Peyton could figure out some way to warn her of the danger. The click from Cecelia's high heels grew louder as she came into view in the dim area.

"Peyton, I'm glad you're still here. We need to discuss the rent of this building."

"Rent?" Peyton would've had no idea what Cecelia was talking about even if her mind wasn't already consumed by the Dennis situation.

Cecelia came closer. "Yes, rent. I just received a call from that other place where I'm on the Board of Directors. So thought I'd come over here and talk to you about rent."

Other place where she was on the Board of Directors? Brearley? Did Cecelia know about Dennis? Had they called her?

"Well, right now is a little…tricky." Peyton couldn't figure out how to signal Cecelia. "I'm busy."

Cecelia moved closer until she was standing right in front of Peyton. "Fine. I'll come back later." Peyton felt something being passed into her hand. A hammer. This would even the odds with Dennis… slightly. "Don't think you'll get rid of me easily, though. I'm staying on this until things are taken care of."

Cecelia tilted her head to the side. Peyton didn't know exactly what that meant, but Cecelia was aware of the danger—that was all that mattered. Peyton needed to get back to Dennis before he did something stupid.

"No, I would never assume I could get rid of you. We'll talk later. Goodbye."

Cecelia turned and walked back the way she'd come in the front door, and Peyton sucked in a breath, walking back toward Dennis, hammer in hand.

She would only have one chance to surprise him.

She didn't hesitate as she rounded the corner—she swung for his head. But Dennis was quick and blocked the hammer before it met its intended mark. He howled in pain as his arm took the brunt of the blow. Peyton jumped to the side and swung again. This time she caught him in the head, and he fell to the floor.

Out of the corner of her eye, she saw Cecelia, who had kicked off her shoes in an effort to double back to help, rushing over to untie Renee. Peyton dropped the hammer and ran over and picked up Jess as Cecelia loosened Renee and helped her stand. The four of them quickly ran toward the exit.

Peyton had only taken a few steps when something grabbed her ankle. She screamed and saw that Dennis had scooted himself across the floor.

Peyton tried to stomp on Dennis with her other foot but couldn't get him to let go. She cried out, and the other women turned back to her. Peyton thrust Jess into Cecelia's arms.

"Go! Get them out of here!"

Peyton could see the hesitation on Cecelia's face.

"Please, Cecelia. Get Jess out of here!" Peyton tried to get her ankle free from Dennis's grasp again but couldn't. He grabbed her other foot, and she tumbled to the floor.

She watched as Cecelia clutched little Jess to her with

one arm and grasped Renee's wrist in the other. The woman ran as fast as she could, dragging Renee with her.

Peyton let out a ragged sigh of relief. Her daughter and mother were safe. But the relief was short-lived.

Dennis struggled to his feet behind her, and she had no weapon. He let go of her leg, wrapped his hand around her wrist, and grabbed for the knife that had fallen to the floor with his other hand.

Oh God. She'd never seen him this angry.

He was going to kill her.

All of a sudden, the warehouse went pitch black. A moment later, Peyton heard the back door open and knew the women and Jess had gotten out. Cecelia had tried to buy Peyton some time by cutting the lights on the power box by the door.

As the door closed behind them, it was dark once more.

Peyton let her body fall to the floor, as she twisted her arm. Dennis wasn't expecting the darkness or the movement and released his grip.

Peyton rolled away quickly and scampered for the crates they'd been packing yesterday. The darkness was the only protection she had.

Chapter 29

As soon as he arrived at Renee's house, Cade knew the situation had gone from bad to worse. He couldn't see Peyton's car anywhere. Couldn't get her back on the phone.

And Renee's door was wide open.

He tried Peyton's phone again, but it went straight to voicemail. Where was she?

And if Dennis wasn't here with Renee and Jess, then where were they?

Cade fought to keep a clear mind. There was no room for panic. His family was in danger.

Cade's phone rang. He looked down and saw the call was from Cecelia. He sent it straight to voice mail; she wasn't who he wanted to talk to right now.

He ran up to look inside Renee's house—to see if there was anything that would point him in the right direction. His phone rang again, Everett this time.

He answered tersely. "Ev, what?"

"Mark filled me in on the details about Dennis Redman. Where are you?"

Cade rammed his fingers into his hair. "I'm at Renee Redman's house. Peyton was supposed to meet me here, but she's nowhere around."

"Fuck. Look, Mark is twenty minutes out. One of the deputies is already over at the school. Sheriff Gavin is headed your way too, but it'll take him a while. I'm in town and will wait for instructions from Mark."

"Peyton wouldn't have left here unless she was forced to. I'm afraid she's trying to face Dennis on her own." Terror coursed through his veins at the thought.

His phone beeped with another call. Cecelia again. He might as well talk to her; she was one more set of eyes. "I've got to go, Everett."

"Alright. I'll see you soon."

Cade clicked over to the other line.

"Cecelia, I can't talk right now We have—"

He stopped mid-sentence. All he could hear was crying and deep breathing.

"Cade? Cade?" It was hard to hear Cecelia over the wailing.

"Cecelia, what is going on? I can barely hear you."

"It's Jess, Cade. She's crying. Dennis had them at the warehouse you've been using for your film shoots. Renee and Jess got out with me, but Peyton didn't make it. She's still inside with Dennis. Jess wants to go back in and help her mom."

"What? You have Jess?"

"Yes, we're outside the warehouse. Dennis had them. Renee is hurt, but not too bad. Jess is okay but scared and crying."

He could hear Jess screaming for her mom as he ran to his car and threw it in drive, keeping the phone on speaker.

"Cecelia, put the phone up to Jess so I can talk to her."

Cade could hear Cecelia try to explain that Cade wanted to talk to her. Jess quieted a bit.

"Jess? It's Cade, sweetie."

"Cade! Mom is in with the bad man. I have to help her. He'll hurt her."

"Jess, listen to me. I'm on my way. I'm not going to let anything happen to your mom. But you need to stay outside with my aunt Cecelia and your granny. But I'm coming, I promise."

He drove through town faster.

Cade could hear Jess's shaky breaths, but at least the wailing had stopped. "Pinky promise. Ethan says those are unbreakable."

"Pinky promise, beautiful. Pinky promise." He took a turn way too fast but didn't care.

"Is Cecelia really your aunt?" Jess whispered. "She helped us. Got us away from the bad man."

"Cecelia loves you, sweetheart. We all do. We'll talk about it after I get your mom out, okay?"

"Okay."

Cade gritted his teeth and kept his voice calm. "Let me talk to Cecelia. I'm almost there."

"Cade?" His aunt's voice rang out.

"Get Jess and Renee as far from the warehouse as you can. As soon as we hang up, call Gavin Zimmerman and tell him to call my security guy Mark immediately." He wasn't going to have time to make the calls himself. "I'm going to rush the back door as soon as I get there."

Rushing in without backup or a weapon wasn't the best tactical plan, but Cade didn't care. He wasn't leaving Peyton in there alone with Dennis a second longer than he had to.

"I'm sorry I had to leave her, Cade. I swear I didn't do it on purpose. I was doing the best I could."

"You got Jess out. I know that's what Peyton wanted. She's tough and smart. Having her mom and Jess gone opens up her options."

"I pulled the main breaker on my way out. I hope that was the right thing to do. I thought darkness might work to her advantage."

That was smart—Peyton definitely knew the building better than Dennis. "Let's hope so. I'll be there in less than two minutes. Call Gavin."

He disconnected the call and drove as fast as he could, praying he wouldn't be too late.

THE DARKNESS WAS Peyton's friend, especially now that Jess and Renee were out. She just needed to keep Dennis in here a few more minutes to make sure he didn't decide to go after them.

She crawled away from him as silently as she could as he muttered filthy expletives. And thanks to her mom's drunken mishap, Peyton knew this end of the warehouse pretty well—much better than Dennis.

"I'm going to kill you, bitch. Finish off what I started five years ago. Except I'm not going to do it fast with the gun. I'm going to use my knife. Prison taught me that."

Peyton swallowed a gasp when a small beam of light flashed in the direction of where she'd just been. He must've remembered his phone had a flashlight.

She pulled her legs back behind a crate, ducking lower so he wouldn't be able to see her easily. But she couldn't hide here forever. He was between her and the back door, and in order to get to the front door, she'd be completely exposed.

She might be able to outrun the knife he was threatening her with, but she wouldn't be able to outrun his gun.

Her weight shifted against the crate and made a noise. Dennis's light spun in her direction. He now knew where she was.

Peyton gripped the hammer she'd found again as she was crawling away. It wasn't much of a weapon, but it was all she had. And Dennis's desire to cut her rather than shoot her, regardless of how terrifying, worked to her advantage.

Running wasn't an option. She had to go on the offensive.

That wasn't a great option either.

She got onto her feet, still crouched behind the crate, straining to hear so she could move at the best possible moment. When she could hear his heavy breathing, she jumped.

He was more prepared for her this time. He blocked her with his left arm, his right swinging the knife down in an arc.

She jumped aside and felt the sting on her arm rather than her torso where he'd been aiming. Without hesitation she threw her arm with the hammer out in his direction and managed to knock the flashlight out of his hand.

Dennis let out a howl of fury and flew at her again. She swung the hammer high and caught him, but she had no idea where.

She didn't wait to see. She ran toward what she hoped was the exit, dodging equipment and boxes in the dark, praying she wasn't trapping herself further. The darkness had been her savior but might now be her downfall.

She sobbed in relief when the back opened and offered some light.

"Peyton!" Cade yelled.

"I'm here!" She cursed when she tripped over some fallen crates. She could hear Dennis moving behind her, much closer than she'd thought. She must not have knocked him out.

Cade ran toward her—but in the light from the door he was making himself the perfect target. "No, Cade, get back. Dennis has a gun."

Cade kept coming. She could see his silhouette.

"Somebody's going to die, bitch!" Dennis yelled, even closer now.

Peyton pushed herself to get to Cade, terrified Dennis would take the easier shot at him.

She wasn't going to get to him in time.

She was almost to Cade when a gunshot rang out in the warehouse. Peyton screamed, still running to Cade.

He caught her as she leapt toward him; she was amazed to find him unharmed.

"Are you okay?" They both asked each other at the same time. Each of them thought the other had been shot. Neither of them had.

In the dim light, they could see Dennis had taken the bullet.

Cade kept hold of her hand and pulled her over to the electrical box, flipping the power back on. Only when they could see Dennis was dead, a hole in his torso, did he let go of her hand.

Everett gave them a shaky wave from the other side of the warehouse. He'd come through the front door, and they'd had no idea.

"Mark told me you were here." Everett stared at Dennis's body. "I thought maybe I could help out. I didn't plan— He was going to—"

Cade ran over and took the gun from his friend's trembling hand. "Thank you, Ev. You saved our lives."

A moment later, chaos erupted around them. Law enforcement poured in from the front door; Mark and his security team from the back. She, Cade, and Everett were escorted out to let them do their work.

"Mommy!" Jess threw a fit when a deputy wouldn't let her through, so Peyton and Cade ran over to where their daughter stood with Renee and Cecelia.

Peyton scooped her daughter up in her arms and pulled her close, then wrapped an arm around her mom too. Cade's arms surrounded them all a moment later.

Peyton peeked out from Jess's neck and saw Cecelia standing stiffly, just watching.

Cecelia had saved them. Risked her own life to do it.

Peyton reached out and grabbed Cecelia to pull her in. The woman remained stiff and Peyton thought for a second she'd made a mistake. But then she felt Cecelia's thin arms come around her.

"Family first," Cecelia said. "Always."

Chapter 30

It was a family dinner, but as Cade was coming to understand, family didn't always mean your blood relatives.

He looked across the table at his aunt. But sometimes it did.

They were at New Brothers pizza which had been Jess's choice after they'd sat down with her this afternoon and told her Cade was her father.

Their near-genius daughter had taken it all in stride.

"This will make our family tree assignment much easier," she'd said calmly.

"I'm glad you feel that way, rug rat." Peyton had ruffled her daughter's hair, then walked into the kitchen, leaving them alone.

Cade had almost called Peyton back. Were they really going to let the entire conversation be two sentences: *I'm your dad. That's great for school projects.*

Jess was smart, but she was only four. Maybe she didn't really understand exactly what they were saying.

As soon as Peyton left, Jess slid a little closer to him.

Then he understood. Peyton had gauged their

daughter and figured out Jess needed a little time alone with him. She'd been able to do that in one sentence because she knew her daughter so well and was such an amazing mother.

"Mom is giving us time to talk," Jess explained when he looked at her.

Great, a four-year-old had figured it out quicker than he had. "Yeah, your mom is pretty fantastic."

"Are you going to marry her and live here or will you be like Fiona's mom and dad. They're divorced and live in separate houses. She sees her dad on weekends."

He reached out and pulled her into his lap, delighted when she snuggled against him. "I love your mom. I want to marry her. But I did some pretty stupid stuff and we have to work things out."

Jess looked down at her hands. "Stupid stuff like not want me?"

Now she sounded like an insecure kid rather than genius.

Cade placed her on the couch and got down on one knee in front of her. This was too important not to do eye to eye. "I will *always* want you. No matter what happens between your mom and me, I want you to know that you will always be my daughter. There was a misunderstanding, and I wasn't around for a lot of years. But now that I'm here, I am never, ever, ever going away. Okay?"

She grinned at him. "Okay!"

"Can we high-five?"

She rolled her eyes. "No, we've got to knuckle touch. Don't be so old. . .Daddy."

His heart felt like it would beat out of his chest at the sound of the word.

Jess looked up from where their knuckles had bumped, obviously to gauge his reaction to her use of the word.

"*Daddy*. I like that. Calls for another knuckle touch."

That memory would be burned into his heart for the rest of his life.

Almost everyone around the table at New Brothers now either already knew or had already figured out the news of Jess's parentage before he and Peyton made the announcement.

Cecelia and Renee both knew, as did Baby and Mark. Finn and Charlie had both been surprised, but they'd taken it in stride.

Riley wasn't here, which had upset Peyton. They'd invited her, of course, because she was every bit a part of this family. And Cade owed her more than he could ever repay for being such a protective friend for Peyton over the years.

Riley had claimed she couldn't make dinner because she needed to prep for tomorrow's multi-day adventure race where she would be medical support.

But both Cade and Peyton thought it had more to do with the fact that she'd broken up with Boy Riley three days ago, completely out of the blue. Peyton said Riley had been acting weird all week.

Not feisty, normal-Riley weird. . .*Scared* weird.

And she wasn't talking to anyone about whatever was going on.

Peyton would surely be storming the gates soon, but not tonight. Tonight was for celebrating his official announcement of fatherhood. Everyone was thrilled.

Except Ethan.

Cade knew how close the two kids were and hated the thought that Ethan had a problem with him. The boy had always been fine before, so this new attitude was a mystery.

Cade wasn't prepared for Ethan's words right after dessert was served.

"Mr. Cade, could I see you outside?"

Silence fell around the entire table before Charlie and Peyton began talking at once to cover it.

Cade looked over at Finn then Baby. Both men shrugged.

Had he really just been asked to step outside by an eight-year-old?

"Is everything okay, son?" Finn asked. "Anything I can help with?"

Ethan didn't look angry, just resolved. "I'd just like to talk to Mr. Cade for a minute alone if I can."

Cade gave him a smile. "You absolutely can, as long as you drop this Mr. stuff. Shall we go outside?"

Ethan nodded stiffly.

They were silent as they walked out. Cade led them across the street and over to one of the benches in the small park at the center of town.

"What's on your mind, Ethan?"

"I have a learning disability," Ethan said. "A form of dyslexia."

Of all the stuff Cade thought might come from Ethan's mouth, this would not have even made the top one hundred. "I'm sorry to hear that."

"It's okay. That's how Mom and Dad met. By Mom, I mean Charlie. She was my tutor, then she and Dad fell in love."

Cade nodded. "Yeah, I think Baby told me something about that." He still had no idea what the boy's point was.

"My real mother, my biological mother, did drugs. That might be part of the reason I have the dyslexia."

"I see."

"My dad wasn't around to protect me when I was little. He didn't know about me either." Ethan held out a hand as if to stop Cade from whatever he was going to say even though Cade wasn't about to say anything at all. "He came and got me as soon as he found out about me. Took me away so I never had to be in the bad places again."

Cade nodded. "Your dad loves you very much."

"Not having a dad around is hard. But I've been looking out for Jess. I'm not her dad, but I've tried to make sure she was okay. That nobody hurt her." He looked down at his hands. "A couple times I haven't been so good at that, and I'm sorry."

Cade slipped an arm around the boy's shoulders. "Are you talking about when that guy came after Dorian and Ray? Used your dog to lure you away?" Cade hadn't been there, but he knew the story.

"Jess could've gotten really hurt bad."

"You've done a good job taking care of Jess while I wasn't around, and I want you to know how much I appreciate it."

Ethan looked up at him, then back down. Evidently he wasn't quite finished with whatever he had to say.

The kid finally cleared his throat. "Being a dad is a big responsibility, and if you're not in it forever, I think you should just move along now. We'll make sure Jess is okay."

Ethan looked stiff like he wasn't sure if Cade might yell at him or even smack him around.

Cade had been a part of enough contract negotiations to recognize when someone was putting everything on the table.

He leaned forward and rested his forearms on his knees, steepling his fingers. "It sounds like I owe you a debt of gratitude, Ethan."

Ethan's eyes flew to Cade's. Obviously, that hadn't been what he'd expected.

"Jess hasn't had a father around, and you've been

looking out for her. There's no way I can ever repay you for that, so I want to thank you, man to man."

"Jess is very special."

It occurred to Cade that in another ten or twelve years he might be having to run this kid off with a shotgun. That the love Ethan had for Jess was going to grow and morph as the two of them got older into something a dad didn't want to think about.

But right now, it was beautiful and innocent and pure.

"Jess is definitely special. And you are too."

Ethan shook his head. "Oh no, I'm not nearly as smart as she is."

Cade sat back and chuckled. "I have a feeling none of us are as smart as she is. But you're still special and I'm not going anywhere. I'm in this dad stuff for the long haul."

"You're sure?"

He raised an eyebrow at the kid. "When Jess gets married thirty years from now, and her dad is walking her down the aisle, that will be me."

The kid actually looked a little disappointed. Damned if this wasn't Finn's kid through and through—a protector.

"Now, my job is going to occasionally take me out of town. Peyton and I haven't worked out all the details of that yet. And whether I'm here or not, I'd appreciate it if you'd keep an eye out on our girl. I have a feeling trouble's going to continue to find her as she gets older."

Ethan nodded solemnly like this was something he'd already considered and was planning for.

"Now, are you ready to go back inside and have some dessert?"

Ethan pointed over to the door of the restaurant. "Dad just stuck his head out. He's probably going to be pretty pissed at me."

Cade slid his arm around Ethan's shoulders and pulled

him in for a bro hug. "I think your dad will be pretty darned proud of everything you said. Standing up for someone you care about, someone who needs protection? That's the sign of a man. Your dad and uncle would be the first ones to commend you for it."

They stood together and walked back into New Brothers. Everyone watched them as they rejoined the table but resumed talking and laughing when it became obvious everything was fine between the two of them.

Cade reclaimed his seat next to Peyton, linking his fingers with hers. He grabbed Jess and lifted her onto his lap with one arm.

This was the first of many family dinners to come.

Chapter 31

"Because the violin, cello, and harp are all in the same family. So it's really like playing the same instrument."

Jess hadn't stopped chatting since they'd left Renee's house fifteen minutes ago.

In the two weeks since Dennis's death, Peyton had been trying to spend more time with her mom. She'd had no idea how lonely Renee had been. Peyton had spent so much time just trying to survive herself over the past few years, she hadn't really thought about her mother.

Renee said she was ready to give up drinking for good. She still had a long way to go in terms of recovery, but now this was something they could tackle as a family.

Cade, because he was Cade, had already offered all his resources for whatever Renee needed. A clinic. A therapist. The number for a local AA group.

God, how she loved him.

"Daddy plays guitar and a little piano, and Granny told me that Grandpa, your dad—is it okay if I call him Grandpa even though he died?—played the bass guitar."

"Yes, it's fine for you to call him Grandpa. I'm sure he

would've liked that. I wish you and I both would have been able to know him better."

"And Aunt Cecelia said Daddy's grandmother played the piano too."

"Sounds like you've got musical ability coming at you from every direction, kid." No wonder she was already playing classical pieces in preschool.

"I think I'm going to do my family tree project with the music theme. I'll need pictures of everyone, but. . ."

Jess trailed off as the car stalled and Peyton muttered a curse under her breath as she pulled over to the side of the road.

"Language, Mom."

"You need a new car. Yours is junk." Peyton did her best impression of Cade.

"Looks like Dad was right."

Peyton slapped her hand on the steering wheel and tried turning the ignition again. Nothing. "Yeah. And now I'm never going to hear the end of it.."

He'd wanted to buy her a new car last week, but she'd stupidly resisted. It was a balance they were still trying to figure out.

She looked down at her phone and saw there was no signal.

Of course not. Everett, on his way out to Reddington City to fly back to Nashville had texted her to warn they were working on a patch of road and had Highway 178 down to one lane. So she'd taken the back roads.

When she looked around, she had to laugh. Here she was, back almost exactly where she'd started five years ago: with a broken-down car on the back roads near Cade's lake house.

Jess continued spouting details of her planned family tree project. Peyton checked her phone for a signal again, just to be sure. Nothing. Fortunately, Cade had installed a land line in the lake house since he'd warned her he planned to sneak her off there regularly to use their X-rated swing.

"Field trip time, kiddo. We've got to walk to Dad's lake house, so we can call for help. There's no cell phone signal here."

"Dad has a lake house? How did I not know about this?"

Peyton rolled her eyes as Jess jumped out of her booster seat and they began walking. So much for this being her and Cade's secret. Jess was already making plans to come back.

She was still chattering away when they made it to the house. She was glad her daughter, for all her genius, was too young and oblivious to recognize Peyton's blush as she ran over to the swing and jumped on it. This new one squeaked every time it moved too much. Cade had joked it let out a squeal to rival hers when it got excited. Then had proved it to her. X-rated indeed.

She was so caught up in her thoughts—her *dirty* thoughts—she was caught completely off guard when the door opened as she reached for the knob. She let out a shriek, scaring both Jess and herself.

"Hey! It's just me." Everett gave them a big smile and a wave as he joined them on the porch.

Peyton threw a hand up to her heart. "Holy crap, Ev—"

"—Language, Mom—"

"—you scared me."

Peyton laughed and sucked in a breath. She obviously hadn't quite recovered from the whole Dennis situation.

She was still trying to get her racing heart under

control when Everett turned toward Jess with a shooing motion.

"Whoa, look out there, kiddo, there's a bee."

Jess immediately jumped down and started screaming. "Where? Where?"

"Be still!" both Peyton and Everett said at the same time. Peyton didn't see the bee, but Everett was swatting near Jess's arm.

"Ow! Mom, it stung me!" Jess grabbed her upper arm and began to cry.

"Oh no, baby." Peyton crouched down in front of her. "Let me see."

It took a couple of minutes of hugs and reassurances that the bee was gone before Jess finally peeled her fingers off her arm and let Peyton see. Peyton couldn't see anything at all on her daughter's arm. She wasn't even sure Jess had been stung.

Her child was a little prone to the melodramatic.

"Does it still hurt?" Peyton kissed her arm.

Jess shook her head slowly. "No. But that's probably because of the anaphylactic shock."

Peyton heard Everett try to swallow his laughter.

"Anaphylactic shock, huh? Well, I think you're going to be okay."

Jess looked down at her arm to check the damage for herself and finally nodded. "I don't like bees. I'm going to tell Daddy."

Peyton smiled at her. "I don't blame you. Let's call him and get out of this crazy place."

Jess's eyes brightened at the thought of sharing her trauma. "Good idea."

Jess climbed back on the swing. Peyton went inside and picked up the phone in the kitchen, letting out a real curse when there was no dial tone. "Seriously?"

"Hey, Everett," she called out. "Do you know what's wrong with the phone?"

Why was he even here anyway? She walked back outside. "I thought you were going back to Nashville?"

"Change of plans." He gave her a sad smile.

"Oh, I'm sorry to hear that. Do you know what's wrong with the phone?"

"I disconnected it."

Maybe this was some sort of weird music-writer thing. "Could you reconnect it so I can call Cade and get him to come get us?"

"I'm afraid not."

She was getting a little bit uncomfortable. "Okay, well, Jess and I'll just walk until we get cell phone signal. No problem."

It would be a couple miles, a long way for little legs, but Peyton would rather do that than stay here in a situation she was uncomfortable in.

She realized the porch swing wasn't making its infamous creaking noise at the same time she looked over at Jess.

It wasn't making a noise because the swing wasn't moving. Jess was sound asleep on it.

Peyton rushed over there. "Wake up, kiddo. We've got to get going."

Jess didn't so much as move a muscle.

"Jess." She shook her shoulder. "Jess, come on."

Nothing.

"I'm not a horrible person, Peyton." Everett said from behind her. "I would never want Jess to be scared or in pain."

"What are you talking about? I think she's had some sort of reaction from the bee sting."

She could see Jess's chest rising and falling with each

breath, and her color looked fine, but she wasn't waking up at all. Even when Peyton helped her sit up, she slid back down. "I really need that phone."

"I practiced on the cats. I euthanized probably two dozen to make sure I would know what I was doing."

Cats? What was he talking about?

Oh shit. *Cats.*

She turned to face Everett. His handsome features held an easy smile, like they always had. But something wasn't right.

"What have you done? Why is Jess sleeping?"

He pulled an empty pressure syringe out of a little case from his pocket. "The bee sting wasn't a bee sting. She should be out long enough to not remember anything."

"Are you the one who cut up those cats? Are you Cade's stalker? But he told me yesterday it was Dennis's old cellmate or something."

"That's what I made him believe, but no, not true. And those cats didn't feel a thing. Jess won't feel a thing either. She was scared after what happened with Dennis. I'm not a monster. I didn't want that to happen again."

Oh God, she had to get out of here. She reached down to pick up Jess. That's when Everett lifted the gun in his hand. "I'm sorry. I can't let you go. You have to stay here, with her. It all has to look like an accident. That's the only way."

"The only way for what?"

"The only way to get Cade back to where he needs to be. He's gotten off track because of you."

"Everett. Don't do this."

"I know, this seems so extreme, doesn't it? And the thing is, I don't have any problem with you. Of course, your dumbass stepfather was supposed to have taken care of this entire situation for me. That was our deal. I helped him work around his parole officer by providing him a jet to get out here from Cheyenne, and he would make sure Cade had enough grief to get him refocused. Twice he was supposed to kill you and twice he failed."

"You shot him on purpose," she whispered.

"I couldn't very well have him explaining to everyone that we'd been working together. So yeah, I showed up and saved the day."

He gestured for her to sit down next to Jess. "I'm the details man. You can ask Cade himself. I can see all the steps that need to be taken to make a plan come together. I had to tinker with your engine to make sure it would stall at the right time. I had to tell you there was traffic on Highway 178 so you would take these back roads. I had to tell Cade and Mark that I was back in Nashville so that they would never suspect me, if they suspect foul play at all."

"What are you going to do?"

"A tragic fire. A gas leak. You and Jess came by for something on your ride home and in the most tragic case of bad timing, lost consciousness in the gas leak and burned in the fire."

"Jesus, Everett."

He shook his head. "It's not going to hurt. You'll be asleep."

He said that as if that made up for the fact she and Jess would both be dead.

"It'll just be one of those tragic stories."

"Everett, you don't need to do this. Between the two of us we can talk Cade into touring. Writing. Whatever it is he needs to do."

"I don't care about touring." He snapped his head back and forth in sharp, rapid motions. "Touring is secondary. I want Cade to let out the full creative genius I know is inside him. Don't you understand? Some men aren't meant to be happy. They're meant to be *great*. When Cade's happy he doesn't create the same way he does when his mind is filled with pain or anger."

Everett's eyes were so earnest. Peyton reached a hand out towards him. "We can help Cade find another way to tap his creativity."

Everett stepped back. "I tried getting him to create when he was comfortable and content. It didn't work. So I had to move on to uglier methods. Do you know all the things I've done to help get Cade to the creative place he is?"

Her heartbeat was racing, nearly exploding. "It was you with the cats and everything, wasn't it? Not Dennis."

"Yes. All of it. I started with small annoyances…graffiti and killing off bushes. Stuff to get him angry. Then I had to move on to hurting a member of his staff. But it was necessary, and I would've kept doing it. But this is better. *This* will give him all the creative motivation he needs for a lifetime. Can't you see that? I want to help Cade be who he's supposed to be."

Everett believed that with every fiber of his being. He might be crazy, but he was committed to it. "Everett. . ."

He walked toward her, gun in one hand.

A second syringe in the other.

"I'm sorry, Peyton. I truly am sorry you have to pay the price. But Cade can't be great *and* happy. He's never going to be great with his perfect little family. So his perfect little family has to die."

Chapter 32

Cade sat in his living room, leaned back on his leather couch, and sipped the eighteen-year-old single malt he'd bought at Glengoyne Distillery in Scotland when he'd visited there a couple of years ago.

He needed to take Peyton there. Not because she was such a big whiskey drinker, but because she'd like Scotland in general. She'd like the distillery tour also. They could do the masterclass where they made their own unique blend. She'd like the nuances that went into that.

Maybe he'd take her there for their honeymoon.

As soon as he could talk her into marrying him.

Baby and Mark were enjoying the whiskey with him. He wished Everett was here, but he'd left Cade a voicemail a couple hours ago from the airport. He was on his way back to Nashville to give Cade some privacy with Peyton and to get back to his own work.

Cade still needed a chance to sit down with his friend and try to impart his vision. The new vision. Everything had changed, but Cade wasn't going to leave his friend in a lurch. He wasn't willing to tour right now, but they would work something out.

Cade wasn't withdrawing completely. He had some ideas about mentoring new artists, but maybe doing it from out here.

Lance thought it was the greatest idea since sliced bread and immediately wanted to turn it into a TV game show—with contestants vying to win the internship. Cade immediately shut that down. He wanted this to be low-key, intimate.

No angst.

Cade was done with angst. Done with trauma, done with danger.

He wanted to see what he could create without drama and frustration fueling him.

He leaned his head back against the couch and took a sip of his whiskey.

"I'm going to write a song about you, Mark."

Mark chuckled. "About my stunning good looks and sparkling personality?"

Cade opened one eye and glanced over at him. Mark was actually a good-looking guy. But he also had an ability to carry himself in a way that changed his whole demeanor—made him seem sort of plain and ordinary. Which was probably pretty helpful in his line of work.

"No. About timing. About how some things are meant to be."

Now Baby laughed. "We thought he was in love with Peyton this whole time, but really he's been in love with you, Mark."

Cade flipped him off.

"I've spent a lot of time thinking about what happened with Dennis. He was going to kill Peyton; I have no doubt about it. Or me. If you hadn't called Everett to let him know we were in the warehouse, either Peyton or I, or maybe both of us, would be dead."

"As long as you name the song, *Mark, the Awesome Guy*, I have no problem with it. But I'm afraid I didn't call Everett and let him know you guys were there."

"Come on, Mark," Baby said. "Don't ruin it for him. He's a sensitive artist."

Cade sat up a little straighter on the couch. "But Everett told me you called him. That's how he knew to come to the warehouse."

"I was driving at one hundred miles an hour. I wasn't calling anybody. He told me he saw Cecelia and Renee. That's how he knew to go in the warehouse."

Cade set his glass on the end table "Okay. I must've misunderstood."

Except, now Cade couldn't get it out of his mind.

Mark was sitting up straighter too.

They looked at each other.

"Why would he have come in the front door?" Mark asked. "If he saw Cecelia and Renee, the back door would've been the quickest, easiest, and most logical place for him to enter to assist."

Cade rubbed a hand down his face. "Telling me you called him would justify why he'd come through the front door. Something about this isn't right."

Mark was immediately on his feet. "I need to check connections between Everett and Dennis. Shit. I should've followed my gut."

"You suspected something earlier?" Baby asked.

"I wasn't so much suspicious as I was confused. Everett said he'd found a connection between Dennis's cellmate and Nashville—a nice little wrap up for our stalker there. I wanted an actual name so we could be on top of it but had come up with nothing. I thought I'd wait for things to calm down a little bit and get more details from Everett."

Cade felt sick. "So what you're telling me is that we may have caught Everett in two separate lies concerning Dennis Redman."

Both Baby and Mark looked grim. None of them had to point out the obvious. One lie could be overlooked as a misunderstanding or miscommunication. Two couldn't.

"Give me one hour. I need to call in backup." Mark left the room at a run.

Cade looked over at Baby. "I can't wrap my head around what's happening right now."

Baby pointed to Cade's phone. "See if you can get your friend on the line. Sometimes circumstances seem damning, but when we hear the whole story it makes sense."

Jesus, Cade hoped that was true.

His call to Everett went straight to voicemail. He tried again a couple minutes later with the same result.

"He's on the flight back to Nashville. I won't be able to talk to him for a while."

Cade kept trying. Tried texting and messaging—both of which Everett should've gotten through the plane's Wi-Fi.

And meanwhile continued to pray it was all a mistake. Some misunderstanding that Everett would be able to explain away—some crazy-ass story that would have them all in tears they'd be laughing so hard.

True to his word, Mark called Cade back to his office an hour later. Baby followed.

Mark's face was somber.

"Do you know Kendrick Foster? He does part-time computer work for Linear."

Cade nodded. "I saw you a few weeks ago at the

Eagle's Nest when all the girls went out. Thanks for your help tonight." He shook Kendrick's hand.

Baby gave him a little wave. "Hey, Blaze."

Kendrick rolled his eyes. "Never gonna live that down."

Cade wanted to ask what they were talking about, but it would have to wait for another time. Mark knew that too.

"What we found isn't good."

Cade scrubbed a hand over his face. "How bad is it?"

"How much time do you have?" Kendrick asked.

Shit.

Mark grimaced. "The day before the warehouse incident when Renee Redman thought she saw Dennis—she actually did. And the car that almost plowed into Peyton? Also Dennis."

Cade shook his head. "How? The guy was in Cheyenne. That's five hours from here. No way he could get there and back in time to be at his parole meetings each day."

"Unless you have a friend who's flying you in a private jet," Kendrick said.

Cade looked at Mark, hoping he'd say something different. Everett could've used the jet two or three times and none of Cade's accountants would've thought twice about it. Cade's entire team occasionally chartered a jet to get somewhere quickly. Hell, Everett probably could afford to charter his own jet a few times if he wanted to.

"You're sure?" He was looking at Mark, but Kendrick answered.

"A second unidentified male passenger was listed on all the flights."

"Shit."

"Even better," Kendrick continued. "I don't know

where your friend is right now, but he's not on his way to Nashville. At least not on any commercial flight or charter jet using your or his accounts."

"So caught in another lie," Cade muttered.

"Why would he get involved with Dennis Redman?" Baby asked.

Cade felt like the whole world was crashing in on him. "Because he was trying to get rid of Peyton. He knew she was the reason I wouldn't tour. He thought she was the reason I wasn't writing."

"Also might be because he's financially leveraged everything he has on this upcoming tour," Kendrick said. "I'll have to dig deeper if you want specifics, but your boy is broke-broke."

"I think canceling the tour pushed him over the edge," Mark said.

Cade grabbed his phone and immediately dialed Peyton.

Voicemail. Fucking voicemail.

"I've already tried tracking Peyton and Everett's phones—no go, which means their phones are off. I've already got men on the way to Peyton's house. They should be reporting in within the next five minutes."

The next five minutes did not bring any good news. She and Jess weren't there.

It was eight o'clock on a school night. Peyton wouldn't be out gallivanting around. Panic clawed at Cade's gut.

Everybody galvanized into action. Baby called his brother to get the Linear guys on the situation.

Mark directed his team, spreading them out all over the county to look for the girls or Everett. He followed that up with a call to Gavin so that law enforcement was working on the same page.

Kendrick, somebody Cade hardly knew, touched base

with some of his computer friends, including Neo, who'd been at the Eagle's Nest that night also. "We're looking at traffic cams, ATM cameras, and security footage from anything we can hack. We'll pick him up."

But would it be in time? What possible good reason would Everett have to keep Peyton and Jess alive if he'd already decided that they needed to die?

Baby squeezed his shoulder. "Finn's got the guys out. They're going to scour the town. Peyton is one of our own, and so is Jess. You can damn well believe nobody is going to let anything happen to them."

Cade nodded, struggling through the fog that wanted to surround him. He didn't even know how to process this level of betrayal.

"He called me *brother*," Cade murmured. "He left me that voicemail today saying he was on his way to Nashville. I was happy he was moving forward. He told me he was happy *I* was moving forward. And called me fucking *brother*."

"I know," Baby said.

Cade shook his head. "He called me from the airport, and I could barely hear him over the annoying noises."

Except he hadn't been calling from the airport, had he? And that annoying sound hadn't been a squeaky conveyor belt like Everett said.

"Kendrick, can you recover a deleted voicemail?"

Kendrick didn't look up from the screen he was studying, nor did his fingers leave the keyboard. "Depends on how many you've had since then. How long ago was it? I can probably get back something from a month or two—"

"From an hour ago."

Kendrick made a face. "I don't even have to hack anything to do that. Let me see your phone."

A minute later Everett's message was playing again.

Hey Cade. I'm at the airport, heading back to Nashville. Now that all the danger is gone, I figure you and Peyton and Jess deserve little time to be just a family. I'm happy for you. I'll get to work, and when you're ready we can move forward with whatever direction we need to go. Love you, brother. Haha. Sorry about the squeaky conveyor belt.

"What a fucking asshole," Baby said.

Cade shook his head. There was something. . . "Play it again."

"Cade—" Mark said

"Play it again."

This time Cade didn't listen to the words. He listened to the sounds in the background.

"That wasn't a squeaky conveyor belt at all. I know where they are."

Chapter 33

Her own coughing woke Peyton up. The breath she took made her lungs feel like they were on fire. She forced one eye open, but that didn't seem to help her see at all.

Smoke. There was so much smoke That's why she couldn't see at all.

It took her addled brain a minute to figure out exactly what had happened. Then she remembered. Everett. The drugs.

Bastard had said their deaths wouldn't hurt. That they wouldn't be awake at all.

He should have practiced on more damn cats.

At least Jess was still unconscious. Peyton prayed she'd stay that way.

She forced her body to move. They were lying on the bed. She had to get them out of here.

She threw herself to the side, her body still mostly unresponsive, falling off the edge of the bed. The hard landing at least gave her a little more feeling in her muscles. She grabbed Jess, dragged her off the edge, and crawled and dragged her into the bathroom.

She stuffed a towel under the crack of the door to limit the smoke coming in and sat trying to catch her breath through all her coughing.

They had to get out. She had to force her body to work and get them out right now or else they weren't going to make it out at all. The fire was moving too fast.

She forced herself off the ground and got all the towels she could find in the darkened bathroom. The water was still on so she wet them and began to wrap them around Jess. It was all that was going to protect her from the blaze.

Wrapping the last towel around her own face, Peyton hoisted Jess up over her shoulder. She was going to have to stay as low as she could and still try to balance her unconscious child.

Gritting her teeth, she opened the door and moved out.

Two steps later, she fell to the ground with a sob. The smoke was worse, the heat was worse. There was no way she was going to make it walking.

Peyton flattened herself on the ground, keeping Jess on her back, and belly crawled as best she could toward the door.

She didn't want to die here. Didn't want her daughter to die here. Not now. Not when their family had finally become united.

Peyton continued to stretch and pull along the floor, resituating Jess every few minutes. When her hand hit a wall she stopped, a sob of relief escaping her. They had to be near the door.

But when she stretched up and felt a set of drawers she knew she was in the kitchen. She hadn't crawled in a straight line and now she was even farther from the door.

There was no way she was going to make it. She'd spent the last of her energy making it here, and it was getting more difficult to breathe. Peyton twisted until Jess rolled off her back and wrapped her arms around her precious daughter.

She would rest, just for a minute. Then she would try again. She buried her face in Jess's towel-wrapped neck and closed her eyes, letting the pull of the drugs in her system drag her back under.

"Peyton!"

She'd almost convinced herself she'd imagined the sound of her name when it came again. "Peyton! Jess!"

The names were cut off by coughing.

Cade was here.

"Cade!"

The word came out as nothing more than a hoarse whisper. He was never going to hear her like that.

Shifting to the side, and using the last of her strength, she yanked open one of the drawers and pulled out a pan. She reached up and started slamming it on the countertop. It was the loudest noise she was going to be able to make.

"I hear you! I'm coming!"

He burst through the smoke like the hero she'd always imagined him to be in the films she'd created in her mind.

He didn't say a word, but he didn't have to.

He put Jess in her lap, then swept them both up into his arms.

They weren't even to the door when somebody took them from Cade's arms and finished carrying them outside.

Baby, she thought, or maybe Aiden? Somebody else helped Cade. A few moments later, all three of them lay on the ground outside, finally able to breathe in the fresh air.

Everyone rushed around them, discussing how to get water from the lake up to the house to save it. "Just get the swing," Cade choked out.

"Roger that." That was definitely Zac Mackay. It wasn't long before Annie was there checking vitals.

"Jess?" Peyton croaked out.

"She's okay. The ambulance is on its way with oxygen for all of you, but you're all going to be fine. Jess will probably wake up and be none the worse for wear except for maybe a sore throat."

Peyton turned to face Cade lying on the grass beside her. "It was Everett."

"I know. I'm so sorry."

Baby crouched down. "We just got word from Mark. Gavin arrested Everett on his way into Reddington City. He's in jail."

Cade reached out and trailed a finger down her cheek. "Everett was the one helping Dennis too. All to try to manipulate me. I'm so sorry, Peaches." His voice was hoarse. Tortured.

She wanted to tell him it wasn't his fault, that she understood, that they were in this together no matter what. But all that came out was a croak.

Jess chose that moment to open her precious blue eyes. She didn't even question why they were lying on the ground in the dark, or why nearly every adult she knew was running around her. She just looked at Cade and held out her arm.

"Daddy, I got a bee sting. Can I get an ice cream?"

Chapter 34

"Are you sure you want to do this?"

Peyton reached over and took Cade's hand. It had been a hard week for him. Coming to grips with Everett's betrayal, dealing with the media fallout, struggling to find a new normal.

Peyton had been by his side trying to help him any way she could. They still hadn't made any formal announcements about their relationship, and she still wasn't ready to make that leap into the public eye.

Even though both of them knew it was just a matter of time.

Peyton didn't mind making the rest of the world wait, but both of them were ready to become a full family.

A legal, married family.

So here they were, on the way to City Hall in Reddington City, about to be married.

Jess was in the back seat, between Renee and Cecelia, chatting away. Peyton and Cade had decided that today's ceremony would legitimately be family only. It made Peyton a little sad that the people from Linear Tactical who meant so much to her wouldn't be there on this special day, but she understood it wasn't possible.

"Am I sure I want to do this? Absolutely." She squeezed his hand. "Today is about you and me starting our life together. There will be plenty of time to get the gang in on everything."

Another wedding. A big wedding. They'd already talked about it.

Today was for them.

"And so now we're going to move in with Daddy, and I will have my own room that I am going to paint black."

"Black?" both women—grandmother, and honorary grandmother—asked.

"Just kidding. I was thinking neon orange. Good for brain development."

Peyton wasn't so sure that was much better than black. But the fact that Jess was excited about moving into Cade's house was all that mattered.

Cade had arranged a special appointment in the judge's chamber for their nuptials. Neither of them wanted the paparazzi finding out about the civil ceremony.

Cade was still talking about a sabbatical. About staying home with Jess while Peyton went to school or went straight to work, whichever she wanted.

They had time to figure that out.

Cade parked and escorted his gaggle of ladies to a side entrance at City Hall. The judge's secretary met them at the door. She was frowning.

"Judge Harris is not very happy with you. Hurry up and follow me."

Peyton shot a concerned look at Cade but he shrugged, obviously not knowing what was going on either.

"Are we late?" he asked.

They all walked quickly down the hallway to keep up

JANIE CROUCH

with the angry secretary. "No, not late." Her tone was as brisk as her heels on the linoleum.

Peyton was worried, but Cade gave her a grin and a wink that had her wanting to pull her husband-to-be into the nearest closet.

"Save it for the honeymoon you two." Cecelia winked at her. She'd be watching Jess while Cade whisked her away to the beach for three days. He told her it might be acceptable not to have a wedding, but he was damn well having a mini-honeymoon. And then a proper honeymoon later. He wouldn't tell her where.

They got to the judge's outer office and the secretary held out a hand. "Please wait here."

She went around her desk and picked up her phone. "They're here, your honor. Again, I'm so sorry for the inconvenience."

Inconvenience? Peyton mouthed.

Cade shrugged again, then picked up Jess and told her how pretty her dress was and showed how perfectly it matched his tie.

Peyton loved him for that. Loved that he recognized that their sensitive daughter would pick up on the emotional nuances of the room, particularly the grumpy secretary, and wanted to protect her.

Grumpy walked over to the door. She still had quite the disapproving look in her eye. Maybe she didn't approve of famous people? Weddings? Life in general?

"You can go in now. If you can fit."

Peyton's eyes widened as she stepped through the door. Nearly every single person from the Linear team was crammed into the judge's chambers. Peyton looked over at Cade.

"Did you. . .?"

"It wasn't me, although if I had known it would light

up your face like this I would have." He turned to Zac. "How did you figure it out?"

Zac thumped him on the back as they walked in and pointed to the other end of the room. "Don't look at me. It's your fault for hiring the best security guy in the business."

Mark gave a small salute.

"If we could get started Mr. O'Conner." The judge stood up behind his desk. "I certainly don't mind doing a favor for the governor, but I would like to get my chambers back sometime today."

That's right, the governor was Gavin and Lyn's father. They were both smiling when Peyton glanced over at them.

She grabbed Cade's hand, Jess still in his arms, and walked forward, everyone clearing a path.

And there, in front of all their family, blood and otherwise, they became man and wife.

After he kissed her he moved his lips to her ears so only she could hear. "Our echo of forever starts now."

Acknowledgments

Some of the books in the Linear Tactical series are *surprises*...characters who just show up and I know I've got to fit them in somewhere.

Not *Echo.* Peyton and Cade were a planned part of this series from the beginning (Cade is even mentioned way back in *Cyclone*).

Echo is loosely based on the very first book I ever completed, over ten years ago now, which I tentatively titled *Unbreak My Heart* (yeah, like the song). I never expected expected to publish that story in any form, and can count on one hand the number of people who read it.

Something about it just wasn't right. All the pieces didn't fit together neatly.

Looking back on it now, I think the reason *Unbreak My Heart* didn't work was because it was always meant to be Peyton and Cade's story.

For them, it worked perfectly. So I'm delighted to finally bring this particular story to light for everyone to read.

But, as always, there's way more than just me that goes into making a good book.

A special thanks to my alpha readers: Denise Chapman-Hendrickson, Susan Greenbank, Kaitlin Shoemaker, Jessica Peare. Thank you for looking beyond the glaring grammatical and spelling errors of an early draft to help bring out the best story underneath.

To my beta readers: Denise Chapman-Hendrickson, Wendy Sue Stillions, CJ Channings, Shana Bullock Anderson, Kathy Boeckenhauer. Thank you for your encouragement and honesty.

And finally, to Marci Mathers of Moonflower Manuscripts...thank you, thank you, thank you for your attention to detail and outpouring of love over this book. You are an amazing editor and I appreciate you so much!

Off to write more Linear Tactical books!

~ Janie

Also by Janie Crouch

OMEGA SECTOR: CRITICAL RESPONSE (series complete)

Special Forces Savior

Fully Committed

Armored Attraction

Man of Action

Overwhelming Force

Battle Tested

OMEGA SECTOR: UNDER SIEGE (series complete)

Daddy Defender

Protector's Instinct

Cease Fire

Major Crimes

Armed Response

In the Lawman's Protection

OMEGA SECTOR SERIES (series complete)

Infiltration

Countermeasures

Untraceable

Leverage

About the Author

"Passion that leaps right off the page." - Romantic Times Book Reviews

USA TODAY bestselling author Janie Crouch writes what she loves to read: passionate romantic suspense. She is a winner and/or finalist of multiple romance literary awards including the Golden Quill Award for Best Romantic Suspense, the National Reader's Choice Award, and the coveted RITA© Award by the Romance Writers of America.

Janie recently relocated with her husband and their four teenagers to Germany (due to her husband's job as support for the U.S. Military), after living in Virginia for nearly 20 years. When she's not listening to the voices in her head—and even when she is—she enjoys engaging in all sorts of crazy adventures (200-mile relay races; Ironman Triathlons, treks to Mt. Everest Base Camp) traveling, and movies of all kinds.

Her favorite quote: "Life is a daring adventure or nothing." ~ Helen Keller.

facebook.com/janiecrouch

amazon.com/author/janiecrouch

instagram.com/janiecrouch

bookbub.com/authors/janie-crouch

CPSIA information can be obtained
at www.ICGtesting.com
Printed in the USA
BVHW031127230322
632179BV00003B/183